DESTINY'S STAR

Also by Beth Vaughan from Gollancz:

Red Gloves
White Star

DESTINY'S STAR

Beth Vaughan

GOLLANCZ

LONDON

The right of Beth Vaughan to be identified as the author
of this work has been asserted by her in accordance with
the Copyright, Designs and Patents Act 1988.

First published in Great Britain in 2010 by Gollancz
An imprint of the Orion Publishing Group
Orion House, 5 Upper St Martin's Lane,
London WC2H 9EA
An Hachette UK Company

A CIP catalogue record for this book
is available from the British Library

ISBN 978 0 575 08452 0 (Cased)
ISBN 978 0 575 08453 7 (Trade Paperback)

1 3 5 7 9 10 8 6 4 2

Typeset at The Spartan Press Ltd,
Lymington, Hants

Printed and bound in the UK by
CPI Mackays, Chatham ME5 8TD

The Orion Publishing Group's policy is to use papers that
are natural, renewable and recyclable products and
made from wood grown in sustainable forests. The logging
and manufacturing processes are expected to conform to
the environmental regulations of the country of origin.

www.eavwrites.com
www.orionbooks.co.uk

This book is dedicated to my writer's group:

Helen Kourous
Spencer Luster
Marc Tassin
Robert Wenzlaff

who, once a month, give me the gift of
their truths with no exchange of tokens
necessary but with much laughter and joy.

Thank you so very much.

ONE

She frowned, contemplating her choices, considering well. Lives depended on her choice, especially her own.

A blade? Or a mace?

Lady Bethral, Warder of the Castle of Edenrich and Protector of Her Majesty, Queen Gloriana, the Chosen of Palins, tightened the last of the buckles on her armor as she looked over the rack of weapons at her disposal.

'Don't see why you bother even pretending,' Oris grumbled from behind her, his deep voice echoing off the stone walls of her office. 'You're gonna take the mace.'

Bethral looked over her shoulder at the older man, and raised an eyebrow. He shrugged, lifting his chin to meet her eyes. 'You always do.'

'It's true, Lady,' Alad chimed in. The younger man was nearer her height and could look her straight in the eye. He gave her one of his boyish grins, his blond hair falling into his eyes.

Bethral shrugged, then turned back and pulled the mace off the rack, securing it to her belt. 'I like the feel of a mace.'

'Can't understand why,' Oris said. 'A blade's a better choice. What if . . .'

Bethral ignored him as she checked her saddlebags for the final time. Oris was a good man of strong opinion. He did his job well, and if he voiced his opinion of weapons once in a while, it was fair enough.

'There's times you need to slash, then there's times you need to hack away,' Oris continued.

Alad sighed, and rolled his eyes.

Bethral looked around her office. Odd how things had turned

I

out. She'd gone from simple mercenary to this in less than a year's passing.

There was a grumbling sound from the windowsill. The ugly barn cat roused itself, stretching in the sun as it woke from its third nap of the morning. Red Gloves had once said that it looked like a soured boil with its mottled fur. Bethral wasn't sure that was true, but it wasn't the loveliest creature, that was certain.

The cat yawned, showing all its teeth, then started to wash its face.

'Then there's stabbing,' Oris continued. 'What good is a mace if you need to run something through? I ask you—'

In less than a year's time, Bethral had gained a battle mare, a barn cat, and plate armor that other warriors could only dream of. She'd fought beside the Chosen to challenge the usurper for the Throne of Palins, and had stood at Gloriana's side as she claimed the throne.

She had lost her sword-sister, though. Red Gloves had left before the coronation. Bethral had offered to go with her, but Red had stopped her with a simple question.

'Now who's avoiding the call to adventure?'

Bethral wasn't sure she'd made the right choice that night. But here she was, and here she'd serve, until there was no longer a need for her services.

But for now, she'd a task at hand.

Bethral sighed as she picked up her helmet, and slung her saddlebags over her shoulder. The cat roused itself, then leapt to the floor to twine around her legs.

'You'll see to the Queen's safety while I'm gone?' Bethral rounded on Oris, cutting off his speech.

Oris and Alad both glowered at her. 'Been doing it since she was a bit of a thing, back at Auxter's farm.' Oris stiffened, his face getting red. 'No reason to think I'll do anything else.'

'True enough.' Bethral nodded to both men. 'But she's no longer a child you need to watch over. She's the Chosen, the newly crowned Queen, and new to the throne. If any were to—'

'They won't,' Alad said firmly.

'Our oaths on it,' Oris added. 'They'd have to take our blood before hers would spill.'

Bethral nodded, and stepped past them to the door of her office. She'd be gone only a day or two at most. 'Then escort the Queen to the courtyard. I'll stop in the kitchens first.'

Oris and Alad gave her a bow and headed off to the Queen's chambers.

Bethral stood for a moment, thinking. Oris was right, there were times a blade was handy.

She returned to the racks and grabbed her sword. Oris would snort when he saw both weapons on her belt, but that was fine. Hope for the best. Plan for the worst.

Bethral strode back to the door. Her saddlebags were packed well enough, but some trail rations would not go amiss. Just in case.

The kitchens were busy, with servants headed this way and that, carrying trays and pots of kav. The nobility usually broke their fasts in their rooms, summoning food and drink. The staff would have already eaten, and were now about the business of the morning.

Bethral paused, waited for a serving girl to ease through the door with her tray, and then slipped in behind her. If she was lucky, he'd be . . .

She was in luck. He was there.

Ezren Storyteller, also known as Ezren Silvertongue, was not one to eat in his room. He preferred the kitchens, with their wide hearths, warm baking ovens, and servants' gossip.

He was careful to tuck in near the hearth, where he'd not get in the way of those busy with their tasks. The room smelled of warm bread, and there was hot whispering of the comings and goings of the noble lords and ladies.

Ezren stayed quiet, enjoying his bowl of pot oats sweetened with honey and cream, a mug of kav near at hand. He'd made it his habit to rise early and take this place, letting none serve him in bed like a lord. No, this was far more comfortable and far more worthwhile. Queen Gloriana needed his aid, and knowledge was valuable. Very valuable.

'More kav, Storyteller?' one of the cooks asked, holding out a fresh pot.

'Always,' Ezren swore.

The cook laughed, and poured. 'They'll be trussing up a carcass on the spit soon, for tonight's dinner. Mind your clothes when they bring it in. The lads always get blood all over everything.'

'I'll have a care.' Ezren smiled at her and took a sip. He'd have to leave soon, anyway. Evelyn and Blackhart were departing this morning, and Ezren wanted to bid them farewell.

Of course, Lord Marlon would be there as well, for he was going to open the portal for them. Ezren would have preferred not to come into the man's presence, because Marlon was firmly convinced that Ezren needed to die, and by his hand.

Ezren sighed, catching a glimpse of the manacles that he wore hidden under his sleeves. The Lady High Priestess Evelyn had given them to him and explained their nature. They absorbed magic, including the wild magic that cursed him. Evelyn had been chained with them when she'd been captured.

He'd resisted them at first. Too many memories of his enslavement. But at Evelyn's urging he'd put them on, and felt the pressure in his chest ease. Without the chains, they appeared to be heavy bracelets. And they did conceal the scarring around his wrists. Still, they made him uneasy. As if, at any moment, he'd find himself . . .

Ezren frowned at his breakfast. If wearing the manacles rendered the wild magic null, it was worth the cost. The people around him were safe. For now.

Evelyn had told him last night that she had learned they were only a temporary measure. The manacles would not last forever. Eventually they'd absorb all the magic they could, and crumble into so much dust.

Well, that was for another day. For now, Ezren needed to finish eating. He took another sip of kav, then froze.

4

She was here. In the kitchens.

He kept the mug up, using it to cover his face as he let his eyes scan the room. They caught a sparkle of light off plate and a glint of golden hair. There, between the kitchen and the pantry.

Lady Bethral.

It was just a glimpse, and then she was gone, disappearing into the shadows of the room beyond. Moving like a silent spirit, even in full armor.

His . . . no . . . an Angel of Light, who had rescued him and saved his life. Lord of Light, Lady of Laughter, she was lovely. Tall, powerful, with hair like gold and blue eyes like a spring sky . . . and not for the likes of him.

The kav suddenly went bitter in his mouth. Why would she give him a second look? Whipped, scarred, a man unable to save himself from being enslaved. No real skill with sword or dagger, and no equal to her. A storyteller with a broken voice, no longer able to enthrall an audience, much less a woman of her—

'Lord Ezren?'

Ezren turned from his thoughts and saw one of the palace clerks hurrying toward him. 'Lord, there is some question concerning damages done at the Flying Pig Tavern last night. The men were there at your expense, and the innkeeper has presented this bill . . .' The man held out a roll of parchment.

Ezren stifled a curse at the amount. 'Blackhart's men. It has to be. Let us go talk with this innkeeper.'

Bethral paused in the doorway and watched as Ezren held his mug out to the cook, his green eyes sparkling. Something he said made the cook laugh.

She'd been out of her mind when she'd bought him for a copper.

She and Red Gloves had been on their way to another city, looking for anyone who'd hire their blades. Her sword-sister had been frothing at the mouth as they'd purchased supplies, all because a goatherder had told her a prophecy about her birthmark. Red had not liked that one bit.

The slavers had thrown the man down to the platform in the slave market, offering him as meat for dogs. Blind with rage, Bethral had flipped the copper coin onto the platform, then eased him up and over her shoulder. Her sword-sister had squawked like a chicken, but Bethral had just turned on her heel and walked away before she'd killed a slaver. Or two.

She'd leave no man to that death, no matter how impulsive or crazy her purchase had been. Red had complained, but she'd fought their pursuers as Bethral had mounted and fled, the slave in her arms.

The cook moved off, and Bethral slipped into the pantry, not wanting to be caught staring. She took a deep breath of the herb-scented air, then went to where the dried meat and hard biscuits were kept. Bethral grabbed one of the small cloth sacks on the shelf and busied herself filling it.

She'd lost her heart when Ezren had opened his green eyes and stared at her, cradled in her arms and safe from their pursuers. She'd caught her breath at the secrets those eyes held even as he slipped back into unconsciousness.

Bethrel had stayed in Edenrich to see if there was a chance that those green eyes might focus on her.

Ezren Silvertongue had recovered with the aid of magical healing and a grim determination to survive what had been done to him.

Beaten, abused, he'd been as close to death as any man Bethral had seen on the battlefield. But even with his tongue cut from his throat, he'd clung to life with a strength of will that astonished her. And his voice . . .

Bethral had been told that his voice had changed, but all she knew was that his voice sent a small thrill down her spine every time she heard him speak.

Which wasn't often. For Lord Silvertongue had immersed himself in the Court once again, rejoining the life he had lost during his captivity. In particular, he seemed very adept at avoiding her.

Bethral shrugged. What was, was. She could no more change

than that barn cat could change the color of its fur. At least she caught glimpses of him occasionally. If she was careful, she could stand in the shadows and listen to him talk to others. And if the day came that he courted and won a lady of the Court, well . . .

She'd deal with that when the time came.

Bethral sighed, and slipped back through the kitchen without drawing attention to herself. Time to meet Gloriana in the courtyard and then be on her way.

The bright sun blinded Bethral as she stepped through the double doors and into the courtyard.

A quick sweep of the area told her that her orders had been obeyed. Lady High Priestess Evelyn stood off to the side with Orrin Blackhart, who was talking to his men as they clustered near their horses.

The walls were manned, and the guards at the gates of the courtyard were at attention.

Bethral felt a pang of envy that she hoped did not show on her face. Evelyn had found her love, and had fought her way to his side with an unshaken faith in him, despite his past.

'Is it safe?' A soft voice came from behind her.

Bethral glanced back, giving the young girl behind her a nod. 'All's well, Your Majesty.'

Gloriana nodded in return, then started across the courtyard toward Evelyn. Oris and Alad waited by the door, watchful in their own right.

Bethral frowned slightly as she watched the two women hug. This would be a hard day for Gloriana, having to say farewell to the woman who had raised her for over half her life. Evelyn was leaving this day to return to the Black Hills, taking over as the Guardian until the new High Baron could be named.

Hard for the girl, who sat so new on her throne. Bethral frowned again, not sure that her decision to leave for a few days was wise. The bandits who were harassing the main road into the City needed to be stopped, but . . .

Bethral's men were gathered at the other side of the courtyard, near the stables, preparing to ride with her. One was leading her horse, Bessie. The roan mare stepped out with pride, her barding gleaming in the bright sun. Bethral chuckled softly to see the cat walk over to the horse and rub against a foreleg. Bessie nuzzled the small creature, giving it a welcoming chuckle.

Bethral turned back to her duty and followed Gloriana, focusing on Blackhart's men. She didn't know them well, and it paid to be watchful.

Gloriana was still hugging Evelyn. 'All we need now is High Mage Marlon.'

'My father is not known for his promptness.' Evelyn returned the hug with a warm smile.

But Bethral's attention had been caught by one of Blackhart's men. The sight of him confused her. What was he doing in Palins? A big black man, dark of skin, his face and arms covered in ritual scars. Bethral was willing to bet the scars also covered his chest. 'Greetings, warrior,' Bethral said in a tongue she had not spoken in many years. 'You are far from the Plains.'

The black man's eyes went wide. 'You know my—'

A sound from behind her, and without turning, Bethral knew that Ezren had come out of the castle. He emerged into the light, blinking and looking about. 'Blackhart' – Ezren's voice cracked as it rang out over the courtyard – 'about your men and their activities.' Ezren started across the courtyard.

'Uh-oh,' said the short man.

'Told you not to put it on account,' the tall one said.

Bethral had been about to turn, but stopped at the sight of the black man's face. It turned ashen, his eyes wide, as he stared at Ezren.

'About these charges' – Ezren came right up to them, the roll of parchment in his hand – 'it seems . . .' Before he could finish, he stopped with a gasp, as if in pain, clutching at his chest. 'What—'

Bethral risked a glance his way as Evelyn reached for him. 'Ezren, what's wrong?'

Ezren yanked back his sleeve, revealing one of the manacles of a spell chain. Bethral frowned; the metal band looked like day-old bread, crumbling off Ezren's wrist.

A *pop*, and High Mage Marlon appeared out of nowhere. 'Ready?' he said. 'I can't be all day—'

White-hot flames surged around Ezren, exploding with power.

Ezren pressed his hands over his heart, the roll of parchment falling from his hands. He stumbled back as the manacles crumbled away. With a cry he collapsed in the center of the courtyard, barely able to keep his head up. 'No, no, no,' he rasped.

With a roar, more light surged from his chest, a huge column of light and fire that started to spin. A wave of heat and force washed over the courtyard, knocking everyone off their feet and sending the horses into fits.

Fear surged through Bethral, fear for Ezren, but her training made her lunge for Gloriana.

The power had begun to turn, spiraling in on itself with a sound like a thousand running horses. The very stones beneath them vibrated with its fury.

'Rogue!' Marlon bellowed. The big man was on the ground, his silk robes spilled around him like a deflated tent. Bethral wedged Gloriana behind his bulk, and stuffed her between them.

Ezren had rolled to his side, and Bethral caught the glint of his green eyes. White-hot power flared about his body, and the sound grew louder. The power lashed out, hitting the area around him. His eyes closed, and he started convulsing on the cobblestones.

Terror caught Bethral's throat. If his wild magic had gone rogue, everyone in the courtyard would die, including Ezren.

Bethral caught the glance between Marlon and Evelyn, saw Evelyn stop her apprentice from aiding Ezren. Her heart contracted in her breast. Marlon was going to kill Ezren. He was staring at Ezren, reaching out as if to—

Bethral raised up on her knees, reached over, and jerked Marlon's arm to the side. 'NO!'

Marlon didn't struggle. He just turned on his side to look up at her. 'He'll kill us all.'

No. Not while she breathed. She needed to get him away, away from the City, from people. No matter the cost. Bethral jerked her head up and caught Evelyn's gaze. 'Open a portal,' she screamed. 'As far distant as you can.'

The wind whipped at their hair and clothes, and the fury of the power grew.

Evelyn shook her head. 'You'll be killed.'

As if that mattered. Bethral released Marlon's hand, still focused on the priestess. 'As far, as remote as you can,' she yelled. 'Where he'll not kill anyone else.'

To her relief, Marlon nodded to Evelyn. They'd do it. She just had to get Ezren up and through the portal. Bethral took a deep breath, but before she could stand, a pale hand grabbed her arm.

She looked down and saw Gloriana staring up at her, her brown hair tossed by the winds.

'Bethral, no, no! Don't leave me!'

There wasn't time. Bethral had to choose, and she had made that choice long ago. She rose to her feet, fighting the winds. Marlon reached out and wrapped his arms around Gloriana, keeping her down. He was talking, but she was protesting, struggling against him.

The power lashed out, as if understanding Bethral's intent, striking cobblestones with white shards of lightning, as if the magic itself sensed a threat.

A portal appeared behind the fury, its soft curtains a contrast to the chaos around them. It wavered, then solidified as Evelyn and her apprentice concentrated.

Bethral did not look back. She fought her way forward through the waves of raging power around Ezren. The flares danced around her, striking her again and again. She took the blows as she reached his side.

He wasn't dead. Bethral gasped in relief. But he was unconscious, his face turned up to the sky, barely breathing. Once again, as she had that fateful day, she reached for Ezren Story-teller, to lift him from the ground.

But this was no starved shadow of a man. She staggered as she gathered him into her arms, heaving him over her shoulder.

The winds grew wilder still, their roaring almost a scream in her ears. They battered at her, as if to tear Ezren from her.

Bethral bared her teeth, took a step, and then another, trying to walk into the portal. But the magic threw itself at her, and when she tried to step forward, she staggered again, almost falling. Bethral wept in frustration as she strained. She had to—

Bessie was beside her, snorting, nervous, her nostrils flared. Terrified, but standing firm. The cat was on all fours, claws hooked in the saddlebags, every inch of fur standing on end, mouth open in what had to be a hiss of defiance.

Bethral reached for the saddle, pulling herself up and over in one smooth move. Ezren slid off her shoulder, but somehow she managed to keep him in her arms.

The light, the wild magic surged around them. Ezren's entire body convulsed and Bethral struggled to keep her hold. She leaned forward, and cried out to Bessie. 'Heyla! Heyla, girl, go! Go!'

Bessie gathered her hind legs, and started forward.

The raging fury lashed out, striking both at the portal and behind them. A thick strand of impossibly bright white whipped out. Bethral glanced back, saw the strand lashing at the others. It would kill—

The big black man stepped in front of them, naked from the waist up. He stood, arms wide, shouting, 'That which was lost is now found!'

Bessie moved, and Bethral's attention returned to the portal that danced before them. The roan leapt forward, as commanded, bolting into the portal. They surged straight through the raw power. For just a moment, Bethral saw open skies and smelled the scent of wildflowers.

Then the world disappeared in a flash of white. Bethral cried out as Bessie slipped out from under her legs, as Ezren tumbled from her arms.

Bethral fell as well, smashing into pain and the deep darkness of her own failure.

TWO

Gilla's heart stopped when the sky tore open above the Plains.

She'd been tending to the gurt drying racks, turning the pebbles of hard cheese so that they dried evenly. It was boring, a child's task, not fit for one of her maturity. But she'd gritted her teeth and done it nonetheless, because being an adult meant that you did what had to be done without protest, now didn't it?

She cast a quick glance behind her to see if anyone was watching her be responsible. But none of the Elders were in sight.

She sighed as she moved to the next rack, shooing gurtles out of her way. A few had wandered between the racks, looking for sweet grass. '*Muwap*.' One of them shook its head, protesting. This part of the herd had just been shorn, and they looked funny, stripped of their fur.

Gilla sighed again as she continued her chore. It was spring on the Plains. Soon, within days, the theas would be releasing the young adult warriors to seek out the armies of the warlords for service, and she'd qualify, if they felt she was ready. And she was more than ready, more than . . .

The sky crackled. The hair on Gilla's arms stirred, as before a summer storm. The land shook with a pounding of thunder, under a cloudless open sky. She looked up and saw the blue sky tear open to show a white glow beyond.

Her heart froze, the gurtles stilled, everything was silent for a long moment. The edges of the tear pulsed above her, as if waiting.

In the next breath, a horse jumped through the tear, as if

13

clearing the banks of some unseen shore. Gilla had a brief glimpse of two people, one astride in armor, one cradled in the other's arms as they hung there in midair.

They fell in the next instant, plummeting down, loose and free-falling, and disappeared in the tall grass.

The rip in the sky exploded with light, and disappeared.

'*Muwap! Muwap!*' The gurtles around her exploded into action. Gurtles feared what they did not know, and once feared, all they knew was 'away,' as fast as their hooves could carry them. Gilla grabbed at the nearest rack and struggled to stay upright as the gurtles bolted by her, bleating their warnings and running straight through camp.

Cries arose from the tents behind her, but Gilla did not glance that way. She kept her eyes on where the enemy had fallen, and warbled a cry to summon warriors to face this threat. She waited as the last of the gurtles ran past, then drew her dagger and started forward.

The young grasses were already springing back as she moved, their flowers torn and shredded by the gurtles' hooves. She got low, taking what cover she could, and crawled toward the enemy, the hilt of her dagger in her hand, the blade pressed to her forearm. She'd worn her armor this morning, as a warrior should, and her blade was sharp and ready. Her heart beat faster as she moved closer . . .

The horse staggered to its feet, shaking its head. It was huge, a big roan, and wearing armor the like of which she'd never seen, although she recognised the saddle and saddlebags. The animal stood there, its legs splayed out, head low, as if exhausted. Amazing that it hadn't broken a leg in the fall.

Gilla watched for a moment, then eased the grasses back in front of her face, keeping a careful eye on the horse. There'd be others coming, but she wanted to be able to report the danger. She needed to see . . .

Her blood singing in her ears, she slowly raised her head. Two people were sprawled in the grass. The one with the armor . . .

Gilla winced at the sight of that one's leg. Twisted like that, it had to be broken.

The other figure stirred, groaned, and sat up, his hand raised to his head. He was hurt as well, but there was no blood that Gilla could see. No armor, no weapons, either.

He saw the other person and cried out something, then crawled over to remove the helmet. Bright blond hair spilled out, and Gilla could see the still, slack face of a woman. The man grew distraught as he examined her, and raised his head to look around.

Gilla sucked in a breath as his bright green eyes stared directly into her brown ones.

Ezren Silvertongue awoke to pain.

A dull pain, as if his entire body had been wrung out like a cloth. It hurt to breathe, hurt to move. He had known beatings in the time he had been enslaved, and thought he had learned every manner of ways that a body could hurt.

He had been wrong.

Ezren concentrated on breathing for a moment, keeping his eyes closed. He was conscious of the sweet smell of grass crushed beneath him, warm sun, and a gentle spring breeze on his skin. Which was wrong. He was not sure exactly why, but it should be cold . . .

A rasping purr and a wet nose in his ear made him jerk upright.

Lord of Light, that hurt. He wrapped an arm around his stomach and groaned. But the next breath was easier, and the next after that.

The hideous cat from the barn, the one that had attached itself to Bethral's warhorse, sat next to him. With its mottled coat of black, brown, yellow, and a kind of green, it almost blended into the shadows in the grass. Its watery yellow eyes stared at him unwaveringly. Accusingly.

Ezren frowned, staring back. Last he recalled, he had been in the kitchens of the Castle of Edenrich, being presented with a bill for damages at the Flying Pig Tavern. He had taken it up, and gone to confront the miscreants, but now . . .

He looked out on nothing but grass and wildflowers, as far as the eye could see. Wide blue sky that stretched from horizon to horizon and filled his vision. His heart skipped a beat at the sight. He had never felt so exposed as at this moment; one man in an ocean of grass. He looked down, trying to steady himself.

The cat stirred, and slipped into the grass. Ezren watched it go, and then lifted his eyes and saw—

Bethral, sprawled on the ground like a broken doll.

'Bethral.' He lurched onto his knees and crawled to her side, ignoring the rough grass that cut his hands and the pain that lanced through his bones.

She was still as death, and pale, so pale, under her helmet. He fell at her side, and pressed his fingers to her neck. *Please, Lady of Laughter, let her not be dead.*

She lived. Her heart still beat.

Relief flooded through Ezren as he fumbled with the chin-strap, then eased the helm from her head. Bright gold hair spilled out, covering the ground and his hands with its silken glory.

Lady of Laughter, she was lovely.

He had called her an angel once, one of the Angels of the Light, come to escort him to paradise. He had thought himself dead at that time, and had opened his eyes to find himself in a small hut with an angel at his bedside. He had never called her that again, unable, unwilling to try to place any claim upon her. But in all truth she was glorious to look on. Her lovely face, and those bright blue eyes.

Eyes now closed, in a face pale and still. Crumpled, broken, her leg twisted.

Ezren swallowed hard, and looked out at the emptiness around him in bleak despair.

And straight into the startled brown eyes of a young girl hiding in the tall grass.

*

Gilla lowered her head and started to scrabble back fast, crawling away from the man. She was so stupid, to be seen like that. She'd—

A firm hand grasped her ankle, and Gilla froze.

The hand squeezed once, and Gilla breathed again. She looked back and saw Urte's calm face. Relief washed over her. Urte was an elder. She'd know what to do.

Urte crawled forward, followed by Helfers, his dark face so serious. Both in leather armor, armed and grim. Relief flooded through her. Helfers was also a strong warrior, his skill with a sword well known.

They came up on either side of Gilla, until their heads were level. 'Report,' Urte whispered.

'Two people, a man and a woman. A horse, too.' Gilla spoke fast. 'Urte, they fell from the sky!'

'I saw,' Urte offered reassurance. 'Continue.'

'They are not of the Plains. They seem hurt. The woman and horse wear armor. No weapons that I saw. Something small moved at the man's side, but I didn't see it clear.' Gilla stopped. 'He saw me, Urte. I—'

Urte's look silenced her. 'Did he attack you?'

'No.' Gilla shook her head.

'What does that matter?' Helfers whispered. 'They are not of the Plains, and therefore must die.'

Urte ignored him and considered the path Gilla had left in the grass. 'The horse. Hurt?'

'It's up, legs splayed. It looks exhausted,' Gilla said.

'Helfers, to the right. Make no move until I give the command.'

Helfers grunted, and wormed off through the grass.

Urte started to crawl as well, angling away from Gilla's path. Gilla sighed. She'd be ordered back, she just knew it, and wouldn't get to see anything.

Urte looked back at her. 'Go back up there, and wait for my command.'

With a thrill of pride, Gilla obeyed.

The girl had disappeared, but Ezren suspected she had gone to summon others. Frankly, it was the least of his concerns.

He got to his feet slowly, easing up as his muscles protested. A pause to catch his breath, as pain and exhaustion washed over him. Then he staggered over to Bethral's horse.

Bessie stood motionless, her legs splayed, head hanging down. Poor beast. She didn't react as he pulled the saddlebags and bedroll off her back, trying to get to the waterskin.

Ezren cast a glance back toward Bethral, but she was still silent and motionless. She'd want him to see to her horse before anything else, so he knelt by Bessie's head and dug around for anything he could use. Finding a bowl, he filled it with water.

'Come, now,' he said softly, putting his wet hand under her nose. 'Come on, Bessie.'

The cat emerged from the grass and started to rub against Bessie's foreleg, a deep rumble coming from its chest.

Bessie snorted, started to lick at Ezren's hand, and then put her nose in the bowl. Ezren struggled to give her as much water as he could, but the bowl wasn't really deep enough for her to drink.

'Better?' he asked as Bessie lifted her head and straightened her legs.

It was all he could do for now. He crawled back to Bethral's side, dragging the waterskin, saddlebags, and bedroll with him. He fumbled with the buckles and got the bedroll free. He settled the blankets around her as best he could. He didn't dare move her, but she'd stay warmer this way. Besides, he wasn't sure what else to do.

As he tucked the blankets around Bethral, Ezren used the concealment of the covers to pull one of Bethral's daggers from her belt. He stuffed it in the grass by his leg, out of sight but well within reach.

He settled back on his heels and looked down at her.

He doubted there was much in the way of healing supplies in the bags. What he wouldn't give for the Lady High Priestess and her healing magic to be standing next to him. But he might as well wish Edenrich Castle would appear around them.

Not a bird in the air, yet the meadowlarks seemed to be singing all around him. Ezren pulled the waterskin close and wet his fingers. He reached out and stroked Bethral's pale cheek, and blew gently on her face. 'Lady Bethral, wake for me.'

No response.

'Lady Bethral.' Ezren tried to keep his voice soft, but the rasp of it grated in his ears. His finger traced a damp line over her forehead. 'I have no clue where we are, or how we came to be here, but I need you to wake up, Lady. We both know that I am a man used to city comforts. You are a skilled warrior, Lady, used to the trials and travails of the wilds.'

Bessie jerked her head up, and snorted.

The grasses moved, and armored warriors rose to surround them, swords and lances in hand. One of them barked out something in a language that Ezren did not comprehend.

'I do not understand you,' he responded as he fumbled under the blanket for the dagger.

Lady Bethral, wake for me.

She was dreaming. She had to be. She'd heard that husky voice call her name only in soft, sweet dreams.

There was a dull throb in the background of her dream, and it seemed to be her leg. It was a promise of pain to come, and she recognised it well. She'd enough experience with injury to know not to move without learning more. She knew full well it would be bad.

Better to float, and listen to that voice.

But . . .

Duty called her forward, demanded that she respond. But she didn't want to answer. She wanted to listen to the dream, to pretend . . .

Duty was a bitch.

A different voice spoke then, harsh, demanding, in a language she knew. Her eyes snapped open at the words, as fear surged over her.

'Intruders! Explain yourself, or die!'

THREE

Ezren froze as Bethral spat a word, and then yanked him down to sprawl in the grass. With one smooth move she sat up, took the dagger from his hand, and threw it.

Shouts came as the warriors dived for cover.

'Bragnect!' Bethral cried the word again as she twisted around, up on her good knee, drawing her other dagger. 'Stay down,' she hissed, her face gray with pain as she scanned the grass that surrounded them. 'How many?'

'At least four,' Ezren said, trying to remember to breathe as he stayed flat in the grass. 'I have no idea where we are—'

'The Plains.' Bethral cut him off, reaching for her helmet. 'We need to get to my horse and—'

A voice shouted from the grass. Ezren stared at Bethral's face, watching as she hesitated, then called a response.

There was silence then, as if their enemy was considering her words.

'A reprieve?' Ezren whispered. 'What is going on?'

'I confused them.' Bethral kept her voice low, and her dagger ready. 'What happened before I woke?'

'I roused, got water for Bessie, and then tried to wake you when a child appeared in the grass—'

'Child?'

'A young girl. She disappeared as soon as she saw me.'

'A thea camp, then,' Bethral mused. 'Not a war camp.' She glanced at Ezren, then back out at the grasses. 'The children here can be as deadly as the adults.'

'Lady, how did we get here?' Ezren asked. 'I remember . . . I was upset. Something about a bill for damages . . .'

Bethral snorted. 'Blackhart's men. You came out into the courtyard—'

'There was a man, a black man, standing there, covered in scars.' Ezren paused as it came flooding back. 'Lord of Light, the wild magic flared. Those manacles—'

'Failed.' Bethral nodded. 'They crumbled away to nothing.'

'It is a wonder that the Lord Mage Marlon did not kill me.'

'I stopped him.' Bethral didn't look at Ezren. 'When it looked as if the wild magic would destroy us, Evelyn opened a portal, and I brought you through.' Her blue eyes flickered in his direction. 'How do you feel?'

'Sore.' Ezren frowned. 'I am not sure why.'

'You were wracked by convulsions,' Bethral said calmly. 'But I meant the magic. Do you feel like it will flare again?'

'No.' Ezren put his hand to his heart, but felt nothing. 'It is quiet. It would appear that I owe you yet again, Lady. It seems—'

A voice called out a question from the grass. From the tone, Ezren could tell it was making a demand.

Bethral replied. From the sound of her inflection, she was making demands of her own.

The voice responded.

Bethral grunted. 'It seems we might have a chance, after all. Help me with this. I need to remove the armor from my right arm.'

Ezren rose carefully to his knees. 'What if they attack while—'

'They promised not to.' Bethral gave him an odd look. 'While they have odd ways, they have honor, Storyteller.'

He did not doubt that, but didn't say anything. He rose to his knees. 'How do we get this off?'

'There's two straps.' She held out her arm for him, all of her weight on her good knee. This close, he could hear the pain in her rough breathing. 'Just under there.'

Ezren fumbled a bit, but the piece came off to reveal the thick, quilted gambeson beneath.

'Cut it.' Bethral handed him her dagger. 'At the seam, if you can.'

Ezren sliced the sleeve at the shoulder.

'Help me up.' Bethral clenched her jaw. Ezren slipped her arm over his shoulder and helped her to stand. He wrapped his arm around her waist, and let her brace herself against his hip.

Once she was stable, Bethral glanced his way. 'For now, stay silent. I'll explain this later, I swear.'

'I will hold you to that, Lady,' Ezren whispered.

Bethral called out to their unseen enemies, then reached around and tore her sleeve down to display her upper arm. Ezren glanced over, surprised to see a row of tattoos. There were two columns of four lines each, black ink against her skin.

A warrior rose from the grasses and stepped forward slowly, showing empty hands. Ezren watched as she approached. Bethral tensed, but took no further action. Together, they waited as the woman came close, and studied Bethral's arm.

Bethral held her breath until the warrior stepped back and smiled. 'So now those of the Plains fall from the skies? There's a song here, I am certain.'

Bethral sagged a bit against the Storyteller, and felt him take her weight easily. 'And long in the telling.'

The woman considered both of them. 'Bethral of the Horse, I am Urte of the Snake.' She tilted her head to one side. 'You missed with the dagger.'

'No,' Bethral said, keeping her gaze on Urte. 'I did not.'

Urte barked a laugh. 'Is this one also of the Plains?' She jerked her chin at Ezren.

'No,' Bethral said. She could only hope she remembered the right words. 'He is Ezren Storyteller, honored Singer of Palins.'

Ezren frowned when he heard his name, but said nothing.

'Palins.' Urte's eyes flicked off to the distance and back. 'Far from his home, then. What is he to you?'

Bethral bit her lip. Never had the temptation to lie been so strong within her. She'd always believed that honesty was the best course, but . . . how she wanted to claim him as her own. Instead, she chose a phrase that those of the Plains would understand even if Ezren Storyteller did not. 'I am his Token-Bearer. We know not how we came here, and our only wish is to depart in peace.'

With that, the pain hit her hard. Bethral's vision grayed.

'Ah, where is my courtesy?' Urte moved to help Ezren lower Bethral to the ground. 'Sit, warrior of the Plains. I have sent for our elders.'

Ezren lowered Bethral to the ground, keeping a careful eye on the strange warrior. 'Reprieve?'

Bethral was pale, taking deep breaths. There was a faint sheen of sweat on her face. 'Yes. They have sent for their . . . leaders.'

'Lady,' Ezren said as he knelt at her side. The woman warrior knelt as well, but her attention was focused into the distance.

'My mother was of the Plains.' Bethral answered his unspoken question. 'The tattoos on my arm mark my . . . lineage. My membership in the tribes. She taught all of us children the language and the ways of the Plains.' A chuckle escaped her, sounding more like a sob. 'I am going to wish I had paid better attention to my lessons.'

'We need to get you to a healer.' Ezren leaned over and pulled the blanket across the grass to throw it over her shoulders.

'As to that' – Bethral drew a shuddering breath – 'Storyteller, listen to me. They have no healing.'

'Nonsense.' Ezren shook out the blanket. 'Of course they have healing. What do they do when someone is hurt or injured?'

'They kill themselves.'

Ezren froze, looking at her. 'That is madness.'

Bethral sighed as he pulled the blanket around her. 'Storyteller, do yourself a favor. Assume they are right.'

'What?'

'They live in a harsh land, and they live by very different rules. But they live – even prosper. If you want to live, best to accept their ways.'

'And you?' Ezren's voice grated in his throat.

Bethral shook her head. 'They are a nomadic warrior people

24

and they have no supplies or time to waste on the wounded. I'll be expected to—'

The woman warrior called out, waving her arm over her head. Two warriors appeared on horseback, headed in their direction.

Bethral tried to sit up as a sign of respect, but Urte pressed a hand to her shoulder. 'Stay.'

The two elders rode close, and dismounted, walking through the grass toward them. An older man, wearing armor that was a mixture of leather and chain. His skin brown and wrinkled, and he was as bald as could be. His eyes were bright blue and considering.

The other was a woman, also tanned, her hair a bright white. Her armor seemed of even better quality, with more chain than leather. Her brown eyes focused on Bethral's arm. They both drew closer.

Bethral extended her arm for consideration, and the woman took her wrist, studying the tattoos. The woman wet her thumb, and smeared it over the markings. Bethral suppressed a shiver at dampness on her skin.

'So,' the woman said, 'it appears you are truly of the Plains, for all that you fell from the sky. I am Haya of the Snake, Elder Thea.'

'I am Seo of the Fox, Elder Warrior,' the man added. 'We greet you, Bethral of the Horse, and offer you and the Singer shelter within our tents.'

Safe. He was safe, for now. Bethral dropped her gaze. 'Thank you, Elders.'

Haya grunted, as if pleased. Seo paused, and considered Bethral's leg. 'Although, it would be better, perhaps, that our tent comes to you.' He turned, and shouted for others to bring supplies. Warriors went running at his commands.

Ezren still knelt next to Bethral, watching the faces of those around him.

'Your injury, it's a bad one, eh?' Haya asked.

Bethral nodded. 'It is, Elder. But I must see to the Singer's safety before I go to the snows.'

'As to that,' Seo said, 'there is time for talk, Warrior.'

'There have been . . . events,' Haya added.

'Events?' Bethral asked.

'Change is in the wind, Warrior,' Seo answered. 'And none knows if it bodes ill or good.'

'Change?' Bethral blinked away the sweat. 'On the Plains? But my mother said that the Plains is as the land. Unending and unchanging.'

Haya nodded her understanding. 'So it is, and so it has always been. But now one has come that brings change with her.'

'Who?'

'A Warprize.'

FOUR

It was hard to take it all in. Ezren stood watching while people swarmed around them as if from nowhere.

And such people! He was used to the different skin colors and races; Edenrich was a trading city, after all, and held a mixture of all types of people.

But here . . . the contrast could not be greater. Here all the people wore armor and carried weapons, even those he'd normally think of as children. But there was an edge to them, a vibrancy that was missing in Edenrich. In his home, people came in all shapes from fat to lanky and all the sizes in between. But here, everyone was fit and hard. A people ready and able to go to battle.

It was disconcerting, to say the least.

He sat by Bethral's side as a huge piece of leather was spread on the grass, then trampled until it rested flat. Then a pallet was made of large swaths of felted wool, piled high.

Two warriors assisted Bethral and settled her on the pallet. As Ezren spread blankets over her, Seo and Haya settled on stools nearby. Seo angled his stool so that he could see the action, and kept gesturing and calling out commands.

Ezren could read faces well enough to know that his oversight was not really appreciated.

Haya was talking to Bethral in the strange, fluid tongue of the Plains as the activity swirled about them. Bethral listened intently, without interrupting. Ezren listened with half an ear, watching as the warriors worked. They were erecting a tent around them, one of the biggest he'd ever seen, when a familiar word caught his attention.

'Xy?' He crouched at Bethral's side. 'Did she say Xy? As in the Kingdom of Xy?'

Haya looked at him with bright eyes as Bethral spoke. 'Haya says that the Warprize is from the Tribe of Xy. Do you know of it?'

'From old stories of long ago,' Ezren said. 'A far mountain kingdom – it was on a major trade route at one point, according to legend.'

'Apparently the Warprize is Xylara, a princess—'

Ezren shook his head. 'They don't use that title. They would call her a Daughter of the Blood or Daughter of Xy. And if that's her name, she is the first female child of the monarch. They use Xy—'

'Storyteller,' Bethral broke in patiently.

'Sorry.' Ezren shrugged. 'Go on.'

'The Warprize is a healer and has offered her skills to all of the people of the Plains. But she has left the Plains, along with her chosen . . .' Bethral paused. 'Chosen warrior or warlord, I'm not sure which. Haya and Seo can't seem to agree. But he is named Keir of the Cat. Xylara is pregnant, and she returned to Xy to bear her child in that land.'

'Understandable, if the child will be the heir to the throne.' Ezren looked at Haya. 'I take it that there are no healers here. How far is Xy?'

Bethral asked. Haya shook her head and gestured off into the distance, talking rapidly.

'Well, from what I can tell, it's probably months,' Bethral said. 'Apparently there was a senel – a gathering of the elders – and a fight . . .' Bethral sighed. 'She's going so fast, I can't follow it all.'

Haya scowled, clearly angry, and made a spitting sound. That caught Seo's attention, and he glared at her.

'The senel turned into a fight – and they aren't agreeing who won,' Bethral said, closing her eyes. 'But from what I can gather, the Plains is in the midst of a civil war.'

There was the hint of strain in her voice. She was hurting, and Ezren was helpless to stop it. 'I am fairly handy with languages. I have learned a smattering of tongues, so that I can read some stories in their original version,' he said. 'I need to learn this language as soon as possible.'

Bethral gave him an odd look. 'Yes, you do.'

A young girl darted between the workers, carrying a pitcher and some mugs. It was the girl Ezren had seen hidden in the grass. Her brown eyes flashed to his face, then she concentrated on her task. She handed the mugs to Haya and Seo and poured for them. Ezren caught the scent of kav on the air.

The girl turned to him and held out a mug. He took it with a smile, and held it out as she poured. 'Please tell me this is kav.'

'It is,' Bethral said. 'They call it kavage.'

'How do I say "thank you"?'

Bethral told him, and Ezren repeated the phrase to the girl, who looked at him, then glanced at Seo.

Seo gestured, admonishing her.

The girl nodded to Ezren and spoke, then knelt to serve Bethral.

'Her name is Gilla, and she says that you are welcome.'

Ezren took a sip of the hot drink. It was the same as in Edenrich, and yet different somehow. Dark and black, but more bitter than at home. Still, it was kav, thank the Lord and the Lady. He enjoyed it as he watched the tent walls start to rise around them.

Suddenly the girl jumped, dropping the pitcher, and scrambled back. Haya and Seo both reacted as well, pulling daggers.

The cat had appeared by Bethral's head, a dead mouse in its jaws.

Gilla's heart leapt in her throat when the animal emerged from the grasses. She dropped the pitcher, pulled her dagger, and retreated, staying between the beast and the Elder. The animal gazed at her with watery yellow eyes, its mottled fur blending with the grasses. The mouse in its mouth was dead. Gilla could see tiny sharp fangs.

The blonde outlander waved her hands. 'It's all right. It's a cat. Just a cat. It came with us.'

The cat ignored them, stepping lightly to drop the mouse at Bethral's side.

'That is not a cat,' Seo exclaimed. 'It's so small, and yet . . .'

The green-eyed man asked something as he rose to his feet. The woman – Bethral of the Horse – answered him.

The animal . . . the cat . . . couldn't have cared less. It circled around and around, then curled by Bethral's side. A rough, rasping noise issued from the creature. It seemed rather pleased with itself.

Haya and Seo just stared at the animal.

'They are . . .' – Bethral used a word that Gilla hadn't heard before – 'pets. This one lived in the barn with my horse.' Bethral reached out and petted the animal as she spoke.

Gilla frowned. Those were words she didn't know. It sounded like the woman thought she owned her horse and the tiny creature. But that couldn't be right.

Haya and Seo slowly sat down, sheathing their weapons. Gilla followed their example, then retrieved her pitcher. She stood there, staring at the cat.

The cat's eyes were half-closed as it made the rumbling noise. But Gilla had an odd feeling that it was looking at her, as if—

'Child,' Seo snapped, 'don't gawk like a gurtle. Be about your duties.'

Gilla flushed, and hurried off.

But not without a backward glance at the strangers.

The tent was up now, and they'd been given a private section divided off from the larger part. They'd been left alone for the time being. Ezren had offered to see to Bessie, in order to give Bethral a bit of privacy while she removed her armor.

Bethral didn't know how to tell him that two male warriors had assisted her. She had yet to figure out how to explain the ways of the Plains when it came to the sexes. She was going to have to tell him, that was clear, because he would need to know everything he could for his journey back to Palins.

A journey she would not take.

She'd stripped down with the help of the lads and had eased the armor off her injured leg with care. The skin wasn't broken, but the bone was. She could feel it grate within. The pain seemed to throb with every breath she took. It was bearable if she lay flat – standing or walking was not going to be an option.

The warriors had left her after they'd seen to her needs. For now, she was clean and warm. The spicy scent of gurtle fur rose from the pallet and blankets. Bethral was reminded of the old blanket her mother had on her bed back home. She was as comfortable as she could be, given the circumstances.

Time to think it through.

If a rescue was coming, it would have been there by now. Evelyn had probably lost control of the portal. Bethral knew little of such things, but if Evelyn had been able, she would have opened another portal. So she and Ezren would have to deal with the situation at hand.

A situation that had been caused by one of the Plains. That black man, the one in the courtyard in Edenrich, the one with the ritual scarring. He was a warrior-priest, she was sure of that. He'd answered her when she'd greeted him in the language of the Plains, before Ezren Storyteller had lost control. And the magic's surge . . . Bethral closed her eyes, picturing the moment. She was certain that the magic had flared because of the warrior-priest. In recognition of the warrior-priest?

Fear coursed through Bethral. This was a harsh land, and its people lived by a rigid code. If the Storyteller lost control of the wild magic . . . if he attacked someone while holding a token . . . they would cut him down immediately.

Bethral swore silently. How to keep him safe?

She glanced at her saddlebags over in the corner. What she did have was packed in there. She'd planned for a night, maybe two, chasing bandits. There was nowhere near what she and the Storyteller would need in the way of supplies in those packs. And all the gold in the world would buy little on the Plains. These people bartered for goods and services. A gold piece was more like to impress the cat than a warrior of the Plains.

Bethral closed her eyes for a moment and cursed again. The idea that Ezren Storyteller, a man of swift intelligence and powerful ideas, would perish on the Plains, far from home and the people who needed him, made her sick to her stomach. There'd been nothing else she could have done – the wild magic had been about to destroy the castle and everyone in it. But now—

Actually, what made her sick wasn't that he wouldn't make the Plains his home. It was the idea that he'd be traveling without her. The idea of a journey at his side, sharing . . . whatever he was willing to share, for months . . . made her heart beat faster.

But the harsh reality of the Plains would forbid it, as would her common sense. She knew exactly what to expect.

So – they could trade armor, her weapons. The barding might not fit a horse of the Plains, but these people were scroungers. There'd be some use for it. If Bessie was to travel for long distances, she'd not need to bear the weight of the barding. Bessie would carry the Storyteller easily. Bethral would just have to find a way to get him an escort.

Bethral reached for her saddlebags, tugging them closer. The pain flared, and she clenched her jaw tight and breathed through the agony. She flipped open the first bag and started to rummage around, giving herself something else to think about.

Her spare tunic and trous, a few dishes. A small packet of bandages and some remedies that she'd learned to carry over the years. She set them aside for later.

A few candle stubs, flint, and tinder. A bundle of leather cords, always useful. Trail rations, dried meat, some grain for Bessie. A small bottle of molasses . . . Bethral thought all of it could be used to barter for what they'd need. She'd crammed more in these bags than she'd thought – some of it she'd forgotten about.

Then her hand brushed a leather bundle at the bottom, and she stilled.

She was fair certain she hadn't packed that.

Bethral wet her lips, and pulled the package out slowly. She wished she had some bells. Jingling them would keep anyone from entering this area of the tent. But Ezren Storyteller wouldn't know what they meant, and he was the one she didn't want to see this. She'd just have to listen for anyone coming close. This couldn't be what she thought it was—

She pulled back the leather, and then the ragged cloth within . . . and stared.

It was. It was the odd knife that Red Gloves had pulled from Ezren's chest that terrible day. They'd been ambushed, dragged into the swamp and sacrificed, one after the other, until Red had shown up and killed the blood mage and his men.

When Red Gloves had pulled the knife from Ezren's chest, the wild magic had been freed, saving all their lives . . . and cursing Ezren's.

She hadn't packed it. Why would she? She'd been bound to deal with bandits for a day, maybe two. She'd had this in her room, deep in a chest, with a vague plan of destroying it when she had time. Certainly never to let the Storyteller see it again, not if she could help it.

Bethral felt the hair on the back of her neck stir.

Her sword-sister Red Gloves had been the Chosen of prophecy, or so Josiah of Athelbryght had believed. Red had felt differently, yet in the end she'd fulfilled that prophecy and then some.

Bethral hadn't felt any particular calling other than the challenge of helping Red. There'd been no touch of destiny on her shoulders, and she preferred it that way.

But Ezren Silvertongue . . .

The chill moved down her arms, as if seeking the stone blade. She quickly twisted the cloth and the leather around the knife, careful not to touch the blade. She shoved it back into the deepest part of the saddlebag.

Bethral stuffed the bag between her and the tent wall, where none could get to it without her knowing. Then she settled back and pulled the warm blanket up to her neck.

Her mother had always said that the dead followed the living until the longest night of winter, when they went beyond, to the very stars. Bethral settled deeper into her pallet with a sigh. She'd follow the Storyteller for as long as it took to see to his safe return.

Weariness washed over her, and she let her eyes drift closed.

She'd go to the snows, but the stars would have to wait.

Ezren shouldered aside the flap of their portion of the tent, his arms full of rolled horse barding. Gilla was just behind him, her arms filled as well. They'd been surrounded by curious young warriors as they removed the armor from Bessie, who had promptly rolled in the grass, to the enjoyment of the young ones. Ezren had been afraid that the horse would wander off without a fence or hobbles, but Bessie had started grazing near the tent and showed no signs of leaving.

The tent was amazing, huge and sectioned off with walls. He'd never heard of such a thing, but then he'd never seen anything like this place.

The young warriors had been of both sexes and many different skin and hair colors. All were armed to the teeth and bore tattoos on both arms. Ezren had used the time to try to learn names and some words. He'd have to ask Bethral about the names, because they seemed to differ depending on who was asking. Some gave their name, some their name and tribes. There had to be a reason – he'd have to ask Bethral . . .

When she woke.

She was lying on the pallet, covered with a blanket, her long hair spread out around her head. The lines of pain were smoothed away, leaving her lovely face peaceful and serene. The skin of her neck and shoulders looked so soft . . . Lord of Light – she was naked under that blanket.

Gilla jostled him from behind, her load of armor poking him in the back. Ezren stepped aside, and she darted around him, glancing at Bethral and then at Ezren's face. She gave him a shy smile, then quietly placed her armload against the tent wall.

Ezren added his pile to hers as Gilla slipped out. He knew she'd be back – there was another armload of the barding outside.

He hated to have to do it, but they couldn't wait much longer. 'Lady Bethral,' he called, his voice rasping in his throat.

Her eyes snapped open and she looked around, almost as if she expected trouble. 'Storyteller?'

'I need you to ask Gilla for some things, Lady,' Ezren said softly. 'We need to set your leg.'

She stared at him for a moment, then frowned. 'Unless you have some skills—'

'I do not,' Ezren said. 'But I know that the leg needs to be kept straight. If nothing else, it might ease some of the pain.' He looked over at the saddlebags. 'Do you have anything for pain?'

'I'm not sure that I should take anything,' Bethral said.

Ezren stared at her. 'We have been offered the shelter of their tents?'

'For now. But it's still just a respite, Storyteller. If Evelyn had been able to find us, she'd have opened another portal by now. We're on our own.'

Ezren pulled the saddlebags closer.

Bethral struggled up on her elbow, reaching for the bag. 'I'll get it.' The blanket slipped from her shoulders, and Ezren forced himself to look away as it slid down to reveal the creamy skin of her breast.

'Sorry,' Bethral said. 'They're not much for bedclothes.'

'That has been made clear.' Ezren kept his eyes down. 'Some of the young warriors were cavorting by the stream when I watered Bessie. They have different ideas about modesty here.'

'And sex,' Bethral said, retrieving a small wooden box from a saddlebag. 'You need to understand that—'

A polite cough, and Gilla entered, her arms full of barding. She gave them both a curious look but said nothing as she set down her bundle.

35

'Ask her for two stout sticks – and strips of cloth,' Ezren said. 'As you say, there is little hope of rescue, so we will do what we can with what we have.'

Bethral spoke to Gilla, who replied quickly and then disappeared.

'We will talk,' Ezren said firmly. 'For now, let me give you a dose of something for pain and see what we can do about that leg. Time enough for stories on the morrow.'

'It's important that you understand their ways,' Bethral said, pushing the saddlebags back behind her. 'I don't want you wearing a weapon.'

'Why not?' Ezren frowned. 'Everyone else is.' And he meant everyone. Even the younger children were armed with daggers and swords. 'I was taught basic skills. I admit I am not a soldier, but I can handle a blade. Not with your level of skill, admit—'

'You need to stand out. To look different because you are different,' Bethral said. 'Just – please trust me on this. These people are dangerous.'

'Dangerous?' He looked around. 'How so?'

Bethral's hand came out from under the blanket and wrapped around his ankle. 'This is a thea camp – a nursery. They brought the tent to us – they didn't take us into the camp. When you went out to Bessie, even then I was being guarded. Yes, they have offered us hospitality, but if we were to be seen as a threat, they would not hesitate to kill us.'

Gilla coughed, then entered, carrying two wooden swords that were splintered on the edges and a bundle of rags. Haya followed behind, her bright eyes taking it all in.

Ezren carefully folded back the blanket to reveal Bethral's lower leg. The toes were at an odd angle, just slightly off. The skin was unbroken, and he thanked the Lord of Light silently for such favors.

Bethral had removed a small bottle from the box and taken a sip. She fumbled as she tried to stopper the bottle, and Ezren reached over to aid her. Her fingers felt cold, and she gave him a startled glance at his touch.

'Tell Haya that you are cold,' Ezren said as he put the box back in one of the saddlebags. 'We need to make sure you stay warm.'

Bethral took a breath and then nodded, starting to talk. Ezren settled back on his heels and sorted through the strips of cloth. He watched Bethral's face as Haya spoke. At one point, a faint blush traced over her cheeks as Haya questioned her. Bethral glanced at Ezren, then away, as she responded. 'She's sent for a brazier and more blankets,' Bethral said. 'She wants to watch you heal me.'

There was something more there, but now was not the time to press the issue. 'You had better explain—'

'I have.' Bethral's eyelids fluttered. 'But she wants to watch anyway.' She forced her eyes open. 'There will be a gathering here later – the evening meal. She invites us both, but understands that I can't attend.'

'That will be fine,' Ezren said. 'And I will be careful. But first . . .'

'Yes.' Bethral nodded. 'I'm ready.'

'I am not,' Ezren said. 'I would feel infinitely better if I knew what I was doing. But—'

He gripped her ankle, pulled and twisted, trying to line up the toes with her knee.

One gasp escaped Bethral, then she clenched her jaw and pressed her lips tight. Ezren set his own teeth and kept trying, pulling and easing the foot to what looked like the proper position. He moved fast once he had it in place, using the cloth strips to bind the swords to her lower leg while trying to keep the foot still.

Bethral was pale when he finished, and Ezren felt fairly shaky himself, but the limb seemed straighter. 'Any better?' he asked.

Bethral gave him a soft, fuzzy smile. 'There's less pain.'

Ezren wasn't certain if that was the drugs or the bindings, but he was glad for any improvement. He reached for some of the pillows and used them to brace Bethral all around, so she wouldn't shift in the night. 'Sleep, Lady.'

Bethral yawned as he tucked the blanket all around her.

Haya said something quietly, and two warriors entered with a brazier of coals and extra blankets. Ezren stayed next to Bethral as they created a second pallet and set the brazier between the two. The room warmed immediately.

Ezren looked down into Bethral's face. She had cried out only the once, although he had to have hurt her. Such a lovely, brave woman. She'd been hurt because of him. Because of his failure to deal with—

A hand settled on his shoulder. Haya looked at him, compassion in her eyes. She gestured for him to come with her as Gilla held open the tent flap.

His regrets would have to wait. With one more look at Bethral, Ezren rose, and followed Haya.

FIVE

Haya had already made her decision as to how she would treat this stranger from the sky. She placed the city-dwelling Singer on a stool next to hers. Seo raised an eyebrow as he settled on his stool, set on her other side. 'You honor him?'

Warriors were coming into the tent now, so Haya kept her voice low. 'What harm? I am told he is a Singer, and I offer him honor. If he is not, then he will have offended me and I have reason to kill him. Either way . . .' She shrugged.

'Yet your token is not displayed.'

Haya looked at Seo out of the corner of her eye. 'Well . . . there is honor, and there is honor.'

Seo snorted. 'Good to know that you have not lost all your wits. Even if you invited all but the gurtles to see your guest.'

'Warriors only, and the children we might release to the armies soon.' Haya gestured to a server for kavage. 'Their curiosity is close to killing them. If I didn't, they'd be finding reasons to visit this tent for days.'

'True,' Seo said in agreement. 'Besides, the young need to see that city dwellers are people much like us. All knowledge is good.'

Haya accepted kavage, and they talked of trivial matters, surrounded as they were by warriors and young ones. The tent was crammed for the meal and people came and went, rotating their duties so to see the city dweller from the sky.

The Singer . . . Ezren . . . seemed to understand that he was on display, and it did not faze him. But he was watching every-one around him. Those green eyes followed every move when the servers began to work their way through the crowd with pitchers and bowls of water for the hand-washing ritual. Ezren focused on her as Haya was offered water for her hands – and he copied her movements. There was sharp thinking behind that smile. She'd heard that city dwellers ate with metal, but again he watched her using her fingers and the flat bread to eat, and he didn't hesitate to do the same.

He'd no fear of the unknown. He sat smiling, drinking kavage, and trying different foods. Those nearby delighted in his responses and at one point roared with laughter when he tried some of the spiced meat. The burn caught him by surprise, but after a gulp of kavage, he took more and really seemed to enjoy it.

Nor was he stupid. He was asking what things were called and people's names, and picking up a fair number of them quickly. He was learning their language. She'd have to keep that in mind.

She noted other things as well. There wasn't a lot of fat on this one. In her days in the raiding armies, she'd seen many a city dweller fleeing her blade. This one was thin, and there was scarring at his wrists. Deep scarring that meant he'd been restrained for some time and struggled against that restraint.

At one point he rose, gave Haya and Seo a bow, and stepped through the crowd. Haya expected him to leave the tent, but instead he went to check on the woman. He just stuck his head in, and then returned to his place, apparently satisfied. He cared for her, that was clear. As to what he was to her, or she to him, well, that could wait.

The meal wound down, as the warriors took their leave and the room cleared. Seo stood, and that was the signal to the last of them that the meal was over. The young would clean and clear.

Ezren stood and stretched as well, then bowed to Haya and Seo. 'My thanks, Elders.'

'Our thanks as well, Singer.' Haya responded. Seo gave the man a nod, and Gilla led him off. The young one would see to his needs.

Seo yawned. 'Time to seek my bed.'

'Share mine,' Haya offered.

'Share or talk?'

Haya smiled. 'Share then talk.'

Seo smiled and reached for her hand.

Gilla and her friends got the cleaning duties. Again. She sighed as she scrubbed a pot with clean sand, up to her elbows in hot water.

'You truly saw them fall out of the sky?' Cosana paused in her drying to stare, her large brown eyes wide in her heart-shaped face.

Gilla nodded, rubbing the pot with the tips of her fingers, looking for any burnt food.

'That must have been something to see,' El mused as he scrubbed another mug. Gilla wasn't sure which was worse: scrubbing cooking pots or mugs. The pots were hard, but there were so many mugs. When she was a warrior, there'd be none of this for her.

'I don't believe it,' Arbon muttered, shaking his black-blue curls at her. He was drying mugs and placing them in their storage baskets.

Gilla dropped her pot back into the water and reached for her dagger, baring her teeth at him.

'Stop,' Chell said calmly, stepping between them. The tall, thin black girl gave them both a commanding look with her dark eyes, made even more powerful by her short clipped hair. 'Arbon, you are an idiot. Do you hold her token?'

Arbon glared at both of them from under his curls. 'She's no right to take offense. We're still children.'

'By a day or maybe two.' Chell started to stack the clean, dry cooking utensils. 'But once we are released, you'll be fighting every hour unless you watch your mouth. Think before you speak.' The tall black girl looked at Gilla. 'And you don't need to be so quick. It is hard to believe.'

Chell was always the sensible one. Gilla released her dagger and returned to her pot. 'There is truth in that. But it is what happened, and I wasn't the only one who saw. Urte saw as well.'

'Tell us again,' Lander demanded as he added hot water to the washing. 'Tell every detail. It's something to sing about.'

Gilla looked at Cosana, and they both rolled their eyes and smiled at each other. The others did the same, used to Lander's ways. The big blond had always wanted to be a Singer from the day he'd learned his first chant, and he always wanted to know what had happened.

Ouse came up with kettles of hot water in each hand. He smiled at Gilla, his red hair and freckled cheeks made even redder by the setting sun. His brown eyes crinkled as he spoke. 'Tell him, Gilla, or he will pester you to death.'

'A death to sing about,' Tenna spoke up from the other side of the fire.

That made them all laugh, as Tenna always did. She looked so sweet, with her angled eyes and straight black hair trimmed with bangs, but she had a wicked sense of humor.

Gilla obliged, telling it again, telling Lander all the details.

'He looks so normal,' Cosana commented. 'I'd thought city dwellers short and fat.'

'They're supposed to stink, too,' Tenna said. 'But the War-prize didn't, did she Gilla?'

'Gilla has all the adventures,' Lander complained.

'I only saw her for a moment,' Gilla said. 'And only long enough to point her in the direction of the Heart. But come to think of it, she wasn't very tall, either.'

'Maybe only a few are short and fat.' Arbon stood, towering over Gilla.

'I doubt the woman is short,' Chell said. 'She looks long on her pallet.'

'That horse is huge,' Ouse said.

Gilla frowned as she scrubbed at a stubborn spot. 'Yes, and then there is the cat.'

'Cat?' they chorused.

She rolled her eyes and explained. 'The last I saw, it was sleeping next to Bethral.'

'You get to see everything,' Lander complained.

'Is this the last of them?' El straightened and handed the last mug to Cosana. 'Please tell me this is the last of them.' He focused his smiling brown eyes on Gilla.

A chorus of 'ayes,' and they all set to work to finish the cleaning and clearing. Once they were done, they were free to seek their tents.

'Share mine?' El asked Gilla as they walked toward their tiny tents.

'No, thank you,' Gilla said, evading his hand.

El shrugged, and turned to another.

Gilla walked off alone, pleased. Once her duty to the tribe had been fulfilled, she'd earned the right to her own small tent. She enjoyed the solitude and the quiet.

She crawled in and started to prepare for sleep. Alone. The others thought her odd, not sharing, but she didn't care. She'd done her duty to the Tribe and now she was free to decline as she willed.

At first, she'd been excited about sharing, learning the ways of pleasure between partners. But after that it seemed to her to lose some of its allure.

The Singers sang of the special joys of bonding, of the love between two people who committed to each other, and each other alone. That was what she wanted – a commitment from a partner she respected. Someone who wanted to walk by her side for the rest of her days.

She sighed as she settled on her pallet and pulled the blankets up. Bonding was only for those who had done service in the armies of the warlords. And truth be told, she hadn't met anyone who she was interested in bonding with. It would take time – maybe even years.

She was certain it was worth waiting for, so wait she would. Who knew what the winds would bring? The others had their plans, but she was content to wait and see.

She closed her eyes, and tried to sleep, but a pair of green eyes flashed in her mind. That Singer was good-looking. Old, but he had a nice smile. Were the city dwellers bonded? She doubted it, given that Bethral had asked for separate pallets. Of course, she was hurt, but still . . .

Gilla huffed at her own silliness and turned over on her side. She closed her eyes, determined to sleep. There'd be answers in the morning, and maybe, just maybe, they'd be made adults on the morrow. Gilla shivered in excitement. To leave the thea camp and go out in the world. To be able to challenge and—

Winds, she'd never get to sleep at this rate.

Seo pulled Haya in close as the night air cooled their overheated bodies. He nuzzled her neck, licking the soft skin by her ear.

Haya hummed her appreciation, then fixed him with her bright eyes. 'We need to talk.'

Seo groaned. 'You've worn out my body, my lovely one.'

'I need your mind.' She arranged herself in his arms. 'And the privacy of the night.'

Seo gave her a sharp glance. 'You'd not bothered with my mind before you offered the shelter of your tent to the strangers. Why ask now?'

Haya stroked his cheek. 'Because I still have decisions to make, wise one. I know how you feel about Keir of the Cat and the changes he would bring.'

'Young colt.' Seo frowned. 'He's full of fire, ready to sweep all the Plains with his changes. Now this division within the Council of Elders, Elder fighting Elder, Warrior-Priest fighting Warrior-Priest. What good comes of his changes, eh?'

Haya reached over and smoothed the lines of his forehead. 'Yet, you stared at the strangers's horse until I thought you'd forgotten to breathe.'

'It is lovely,' Seo agreed. 'So big! I wonder what its young would be like, bred into our herds. And that cat – small and fierce.'

'I do not know what to make of this. I'd already sent for the warrior-priests who would conduct the rites for the children. But this matter,' – Haya sighed – 'it raises concerns for more than just the Tribe of the Snake.'

'It does,' Seo agreed. 'So?'

'If the Council had not been sundered, I would send for the Eldest Elders of the Plains,' Haya said. 'All of them, including Wild Winds. They could make decisions about the strangers.'

'Hmmm.' Seo paused. 'Eldest Thea Reness went with the Warprize to Xy. Eldest Singer Essa is somewhere close to the Heart, he always is. There is no Eldest of the Warriors, not since the sundering. And the Eldest of the Warrior-Priests . . . To summon Wild Winds? Is that wise?'

'I don't know from wise,' Haya replied. 'But I'd have this information open to the skies. No sense trying to hide it – the tale is probably already on the wind.' Haya shivered a bit, as her skin cooled. 'Besides, I want to know more about Keir and his actions. I must decide where to send the young soon. Do I send them to the Heart of the Plains, for the spring contests, as if nothing had happened? Do I send them to serve under Osa of the Fox, and avoid all conflict? Or do I send them to Keir or Antas directly, and choose a side?'

'You could split them up, sending some to both,' Seo said.

'Which is like riding two horses at once.' Haya growled. 'I do not see my way clear in this. I would have preferred to talk to Reness. She was ever the sensible one.'

'As the Elder Thea of this camp, it is your choice. None can overrule your decision,' Seo said absently, his thoughts wandering.

'What is it?' Haya asked.

'I . . .' Seo's voice trailed off for a moment as he considered. Haya watched him, waiting.

'Perhaps it is nothing, but I am uneasy.' Seo frowned. 'Maybe it is just this talk of change, but . . . I would move the main camp.'

Haya's eyebrows rose. 'How so?'

'It is a feeling. If I leave you here with the strangers, a handful of warriors and the young, I could move the life-bearers, the babies, and the others off a few miles. Not to separate, but to' – he hesitated – 'to keep the littlest ones safe.'

Haya put her hand on his cheek. 'Your instincts have always been good, warrior.'

Seo kissed her, then pulled the blankets up over their bodies. 'Let us sleep on the matter, since that is all the wit I have left to do.'

'I'll hold off on any decisions for a while. There's time.' Haya decided. 'After the Rites.'

'The young ones may explode with not knowing.' Seo yawned. 'Call a senel and speak with the warriors. Consider the truths of all, then make your decision.'

Haya nodded. 'In the meantime, the Singer of the City and his token-bearer will be my guest. We will see if they can learn our ways.'

'They will learn, or they will perish. So it has always been,' Seo growled. 'Now sleep.'

Haya huffed out a breath, but she closed her eyes, content.

SIX

'Five children?' Ezren sputtered. 'Each?'

'That's what those tattoos on their left arm mean. That's how they keep track of their duty to the tribe,' Bethral said calmly. She *had* shocked him, but he had to know the ways of these people if he was to survive.

She watched him consider her words. Once she saw that he was really listening to her, she continued. 'Once they have met their obligation, only then are they acknowledged as adults and released for service in the armies of the warlords.'

'But that's—'

'No, Storyteller.' Bethral raised a finger to make a point. 'Assume they are right and you are wrong.'

Ezren frowned but said nothing, waiting for her to continue.

They'd been served their breakfast and their needs had been seen to at dawn. The warriors had rolled up the outer wall of their sleeping area to let in air and sun, and so they had a view of the activity of the area around them.

Bethral sat on her pallet, braced by her saddle, her legs stretched out before her. Once the warriors had left them, Ezren had fussed, using pillows to support her legs and back. He'd checked the splint he'd rigged. Her leg had swollen during the night, and he loosened the ties before settling next to her.

The cat had wandered in and claimed a patch of sunlight by Bethral's feet.

Everyone in the camp was working at something, coming and going. Bethral had pulled her sharpening stone out, and started working the edges of her blades, laying her sword and two daggers next to her.

The fact that her weapons were ready if needed was also a practical benefit.

She drew in a breath, considering what next to say. He had to understand, and she'd repeat herself until he did. 'This is a harsh land, and the people of the Plains live hard lives. But they live them, which means that their way of life allows them to survive. It is not our way, that is true. You must respect it or—'

'Die.' Ezren was sitting cross-legged on the ground next to Bethral, the breeze playing with his hair. It was getting longer, starting to curl softly at the back of his neck. Bethral looked back at her blade and started to work it again.

'Still . . . that they bear so many, then ride off, leaving the babes behind . . .'

'They are a warrior culture. They raid the lands that surround the Plains and take what they need,' Bethral explained. 'Those armies are their supply lines. The young need to provide warriors to replace those that are killed.'

She continued to run her stone down the length of the blade. The Storyteller sat silent, looking out over the grasses, thinking, taking it all in.

'Very well,' Ezren said. 'They have different attitudes toward sex, child rearing, and marriage. They do not marry – bond – until they have earned a reputation for military service. Everyone is free to sleep with everyone not of the same Tribe, regardless of gender.'

'Yes. Do not be shocked if you see men kissing men.'

'That's not so shocking. It is not common in Palins, but not an issue except for the noble houses, where the bloodlines must be preserved.' Ezren drummed his fingers on his leg. 'I wish I had paper, to write this all down.'

'No written language, so—'

'No paper.' Ezren flashed Bethral a smile. 'And they have perfect memories. They remember what is said, all of them?' Ezren ran his fingers through his hair.

'Mother said those of the Plains never forget.' Bethral smiled. 'It made it hard for us kids sometimes.'

48

'I would hear that story someday, Lady.' Ezren's green eyes focused on her face.

Bethral held her sword up and ran a finger along the edge, looking for nicks. 'Someday, Storyteller. But for now—' She arched an eyebrow in his direction.

Ezren nodded. 'They also take offense easily unless there is a token involved. And those fights can lead to death, but no one thinks twice or will interfere.'

'Always ask for a token if you think your words will give offense,' Bethral said. 'Attacking one who holds your token is a terrible violation of their ways, and they will kill you for it.'

'And a token can be anything except a weapon, but the higher a warrior's status, the more important or impressive a token is.'

'We need to get you one.' Bethral thought about that for a minute. 'Maybe one of the gold coins in my saddlebags.'

'You said they don't use money.'

'They don't. A gold coin is shiny and unusual. So it would work as a token.' Bethral pulled her saddlebag over and started rummaging.

'Fine.' Ezren accepted one of the coins and tucked it into his sleeve. 'So. Perfect memories, five children, quick to avenge an insult with weapons . . . is there anything else I need to know?'

Bethral suppressed a smile. 'Yes. But that is a good start.'

His green eyes flashed at her, as if he sensed her mirth, but then they went wide with what could only be horror. 'They won't expect us to have children – will they?'

A chill ran right down his spine. Lord of Light, would they expect him to . . . breed? He would not—

'No.' Bethral gave him an odd look. 'They will not. They understand that we are from a different land with different ways.' She hesitated, then looked away. 'You can expect invitations to share, Storyteller. You are . . . exotic.'

To them. Not to her. Ezren shook his head deliberately. 'Let us not complicate this situation any more than it already is. How do I say "no" without offending?'

'Just say "no",' Bethral said softly. 'There will be no pressure. Disappointment, though.'

'I can deal with disapp—' Ezren cut off his words as a shadow fell over him. He looked up and saw Haya standing before them. And now he saw her with new eyes.

Haya was a thea, one who raised the children of the Tribe. As Elder Thea her word was law in this camp . . . even Seo, as Elder Warrior, acknowledged her authority. She ruled the camp as surely as Gloriana sat on the Throne of Palins.

Gloriana didn't yet have this confidence or this air of power. Haya wore her armor and weapons with ease, and he could see that they were of the best quality. Her white hair and weathered face spoke of years of experience. Odd to think of a nursemaid wearing a sword.

Ezren stood, and bowed his head to her. He spoke slowly, careful of each word. 'Good morning, Elder Thea Haya.'

She studied him, then gave him a slow smile. 'Good morning, Ezren Storyteller, Singer of the City.' She raised an eyebrow. 'You learn fast, Singer.'

'My thanks, Elder,' Ezren said.

Haya settled down on the grass, facing both of them, and said something to Bethral fairly quickly. Ezren had a feeling that she was complimenting him, but then he caught the word 'token.'

Bethral had set aside her weapons when Haya arrived. She stiffened slightly at Haya's words, but reached within her saddlebag and drew forth a braid of gray horsehair and ribbon.

Ezren narrowed his eyes but said nothing. He knew that bit of hair. Bethral had cut it from the mane of her dead horse, Steel, a large gray gelding that had died trying to protect her during the ambush by the bog. He swallowed hard at the memory of her grief at the horse's death.

She handed it to Haya.

Haya took it and placed it on her knee. They began to talk rapidly. He couldn't follow the conversation, but once in a while he caught a word that he knew. Nothing out of the ordinary, except that they seemed to refer to the weather quite often.

Ezren also knew enough courtesy to stay silent. He kept his eyes on the two women, watching their eyes, their hands, trying to interpret their discussion. There was tension between them, but more on Bethral's part than on Haya's.

Haya leaned back, and sighed. She picked up the token and held it out to Bethral, saying something that sounded like a rote piece.

Bethral waited until Haya stopped speaking, then took the token and responded in turn. He would have to ask about that once Haya left. There was more to the token than just the exchange.

Haya stood, brushing off her trous. She gave Ezren a deliberate nod, then walked off without another look.

Bethral was playing with her token, running it through her fingers.

'Is it going to snow?' Ezren demanded. 'Or did I misunderstand that word?'

Bethral didn't look up. She just tucked the token back in the saddlebag. 'We need supplies, Storyteller. Need to earn our keep, in the eyes of the Tribe.'

'We can trade.' Ezren gestured toward the horse barding and Bethral's armor. 'Much though I hate to do it, we can—'

Now she looked him in the eye. 'It will not be enough. You must tell your stories, Silvertongue.'

Bethral hated to push Ezren, hated that she'd put that look in his eyes, but it had to be done. A singer had value, and to have the Singer of the City sing in this camp would bring them what they needed.

She knew what she asked of him. She'd held his broken body in her arms — she'd been the first to discover that his captors had cut out his tongue. He'd been broken physically, and he bore the scars to prove it. Evelyn had explained that his voice had suffered as well.

But not his spirit or his mind. Ezren Silvertongue, with the help of the healing magic of the Gods, had recovered faster than she'd ever thought possible. And his mind – that quicksilver mind – had aided the Chosen even before his body had recovered. Still, he'd refused to tell stories in Edenrich; he'd written them out instead.

Haya had made it clear that they had a few days at most. Bethral had no choice. Ezren Silvertongue had to return to Palins, to aid the young Queen, and she had to make sure that he was well on his way before she took her own path.

He'd frozen up, his hands clenched in fists.

'The young are being released soon.' Bethral picked up her stone. 'It's normal to grant them adulthood, then celebrate for a few days to let them work off their energy before sending them to serve.' Bethral ran the stone over the blade again. 'Now would be an ideal time to announce a story. You honor them in your timing – and the warriors will honor you with gifts in exchange for the stories. Practical gifts that will give us the supplies we need. We need to prove your value to the—'

'Our value,' Ezren said through his locked jaw.

Bethral stayed silent for a moment. She set the stone aside and reached for her polishing cloth. She worked it over the blade once, watching Ezren in its reflection. 'A wounded warrior has little to no value. There is no shame in this – but right now my only value is to interpret your words. If we get supplies and horses – you can leave.'

'You need time to heal. You can't ride until the bone is set.'

Ah, he was so brave and so stubborn. 'You forget one thing.'

'What?'

'We must get you out of here as soon as possible.'

'Why?'

Bethral looked up and met his glare. 'To protect them from you.'

SEVEN

Now those green eyes cut right through her, bright and angry. Bethral returned the look calmly, not looking away, waiting.

It didn't take long before understanding flooded into his eyes. 'The wild magic.'

'It may not be with you now, Storyteller, but we can't pretend it's not there. If – when – you lose control again, we need to be as far away from these people as possible. For if you explode in the sight of these tents, they will not hesitate to kill you.'

His head was down, his eyes hidden. Bethral drove home the point. 'And who knows how many you might kill in the process?'

He sat, still and silent. Bethral finished the polishing and sheathed her sword. 'You need to tell stories,' she repeated. 'Soon.'

'I cannot—' Ezren stopped at the sound of footsteps.

Gilla was standing before them, looking very nervous, and a tall, handsome blond boy was next to her. When they saw that she had Bethral's attention, both of them knelt in the grass before her.

'Bethral of the Horse, Token-Bearer, we would ask you to give our words to Ezren Storyteller, the Singer of the City.'

Bethral was nodding to the children before Ezren could say a word. They rose to their feet, then knelt again, this time facing Ezren.

'I don't know what they want, but that is not necessary.' Ezren shifted, uncomfortable with this recognition.

'It is necessary,' Bethral said softly. 'The young are required to have absolute obedience and respect for their elders. They are being careful, because they do not know our ways. They wish to ask a favor of you.'

'Very well, then.' Ezren gestured to them. 'I will listen.'

Bethral spoke, then listened as Gilla talked for a moment, never raising her eyes.

'The boy is Lander of the Snake,' Bethral explained. 'Lander wishes to learn our language, and that of any other land you know. He plans to be a singer, and he wants to learn of other lands. He asks that he be allowed to serve you when his duties permit, and offers to help you learn their language in exchange.' Bethral stopped, and asked a sharp question. Both Gilla and Lander responded.

'They have asked Haya's permission in this, and she has consented.'

'He can't think me much of a singer, not with this voice.' Ezren spat out his words, conscious of the bitterness rising in the back of his throat.

'This is the only voice I have ever heard you speak with,' Bethral replied. 'And it's the only voice they know.' She paused. 'None of us has anything to compare it to, Storyteller.'

Ezren stared down at his hands, the scars barely covered by his sleeve. He'd never thought of it like that. She'd seen him only as a crippled slave, his tongue cut out, unable even to control his bowels. Yet, there was a look of something else in her eyes. Dare he think it admiration?

'What shall I tell them, Storyteller?' Bethral said. 'I warn you, Lander may follow you around like a lost puppy.'

Ezren looked at the two kneeling before him, their heads bowed. So young to be so intent, so serious. Had he looked like that to old Joseph Taleteller? 'Yes,' he heard himself say, not really aware that he had changed his mind. 'Tell him I am honored.'

Bethral spoke, and both Gilla and Lander jerked their heads up with wide smiles.

Ezren drew a breath and spoke fast, before his brain could catch up with his mouth. 'And ask him to take a message to Haya for me. I will tell a story tonight.' He couldn't believe what he was doing. The sick in the pit of his stomach grew. 'Tell him to spread the word, then come back here, and we will start to teach each other.'

Gilla and Lander jumped up, their faces filled with delight as Bethral spoke. They raced off before Ezren could reconsider, calling back what had to be their thanks.

'Bravely done, Storyteller.' Bethral lifted her eyes to his. Dare he think there was a hint of admiration there?

More likely she was proud that her 'stray' had grown a backbone. That was what Red Gloves had called him back in the barn when . . . He ran his fingers through his hair and tried to think of other things. 'And what do all those references to snow mean?'

He had caught her off guard, and an embarrassed flush rose on Bethral's cheeks. 'To go to the snows means to die.'

Ezren grunted, then stood, brushing off his trous. 'I thought so. I would remind you, Lady, that I am city born and bred. I need a guide to return to Palins. Alone, I would wander these grasses until I died.'

Bethral's gaze dropped to the dagger in her lap.

Ezren looked at her golden head, and hated himself. It was his fault she was here, injured, forced to sacrifice herself for his worthless hide. Something clenched in his chest at the idea, but he forced it down. Not now . . . not here . . . he'd not fail her again.

'So.' His voice was rougher than normal. 'I am going to go find more kavage. Then you had best help me pick an appropriate tale to tell, Lady. For I doubt very much these people will comprehend Romando and Julianna.'

Ezren strode off, ignoring Bethral's snort of laughter behind him.

And trying to ignore the churning in his stomach.

To Bethral's delight, Haya's tent wasn't big enough.

The young warriors helped Bethral shift to the wooden

55

platform, braced by a mound of pillows. A stool had been placed for the Storyteller, who sat as if facing a tent crammed full of Plains warriors was an everyday event.

They were rolling up the tent walls now, allowing even more people to crowd in, yet still breathe.

Bethral had to admit that she had butterflies in her stomach, since her job was to translate Ezren's words for the crowd. She wished she could figure out a way to stand that would allow her to make sure she was heard, but she wouldn't be able to last through an entire tale. The pain was bad enough just being shifted to this part of the tent.

Ezren Storyteller seemed calm with Lander kneeling on the other side, ready to provide whatever he needed. Those two had been together all afternoon, pacing around the camp. The Story-teller had claimed he thought better on his feet, but Bethral was sure he'd been working off his nerves.

He wasn't the only one with nerves. Status was important to these people, and Ezren's performance as a singer was the turning point. Ezren had decided on a story to tell, but had refused to share the information. He had, however, promised to talk slowly, to allow her to translate as he spoke. Bethral wasn't sure that would work for the telling of a tale, but they'd make do with what they had.

Ezren stood, and waited as everyone sat and grew quiet. He looked around the tent, gathered their attention, and then bowed his head to Haya and Seo, who were seated before him.

They returned the nod, clearly pleased at his civility.

He raised his hand, palm up, as if holding out an invisible gift. To Bethral's shock, he spoke in the language of the Plains. 'May the skies hear my voice. May the people remember.'

There was a stir all around him, then a response rose from all those present. 'We will remember.'

Bethral caught the pleased look Ezren and Lander exchanged before Ezren turned his bright green eyes on her, to see if she was ready. Apparently those two had already started their lessons.

'Hear now a tale of the Lady High Priestess Evelyn, a woman

56

of great power and highest virtue, and Orrin Blackhart, Scourge of Palins, a warrior with a dark and terrible burden. Two people, different as night and day, who came together to fight the monsters that threatened their land.'

Bethral stared at Ezren, wondering if he had lost his mind. That story?

Ezren raised his eyebrows.

Bethral translated, speaking as loudly as she could. There was an odd murmur from the crowd, and she realized that they were repeating her words for those on the outer edges of the group. She relaxed then, and concentrated on Ezren and finding the right words. This wasn't the tale to tell, to her way of thinking.

She need not have worried. Ezren held them spellbound. He didn't seem to act out the story, but he used his body language and facial expressions, changing his voice just enough that the characters seemed to come alive. He even seemed to become one of the monsters, his face slack and expressionless as he described the gray rotting flesh falling off their bones.

It wasn't perfect. Bethral felt that her translation drew attention away from where it should be, on the Storyteller. A few times she had to remember not to get caught up in the story itself.

They didn't care. The audience sat quiet, reacting in just the right places, as they listened to the story. They were wide-eyed as he spoke of Evelyn's kidnapping and Orrin's pending execution. No one breathed as the Storyteller told the tale of magic wisely used, and magic abused horribly. Bethral saw some tears at the final wedding ceremony, when Evelyn's and Orrin's hearts were joined in marriage. Some ideas were universal, it seemed.

At the very end, in the silence after his last words, Ezren lifted his palm again, and spoke again in their language. 'May the people remember.'

Again the response came. 'We will remember.' Then the tent shook as they cheered, with joyous cries of 'Heyla!'

Haya called out her praise as well, then continued, 'My thanks, Ezren Storyteller. You honor us.'

Ezren sat on the stool, and bowed his head to her. His

breathing was even, but Bethral could see a sheen of sweat on his forehead. His face was serene, yet he seemed both pleased and strangely surprised at his success.

Lander brought kavage as the tent slowly emptied, the warriors talking in low voices about what they had heard.

'Well done, Storyteller,' Bethral said.

Ezren glanced at her over his mug. 'Are you sure? No one gave us—'

Bethral pointed with her chin to the far wall of the tent, where a pile of items had been left.

'Ah,' Ezren said, satisfaction in his voice.

The sides of the tent were being rolled down, and the tent secured for the night. Haya rose with a smile. 'I'll have Gilla and Lander place these items by your pallets, and you can go through them as you will. I think you will find that my people have done well by you, Ezren Silvertongue.'

Ezren nodded as Bethral translated for him. 'Your people have given me a gift as well, Haya. I will tell another, if they will listen.'

Haya laughed. 'Oh, they will listen. And I will pledge a saddle and tack to you, for the honor you have done to me this night.'

'Why not a horse?' Ezren complained in his own language. 'If she wants to honor me, why not give me a horse? Why just saddle and tack?'

Bethral shot him a puzzled look, then laughed quietly as Lander and a red-haired lad helped her settle onto her pallet. 'Storyteller, the Plains are filled with horses. No one owns the horses. They just are.'

'But, if you don't own a horse, how do you get one?'

'You call one to you,' Bethral explained. 'If you can't do that, you don't survive long on the Plains.' She caught her breath as she shifted her hip.

'I'd best see to that leg,' Ezren said. He switched to the language of the Plains. 'Lander, what is the name of your friend?'

'Ouse,' Lander answered. 'His name is Ouse, Storyteller.'

'All right, the two of you are going to help us.' Ezren knelt next to Bethral.

The young warriors looked confused, but they knelt as well. Ezren clenched his jaw when he saw Bethral shake her head. 'I don't see why you are bothering to—'

'I told a story, didn't I?' he demanded, reaching out to loosen the bindings on her leg.

'Yes,' Bethral said. 'Yes, you did.' There was resignation in her voice.

'Then you can put up with my attempts at healing.' Ezren gestured for Ouse to sit at Bethral's shoulders and for Landers to grab her ankle. 'I acknowledge that I do not know what I am doing, but it is better than doing nothing at all.'

He finished untying the bandages. 'Now, Lander, I want you to grab her ankle and pull. A strong, slow pull. And you, Ouse, I want you to brace her, so he can pull the leg straight, understand?'

Bethral made sure that they did, translating quickly. Ouse nodded, and brought his arms under hers, hugging her ribs. Lander grasped her ankle and leaned back, a slow, steady pull.

Bethral closed her eyes and stayed silent, but Ezren could see the pain in the lines on her face.

The bone shifted under the skin. Ezren moved fast, retying the cloths and the wooden swords as tight as he could, making sure the toes faced the right way.

Bethral was stoic, but she was pale and breathing hard before they were finished. Once the task was done, she lowered herself to the pillows and sighed with relief.

'I wish I knew what I am doing.' Ezren drew the blankets up to cover her. 'Or that what I am doing is actually helping.'

Gilla and a black-skinned young woman came into their area with their arms full. Bethral craned her neck to look around Ezren. 'Is that a sword?'

Ezren glanced at a long scabbard sticking out from under the pile. Gilla pulled it free and handed it to him, but Bethral reached out her hand to intercept it, looking almost greedy. Gilla said something, and Bethral replied as she pulled the odd wooden sheath free. 'Oh, this is lovely.'

'I have never seen a sword like that before. How can you wield that?' Ezren asked.

'Two-handed. It's a lovely blade, but Gilla says it's not of much use here on the Plains. It can't be used from horseback, and not many are big enough to wield it properly.'

The blade was bright and very thick. The pommel was large, of polished metal. The handle was wrapped in leather, and there seemed to be two sets of crosspieces. 'I don't see how it could be more effective than a regular sword.'

'You can put a man down fast, with one blow.' Bethral stifled a yawn. 'And if you hold it properly, it can punch through armor like—' She lost the battle, and yawned widely.

'We can talk more in the morning. You should sleep.'

Bethral blinked, her eyes watering. She sheathed the sword and laid it next to her pallet. 'I won't argue with that.' She started shrugging out of her tunic under the blanket.

Ezren turned away. 'I will give you a bit of privacy, then.' He left the tent, escaping into the night air, ignoring the odd looks that the young ones gave him. They might be comfortable with naked bodies. He was not.

He saw to his own needs, then headed back to Haya's tent. The stars were coming out in the spring sky, and there was a slight breeze. He paused to look out over the grasslands and the herd of horses that lay beyond.

This land was so lovely, yet so harsh. It was hard to believe that these people could live like this, and yet they did. He could hear laughter from the small tents that surrounded Haya's.

As he walked back, several warriors saw him and smiled, inclining their heads. He returned the greetings, pleased that the storytelling had been so well received. He had done well enough, given that he hadn't told a story to an audience in more than two years.

Still, his voice was not what it had been. And would never be again, although the Lady High Priestess Evelyn had held out some hope for the future. He had to face the fact that it was gone for good

He could accept that now, because he'd been gifted with something important tonight. He'd learned he could still tell a tale, could still hold an audience enthralled, even when his words were being translated.

Pleasure washed through him. It was so good, such a wonderful feeling, to tell a tale, to make the audience weep or laugh, or do both at the same time. He'd missed that, missed performing for an audience. To see their faces, eyes wide as they hung on every word. It was a special kind of power and joy, all in one.

It was a good story, filled with traditional archetypes. Blackhart's restoration to honor, Evelyn having to deal with her internal conflict about Church politics. A classic villainess and horrifying monsters to top it off. There was even a descent into darkness, exploring the dungeons below the keep . . . Classical elements, to be sure.

Still, he needed to improve. Not on the tale, but on the telling. Ezren frowned, looking at the grasses as he walked. How could he improve on the presentation when his voice was so very harsh? Perhaps he could . . .

He shook his head, as if to wake himself. Perhaps he should concentrate on surviving this little adventure before he worried about much else.

He chuckled to himself as he returned to their sleeping area. The sides of the tent had been lowered, and they were isolated once again from Haya's portion and the main eating area. He stepped through the flap, then lowered it, making sure it closed all the way.

The young ones had left. There was a low brazier full of glowing coals between his pallet and Bethral's. Just enough light to see . . .

She was asleep, her hair fanned out around her head. The blanket had slipped down, revealing her soft shoulders. No, those were not the right words. To reveal the soft skin of her powerful shoulders. One hand rested lightly on the pommel of the new sword.

Lust pierced Ezren through, leaving him standing trembling, breathless.

If the Gods of Palins saw into the hearts of men, the Lady of Laughter must be highly entertained that one such as he should desire a lady warrior.

He turned to his pallet, stripped off his tunic and shoes, and slipped between the blankets. He'd leave his trous on for decency's sake. Not to mention avoiding embarrassment if his feeling should be discovered. He turned to face the tent wall, and closed his eyes resolutely. He'd recite the 'Death March of Wils,' an epic poem he'd learned early in his studies. He had memorised all one hundred stanzas in his youth. The unending sufferings of Wils would bring his body under control.

He was on the eighty-third stanza when he finally fell asleep.

EIGHT

'I think he must be gelded,' Lander announced as he stripped off his tunic and trous.

'Lander! How do you know that?' Gilla asked as she pulled her own tunic over her head.

She and her tent mates had decided to bathe at the river's edge after hearing the Storyteller's tale. The night was clear, and the waning moon was bright enough to see by. They'd all walked down together, talking about the story and the Storyteller. Chell stayed back, since it was her turn to guard their gear and keep an eye out for predators.

'Why else does he sleep apart from her?' Lander demanded as he shook out his blond hair.

Ouse was seated on the ground, unlacing his boots. 'City dwellers hide their bodies from each other.'

'Maybe there is a reason.' Lander folded his clothes and set them by his weapons. 'Maybe he is deformed or . . .' He screwed his face up. 'Maybe he is sick.'

'She is hurt,' Cosana pointed out. She'd already stripped and was testing the water with a toe.

'So? You could still share for warmth, if nothing else.' Lander started to wade into the river. 'Why else hide? Everyone is the same.'

Cosana shrugged. 'Their ways are different. Maybe their bodies are, too.'

'Or maybe his balls were cut.' Ouse stood, and followed Lander into the water.

Cosana ran in after him, splashing a bit. 'Best have his token in your hand before you ask.'

Gilla rolled her eyes. 'Best not to ask.'

Lander was waist deep in the center of the river. He turned and glared at her. 'How else to learn about them and their ways, except to ask?'

'Maybe they are of the same Tribe.' El suggested. 'It's hard to tell from their names. Does he bear the tattoos?'

'Not that I've seen.' Gilla waded out, picked up a handful of sand, and started to rub her skin.

'Haya expects a singer and some warrior-priests to arrive in the next day or so,' Chell announced from the shore.

Everyone turned to look at her, startled into silence.

'I heard her tell Urte to watch for them,' Arbon added.

'Do you think' – Cosana whispered – 'for the ceremony?'

'Probably.' Arbon started to scrub Cosana's back. 'She has said that she would make her decisions soon.'

'I hope not,' Lander said. 'I want to learn more from the Storyteller.'

'Where do you think they will send us?' Ouse looked up into the night sky, as if the answer was written in the stars. 'To the Heart?'

'Does it matter?' Chell replied matter-of-factly. 'It's not as if we choose. Besides, we do not fight for rank in our first year of service.'

Gilla looked down at her sandy hands. To be an adult, responsible for her own actions, finally able to make— She swallowed hard.

Her heart beat a bit faster, and she wasn't sure if it was in anticipation or fear.

Or both.

'This is not a good idea.' Ezren stood, his arms crossed. 'What if the person who gifted it to us is insulted?'

They were standing in front of their sleeping area, having finished their morning meal.

Bethral had wrapped the crosspiece of the two-handed sword in cloth, and was trying to use it to support her weight. Her broken leg was off the ground, with all her weight on her good leg and the sword. The tip of the wooden scabbard dug into the earth as she leaned on it.

Haya had provided tunic and trous, and Bethral had strapped on her sword belt. Which was ridiculous; she wouldn't be able to swing a sword and keep her balance. The whole thing was—

'I'm not going to try to walk far.' Bethral tried another quick step. The pommel was jammed under her armpit, and she tried to hold it there as she hopped on the good leg. 'I just want to be able to—'

'The blade will break,' Ezren snapped. He was more concerned about her leg, but he would use any argument that convinced her to be sensible. Her face was strained; she had to be in pain.

'The scabbard should hold,' Bethral pointed out with maddening logic. 'This allows me some—'

'And if you fall?' Ezren pointed out. 'That would do more harm then good.'

'It's worth a try.' Bethral hopped again. 'Better than lying flat all the time. Besides, I'd like a bath. There's a stream—'

'Your wits have been taken by the wind,' Ezren snapped in the language of the Plains.

Bethral gave him a surprised look.

'But do as you see fit, Lady.' Ezren turned and stomped back into the tent to start sorting through the rest of the pile of gear they'd been given. Stubborn woman – couldn't she see the risk if she fell? What if the bone broke through the skin – they'd be in real trouble then. But would she listen to him, a mere storyteller? No, no, and again no. He cursed under his breath and looked over his shoulder.

Bethral was standing still now, looking around, balanced on that stupid two-handed sword. He had to admit that it had not occurred to him that the sword and scabbard could be used like that. It was probably hard for one such as herself to be stuck on a pallet all the time.

But the risks . . .

She'd piled her hair up on her head, and her tunic and trous were a bit too small. The sunlight gleamed on those gold tresses—

Ezren looked down at the pile, cursing himself for a threefold fool. Fool, fool, pathetic fool—

'Come and see, Storyteller.' Bethral called. 'The young ones are practicing.'

Practice is practice, no matter where you are, Bethral mused. She balanced herself with the sword and watched the group of young ones pair off and start to spar.

They were practicing with wooden swords and small wooden shields. Seo walked among them, watching their form. He'd watch each pair for a moment, then move to the next.

'They look well trained,' Ezren commented, coming to stand next to her.

He sounded calmer. Bethral knew full well he was angry with her; his body fairly vibrated with emotion. As much as it hurt to move, it did no good to lie flat all the time. Besides, being on her feet, with a weapon at her side, reminded their hosts that she was a warrior.

Bethral was grateful, though. The sword was much lighter than her mace, and easier to handle if she had to fight.

'Well, that's one use for that huge sword.' Haya came around the corner of the tent.

'The Storyteller was just saying how good the young ones look,' Bethral replied. She had to balance herself again, shifting her weight around. The idea of using the two-handed sword as a crutch was better than the truth of it. It would help, but she couldn't stay upright much longer.

'Of course they do.' Haya flashed a grin. 'They perform for an audience.' She indicated the three of them. 'They also know that I have summoned a singer and warrior-priests for the rites of passage.'

'Warrior-priests?' Bethral frowned. 'Haya, what little I know of them – from my mother's tales – should I ask for your token before I go further?'

66

'No need.' Haya shrugged. 'Take your mother's tales and let them breed and you will find them no less true. I'd prefer their absence, but the rites must be observed.'

Bethral flicked a glance at Ezren. 'There was trouble, back in our land, before we came here. There was a man, a large black man, who carried the ritual scars of a warrior-priest. He knew our language and our ways.'

'So?' Haya raised an eyebrow. 'I could wish you had mentioned this before. Perhaps we should conceal—'

A shout caught their attention. Seo was pointing them out to a large group of riders. The young were poised with their practice weapons, trying not to look impressed.

The riders headed their way, their horses trotting briskly.

The Storyteller's mouth had dropped open. 'Who is that?'

The front rider was dressed in fine leather, and the wing of a bird was tattooed around his right eye. He had long, flowing brown hair decorated with beads and feathers. A singer of the Plains, his eyes bright with curiosity. But as impressive as he was, he was nothing compared with the others.

Warrior-priests. Her mother had said that they walked the earth in arrogance and pride, sure of their mastery of the very winds. They were said to wield the magic of the Plains, but her mother had not been impressed.

The black man she had seen in the courtyard in Edenrich had the ritual scarring over his chest and arms. These warrior-priests were pale-skinned, so they were covered with massive tattoos in red, green, brown, and black. They were all bare-chested, dressed only in trous and cloaks. Their hair was in long, matted locks that fell to their waists.

'Focus on your blades!' Seo roared at his students. 'What do you mean, gawking like gurtles?'

The young ones returned to their sparring as the group of riders drew closer to where Haya stood. They all brought their horses to a halt before the tent.

'Too late,' Haya muttered. 'Remember, Bethral of the Horse,

that you and the Singer of the City have the shelter of my tent.'
She stepped forward and raised her hand in greeting.

'Storyteller' – Bethral stepped between Ezren and the on-
coming group – 'I think you should—'

'Who are they?' Ezren breathed, stepping around her before
she could stop him. 'What are they? Clerics of some kind?
From the looks they are getting, they are powerful figures in
this culture—'

'Storyteller,' Bethral warned, trying to get his attention,
'let's—'

'Haya,' the Plains singer called out, dismounting from his
horse. The beads in his hair rattled as he swung down. 'What is
this I hear of city dwellers falling from the sky?'

'Quartis, you'd smell a story a mile off,' Haya replied. 'How
did you hear—'

There was an audible gasp. Bethral jerked her head around
and saw the lead warrior-priest staring at Ezren, his mouth open
in shock.

Ezren stared back at him, his face alive with curiosity. But
curiosity turned to concern, and he brought his hand up to his
heart. 'What—' Puzzled green eyes sought Bethral's.

Bethral sucked in a breath through her teeth. Haya and the
Plains singer were still talking, unaware of what was happening.

The other warrior-priests were staring now, in open surprise.
The first one had recovered, and his glare was fixed on the
Storyteller. 'You four,' he snapped, gesturing with his hand, 'take
word. Go. Now!'

Four of the warrior-priests turned their horses and galloped
off, each in a different direction.

That caught Haya's attention. 'Warrior-Priest, what is wrong?'

'That man' – the Warrior-Priest pointed at the Storyteller –
'he is coming with me. Now.'

Bethral growled. She stepped in front of Ezren, who was
looking at them all, trying to follow their words.

'He is under the shelter of my tent.' Haya moved back a step,

68

closer to Ezren. She put her hand on the pommel of her sword. 'Why do you—'

'You break the rules of hospitality, Grass Fires.' The Singer stood calmly, looking up at the mounted man. 'Why do you not follow the traditions of the Plains?'

'We will take him.' Grass Fires drew a lance from his quiver. 'Do not stand in our way.'

The Singer frowned, then shrugged and stepped back, taking his horse with him, out of the conflict.

'What is this?' Haya spat. 'Do you doubt the strength of my sword, that you threaten one under my protection?'

The three remaining warrior-priests dismounted and pulled their weapons. Grass Fires remained on his horse and pointed at Ezren. 'Bind him. Quickly.'

'Seo!' Haya screamed, and charged Grass Fires. They met with a clash of swords. Their horses scattered.

The other two warrior-priests headed for Ezren, who started to back away. Grass Fires was dismounting, aiming his lance at Ezren's chest, pulling his arm back for a throw.

Bethral fumbled with her support, as if to shift her weight. One of the two warrior-priests glanced at her, then focused on Ezren. His mistake.

She dropped the two-handed sword, pulled her own blade from its scabbard, and lunged. The splints on her leg held, but the bone grated within. Pain flared up, but it was distant and unimportant. Her focus was all on the enemy.

One warrior-priest tried to parry her stroke, but her blade scored off his ribs and cut into his upper arm. She pulled back, and tried to find the second warrior-priest—

But he'd gotten to her first. He came up behind, and kicked at the splints on her leg.

The old wooden practice swords splintered, and Bethral screamed as bone tore through flesh. She collapsed to the ground. The warrior-priest kicked her sword away and stood over her. A dagger flashed in his hand.

Her death was here.

She pulled her own dagger, determined to make him pay a price for it.

So fast. It happened so fast. One moment he was staring at the oddly tattooed men and women that had ridden up, and then blades flashed, and in the next instant—

Bethral was down, her leg torn in two, with one of the bastards standing over her, brandishing a dagger.

Lord of Light, no! She had been hurt because of him; now she would die for him, and he could not—

Ezren cried out in rage and anger, and the wild magic rose within him, lashing out with hot fury.

NINE

The Storyteller's furious scream caught everyone by surprise. Bethral's enemy made the mistake of glancing in Ezren's direction.

She didn't. She lunged at him, grabbing his trous at the waist. With one hand she pulled herself off the ground. With the other, she thrust her dagger deep into his groin.

He screamed and fell, blood spurting from the wound.

Bethral pushed him off. Pain lanced through her body, and she caught a glimpse of glistening white bone and her own red blood. She looked away, trying to focus past the pain. Her sword lay just out of reach, and she twisted to reach for it. Her fingers touched the pommel as the pain surged again, clouding her vision. It was a fight to stay conscious. She wanted a blade in her hand before—

Wild magic lashed past her.

She jerked her head around. The Storyteller stood covered in fire, his face screwed up in agony. The flames writhed around him, reaching out, seeking—

'Down!' Bethral shouted. 'Get down, get down.' She didn't wait to see if anyone listened. She flipped over, pressing her face to the grass, covered her head. *Spirit of the Horse, protect me.*

Heat washed over her back. She heard a horse screaming, and hooves running off. Her heart stopped at the thought that Bessie had been caught in this nightmare. But she forced herself to stay down.

The heat flared again. The grass around Bethral crackled and fizzed. She tried to breathe through cool soil. For a moment she felt as if a gentle hand had dropped a blanket over her, wrapping her in warmth. The hand squeezed, and her vision blurred as pain surged through her leg. She breathed through it, doggedly determined to stay awake and aware. The feeling was gone in an instant.

It took a bit longer for her vision to clear. She took a breath, listening to the silence around her. There was the smell of smoke and ash and burning flesh.

Carefully, Bethral raised her head and looked around.

The two that she'd attacked lay in the grass, dead. She couldn't see any horses, and no one seemed to present a threat at the moment.

Ezren Storyteller was down, collapsed in the grass behind her. Pale, and still as death. The top of the tent behind him was burnt away, the leather edges smoldering.

Bethral rolled to her side to see better, and lifted her head higher.

There was another body, the warrior-priest they'd called Grass Fires. He . . . it . . . was charred black, the skin and muscle crisped. The smell . . .

Bethral swallowed hard and started to breathe through her mouth.

A rustle of grass, and the Singer . . . Quartis . . . lifted his head to look around.

Footsteps, and Haya appeared, grim and covered in ash and soot. She moved quickly, her sword out and her gaze fixed on Ezren Storyteller.

Bethral sucked in a breath. Haya was going to kill Ezren.

Her sword was gone, but in the grass close by was her makeshift crutch. Bethral jumped up, grabbing the two-handed sword. With one swift move, she ripped the cloth bindings and unsheathed the weapon. She dropped the scabbard and blocked Haya, bringing the bright blade up in a guard position.

Haya jerked to a stop. She stared at Bethral.

Bethral paused, in sudden realisation. She was standing, free of pain. Her leg . . . the trous torn, ripped away. Beneath the fabric, her leg was whole and healthy. Healed.

Haya recovered first. Her eyes narrowed to a glare. 'What monster have you brought into my camp?'

'No monster,' Bethral snapped back. 'Did he violate your hospitality? Did he attack any that did not attack us first?' Bethral eased back a step, conscious that Ezren lay behind her, helpless.

Haya followed, her blade still at the ready. She glanced over the bodies on the ground, at the unharmed Quartis still trying to get to his feet. Her gaze flicked to the burnt tent and back to Bethral's leg. She stopped advancing, but the look in her eyes . . .

Bethral spun, bringing the blade around in an arc. Seo was behind her, close to Ezren. With a snarl, she used both hands to brace the blade, and lunged—

'Stop!' Quartis commanded.

Seo froze.

Bethral diverted the tip of the blade, missing Seo. Her lunge carried her forward, and from the look on Seo's face he knew that the blade would have pierced his chest. They stood, breathing hard, waiting.

Haya growled, 'Singer, you do not have the right—'

'I do not,' he agreed. 'But I have seen enough to want to know more. So let us declare a battle truce among us, that we may see to our dead.'

'So be it.' Seo stepped back, sheathing his sword. 'With any luck, the Storyteller is dead.'

Bethral sucked in her breath, then snarled in rage.

Seo backed away, eyeing her carefully. They all moved off, Haya calling for more warriors to aid her. Bethral waited until they were out of range of swords, then fell to her knees beside her Storyteller. Her mouth dry with fear, she reached out and touched his face.

Pale, and cold to the touch. It didn't appear that anything was broken. She bent over him, her hair falling down, curtaining off the rest of the world. The barest puff of breath touched her cheek.

Her heart leapt in her chest. Alive, he was still alive, praise the skies and the stars and the winds in between. She combed his auburn hair off his face, taking a liberty she wouldn't have dared if he were conscious.

His dark lashes fluttered, and Bethral caught a flash of green. Joy and relief made her laugh out loud. Without another thought, she kissed him.

Lips touched lips, and a thrill shot through her, down to her toes. Like a fine wine, and she wanted more, so much more. His lips moved in response, and she moaned at the sensation. More, she wanted more and—

She jerked her head away, shocked at her daring. Dazed green eyes stared into hers, confused.

A sound brought her to her feet, sword in hand.

The young were all standing there, staring at them wide-eyed.

'Remove everything that is mine from that tent,' Haya growled at Urte. 'Return it all to the main camp. Put it in Seo's tent for now.'

Urte wasted no time, signaling other warriors to come with her.

'Guard them,' Seo said to a group of four warriors standing around him, their lances in their hands. 'Do not approach, do not threaten, but guard them. If they ask for food and drink, provide it. Understood?'

Haya looked around. 'I want the young to return to the main—'

'Too late for that,' Quartis said, pointing with his chin.

Haya looked over, and cursed when she saw the young warriors clustering around Bethral and Ezren. She opened her mouth to summon them, but the Singer put his hand on her arm. 'Wait,' he said.

Haya watched as Bethral shook her head, and waved the young ones away. They moved off, and turned to help the other warriors with the dead.

'She takes no advantage,' Quartis pointed out.

74

'He threw fire,' Haya snapped. 'Did you see what is left of that warrior-priest?'

'I did,' Quartis replied calmly, which set Haya's teeth on edge even more. 'I was on the ground, yet unharmed. Would your blade leave an enemy any less dead?'

Seo growled, his sword still in his hand. 'We'd have been better off killing them when they fell from the sky.'

'As to that, I cannot say. What is, is,' Quartis said as he watched the blonde warrior care for her Singer. 'I'd like to know more before decisions are made.'

'What did that warrior-priest say?' Seo demanded. 'Those four riders tore off in a hurry, and at his command.'

'Two words,' Quartis said. ' "Take word." '

They stood silent for a moment, each in their own thoughts.

'What did they see, that he would send word out in the four directions?' Haya asked.

'We'll have more of them swarming down on us, then.' Seo sheathed his sword. 'And soon.'

Quartis looked out over the Plains. 'Let us get kavage and talk. There isn't much time. I would hear how it happened that they fell from the sky.'

Bethral made sure the young ones had moved off before she gathered up her weapons and struggled to lift Ezren off the ground. She staggered under his weight. He was no longer the emaciated, beaten slave that she'd bought for a copper in the market. She managed to get him to his pallet, and covered him with blankets in an effort to warm him.

Ezren wasn't truly conscious, thankfully. His eyes were open, and he responded to her commands, but he seemed only dimly aware of his surroundings. If the skies were kind, if his Gods were kind, he'd not remember that she'd kissed him.

Once under the blankets, Ezren sighed, then drifted off to sleep. There was a bit more color in his face, and his hands felt warmer.

Then Bethral set about her task.

She packed the saddlebags, both hers and the new ones Ezren had been gifted with. She took everything, trying to sort as she went, but she'd leave nothing behind. Everything had a use, even if only to be bartered away. She noticed some odd small sacks but didn't bother to open them. Everything could be explored later. Right now, she had to be ready to mount and ride in an instant.

As she moved about, she worked her leg, taking the time to stretch the muscles. The absence of pain, the strength in the leg – Ezren had to have healed it with the wild magic. It was the second time her life had been given back to her, and it felt so odd to be healthy again. To have hope again. She'd resigned herself to her own death, but now . . . now, they'd be able to travel together.

Bethral flushed. Not that he'd have any interest in one such as her. A gentle maid of courtly airs, one skilled in the feminine arts, would be more suitable. Still, the Plains were wide and the trip would be a long one. She'd be satisfied to be at his side; to return him to his rightful place in Queen Gloriana's court.

She noted the guards as she moved about. They were not threatening, but they were there for a reason. Bethral couldn't blame Haya for her anger. There was no magic on the Plains except what was wielded by the warrior-priests, and Bethral had a firm idea that they didn't wield fire as a weapon. Otherwise, they'd have guarded against it, wouldn't they?

She paused in the packing, and considered. Her armor was stacked in the corner.

Packing could wait. She stripped off her tunic and trous, and reached for her gambeson and plate. *Hope for the best. Plan for the worst.*

She'd barely finished belting on her weapons when she heard the Storyteller moan. She knelt at his side. He stared at her for a moment, then awareness flooded his face. 'I lost control.'

'You did.' Bethral offered him a mug of water and helped him support his head as he drank. 'How do you feel?'

'Weak.' Ezren licked his lips. 'Sore.' He blinked. 'You – your leg?'

'Healed.' Bethral stood and gestured. 'See?'

He gave her a blinding smile, but then frowned. 'I seem to remember . . . What happened?'

Bethral settled him down as she spoke, and told him what he wanted to know.

Ezren closed his eyes, and his face grew tight. 'I killed—'

'Those who threatened us,' Bethral finished firmly. 'You defended us and healed my leg in the process.' She paused. 'You did not kill anyone who did not threaten us.'

'Why did they attack us?' Ezren opened his eyes. 'He deliberately—'

'We have other things to worry about.' Bethral looked over her shoulder, and then shifted to face the front.

Haya, Seo, and the man with the beaded hair stood there. Haya's face was grim as she took in Bethral's armor. 'You will give my words to him,' Haya demanded.

Bethral stood. 'I will give your words to Ezren Storyteller.'

'We called a battle truce, to see to our dead,' Haya looked down at Ezren.

'That is well,' Ezren replied. 'Even though they threatened me and my token-bearer, I would not have their bodies dishonored.'

Bethral translated, careful to use his words.

'This is Singer Quartis. He wishes to hear your truths, if you will share them with him.' Haya gestured to the unknown man, who nodded

'The Singer honors me,' Ezren replied, speaking in their language. Bethral gave him a quick smile of approval, but noted his exhaustion. He was coming to the end of his strength. 'We will hold a senel tonight, and decide what is to be done,' Haya said.

'Who will speak for us at this senel?' Bethral demanded. 'Will no one hear our truths?'

'The senel is for those of the Plains.' Haya bristled. 'You still have the shelter of this tent,' she added, casting an eye up to what was left of the top. 'We will move you to an undamaged portion.' She hesitated, then continued. 'You harmed none but those that threatened you, and there was no harm to the horses or the young. You did not violate our hospitality. However' – she drew a deep breath – 'I cannot—'

Bethral felt a tap on her foot. She looked down and saw the Storyteller struggling to sit up. 'I missed that,' he said.

She knelt, helping him to stay upright. He listened as she explained what Haya had said. 'Tell Haya the safety of the children is first before all else. You and I will abide by the decision of their people, as long as they do not call for our deaths.' Ezren sagged back against the pallet. 'Tell her we understand, and we thank her.'

Bethral did so.

'You are tired. We will speak later,' Quartis said. 'The senel will be called. We will consider all the truths of all concerned.'

With that, Haya, Seo, and Quartis walked away.

Bethral watched them go, Seo joining the young ones who were clearing the dead. 'I do not like this. Not one bit.'

'No choice,' the Storyteller whispered. 'If nothing else, we need the saddle she promised . . . and . . . directions.' His eyes fluttered as he fought to stay awake.

'I already know the direction to go,' Bethral said softly as she eased him down to the pallet. 'Urte gave it away that first time, when she looked away when I mentioned Palins.'

There was no response. The Storyteller's eyes were closed, and he was already asleep.

TEN

Gilla held her breath and swallowed hard, trying not to purge her stomach. Thankfully, the others looked like they were having the same problem.

'Breathe through your mouths,' Seo said gruffly as they worked. 'It helps.'

She'd dealt with the dead before, but mostly those who had died in childbirth, or babies who had faded away. She'd seen corpses before, but not ones killed in combat. And never one burned beyond recognition.

Seo had directed them to gather the bodies on blankets. It had been Lander who had nudged her and pointed his chin in the direction of the tent. She'd turned and seen Bethral check Ezren Storyteller. Her face had blazed with joy, and then to see them kiss . . . such passion.

Bethral had caught them staring, and they had looked away, because her expression made it clear that city dwellers were private about kisses, too. Gilla had the oddest notion: that had been the first time they'd kissed, but that was not possible.

Still . . .

They'd turned back to their task, using a bloodied cloak to gather up the burned ruins of what had once been a warrior-priest. The blackened skin flaked in their hands, and Gilla shuddered, but they rolled it onto the blanket and took up the four corners. The other three bodies were also taken up.

Seo watched as they waited for his command, his face grim. 'Bring them,' he said as he started to walk back to the main camp.

'Elder, will we offer them to the earth?' Ouse asked after they had walked for a while.

'No,' Seo answered. 'We shall arrange them in a storage tent. They must be seen by the others. When the warrior-priests come, they will decide if it is to be an earth or a sky burial.' He glanced back at the burned body. 'I think there has been more than enough fire.'

Gilla exchanged glances with her friends, each daring the other to ask the questions they all wanted answered. Finally, she couldn't take it any longer. 'Elder, did the Storyteller actually throw fire?'

'You did not see?' Seo lifted an eyebrow.

'No, Elder.' Lander's disappointment was clear. 'We were focused on our blades!'

'As you should be,' Seo snapped. But then, to Gilla's surprise, he continued. 'No harm in telling, since you will serve at the senel. Yes, the City Singer burned this one with fire.' Seo looked at them each in turn. 'You will hear all truths tonight, with the other warriors.'

Cosana stumbled, almost spilling the corpse out of the blanket. 'Other warriors?'

'Warriors,' Seo barked. 'Warriors who honor the fallen with respect and silence.'

Their grins quickly stifled, the young warriors continued with their task.

Sun Setting urged his horse on at a full gallop, as Grass Fires had commanded. His horse flew over the Plains, running hard.

As he rode, he scanned the grasses for the soft glow of magic. He would need as big a source as he could find quickly, if he was to obey his orders. His heart raced with growing excitement that he would bring amazing news.

The Sacrifice had been found, bearing the magic of the Plains.

On the horse ran, as Sun Setting leaned forward, watching the land ahead. Skies above, let there be a source—

There!

Sun Setting jerked the reins, and his horse turned, bucking a bit at the command. Sun Setting patted its neck in apology and allowed the animal to slow.

The glow was a good-sized area, visible under the new grasses. He'd need all of it, and though the teaching of the Elders said that no area was to be drained, he had no choice.

He flung himself from the saddle, pulling at his saddlebags. He fumbled with his small scrying bowl and waterskin. His horse shook its head, breathing hard.

Kneeling in the grass, Sun Setting tore the grasses away and set the bowl in as level a place as possible. He filled it with water, slopping some over the side. The water trembled in the bowl, his hands were shaking so.

The horse came over to investigate, drawn by the scent. Sun Setting cursed, pushing its head away, then caught himself. He needed to be calm before casting the spell.

He stood, and removed the saddle and halter from the animal. He'd release it to find the water it needed. The casting would drain him enough that he would need to rest. He could summon another animal in the morning.

Once freed, the horse lifted its head to scent the air, then started off, leaving him alone in the grasses.

Sun Setting knelt, and waited until his breathing was under control before invoking the elements. He stared into the depths of the water, placed his palms on the ground, and drained the magic from the land. He started the chant as he concentrated, using the magic to bear his message on the wind.

'Hail Storm . . . I seek Hail Storm . . .'

The grasses swayed around him as he focused, seeking . . .

The water clouded, then an image appeared, the face of Elder Hail Storm. His face was covered with the traditional tattoos, but the stylised markings around his eye identified him.

'Elder Hail Storm.' Sun Setting barely dared to breathe, for fear of disturbing the water.

'Sun Setting' – Hail Storm frowned – 'what is it?'

'The Sacrifice,' Sun Setting said. 'The Sacrifice has returned to the Plains.'

*

Wild Winds, warrior-priest and Eldest Elder of the Plains, shifted in his saddle. Riding was becoming harder and harder with his waning strength.

Even that slight movement caught the eye of Snowfall. She glanced at him sharply, as if assessing his ability to continue. He ignored her raised eyebrow, and settled back down into his saddle.

The day was a fine one, and the Plains seemed unusually fair this season. It would be good to conduct a few Rites of Ascension and celebrate the passage of new warriors to adult status. Being Eldest Elder, he seemed to deal more with the arguments and problems of the Plains than with the young ones. He was looking forward to it. A familiar ritual, and a joyous one.

Provided he had enough strength.

Well, that was easily done. He'd make certain he had enough rest before the rite was held. Even if he didn't, young Snowfall would. She who did not even have all of her tattoos yet.

It bordered on disrespect, to treat an elder – an Eldest Elder – as if he were the child.

Were she not the best and brightest of his charges . . .

Lightning Strike stiffened in his saddle, reaching for a lance. 'Rider,' he called out. 'Warrior-priest.'

The others reached for weapons as well. Wild Winds shook his head. So this is what they had come to now, with the Council of Elders sundered. Change was sweeping the Plains, and not for the better. Keir of the Cat did not understand that he and his Warprize were—

'It's Swift Arrow,' Snowfall said. 'Wasn't he with Grass Fires?'

The others did not relax.

The rider came on at a full gallop, not slowing until he was well within speaking range. 'Eldest Elder,' he gasped as he pulled his horse up. 'The Sacrifice has been spotted. He is on the Plains, bearing the magic within him.' Swift Arrow paused to gasp for air. 'There was an attack . . . I do not know . . .'

'Show me,' Wild Winds demanded.

*

'So.' Haya sat on her stool and surveyed the tent crammed full of warriors. 'We sit in senel, and my token is here before me. The city dwellers are secure in their tent and well guarded. You have seen the bodies of the warrior-priests. Seo, Quartis, and I have given you our truths.

'It would seem that there are three paths before us,' Haya continued. 'We can let the city dwellers go on their way, with the tributes that they earned with the City Singer's tale.'

A few of the warriors nodded, and others shook their heads.

'We can hold the city dwellers here, and wait for the arrival of the warrior-priests who may come. We do not know when this might happen, for we do not know where the messengers headed when they rode off.'

More nods to that statement. Haya was fairly sure that warrior-priests would arrive within days, but there was no way to know for sure.

The young ones were circling about, refilling mugs with kavage. Haya watched them as they moved, so serious and intent. Seo had let their intentions slip, and it was clear the young ones wished to be taken seriously.

'The final path is to kill them both, and give their bodies to the sky.'

A clatter as Gilla started, spilling her pitcher. There was a stir as she moved to clean up the kavage and the warrior she'd spilled it on. Haya sighed. Gilla was a strong one, serious and dependable, but she had a soft heart.

'The decision is mine to make. But I would hear everyone's truths. What say you, Seo?' Haya sat, and took up her mug of kavage.

Seo stood. 'Change may be on the wind for the Plains, but not for our traditions. The warrior-priests rode in with Quartis and attacked the city dwellers with no explanation. No insults were exchanged that I know of, no tokens asked for. Even after Elder Thea Haya stated that they had been offered the shelter of her tent, still the warrior-priests attacked – and attacked Haya in the bargain.' He shook his head in disgust. 'I have no love of change, and no love for city dwellers who fall from the sky. But the arrogance of the warrior-priests is as large as the sky itself.'

Helfers stood next. 'The Storyteller threw fire, burning the warrior-priest to a crisp. I have never seen such a thing, but I believe your truths. Can we risk releasing such a weapon onto the Plains?' Helfers looked around. 'What if he throws such fire during the dry season, when the risk of grass fires is high? He could wipe out camps and herds with a wave of his hand.' Helfers shook his head. 'I heard the Singer's tale and was much impressed. Yet, I say they should be killed for the threat they represent.'

Another warrior stood and took up the token, and so it went, well into the night. Haya listened to all, taking each truth, and tried to weigh each truth in balance with the truths of the city dwellers.

Finally, when all had said their truths, she stood. 'I thank you all for the gift of your truths. As Elder Thea of this camp, the decision is mine to make. I will consider all these truths and the safety of our children in making my decision. This senel is at an end.'

She sat down as the warriors began to stream out of the tent, talking among themselves. The young ones were milling around in the back of the tent, arguing about something. They probably were fighting about who would do the dishes.

'Not an easy decision to make,' Quartis said softly.

'No.' Haya sighed. 'But one that must be made, and swiftly.'

'Sleep on it.' Seo stood and stretched. 'Share with me this night, since your tent has no top. In the morn—'

He cut off his words as Gilla approached, followed by the other young warriors.

Haya looked them over. 'What?' she asked sharply.

Gilla sank to her knees, then pressed her head to the ground before Haya. The others followed her action, abasing themselves.

Gilla shook, and swallowed hard. She'd been willing when the others had told her to do the talking, but now her tongue was sticking to the roof of her mouth. 'Elders,' Gilla's voice quavered, 'we would quest.'

'Eh?' Seo's voice boomed over her head. 'Quest?'

'How so, child?' Haya did not sound pleased. 'A quest is a warrior calling. It is not for children.'

Gilla winced at that but plunged on, rushing her words. 'Elder Thea Haya, we wish to quest in aid of the Singer Ezren Silver-tongue and his Token-Bearer, Bethral of the Horse.'

There was a long silence from the elders. It almost killed Gilla to stay still and silent, and wait, trying to look as mature as was possible, pressed to the ground.

'Rise, all of you,' Haya said.

Gilla lifted her head, releasing a slow breath of relief. The elders were willing to listen. They would be heard, and might be taken seriously. She rose to her feet, and the others did as well, staying behind her.

Gilla straightened her shoulders. 'Elder Thea Haya of the Tribe of the Snake, we have thought and discussed among ourselves, man and woman, element to element. We wish to go with the lost ones to see them safe to their home, as guides and guardians. I speak as a woman of the Snake and as Fire, to offer my sword and my aid.'

'Well, they know the ritual,' Quartis said, a slight smile on his face. 'The tradition is that such quests are taken by eight warriors. Four men and four women, one pair for each of the four elements.'

Gilla looked at Lander, for him to speak next, but Haya cut him off. 'Before you perform a ritual you have no right to, best you explain why.'

'Our hospitality is broken,' Gilla said. 'I would restore the name of our Tribe and the honor of our tents.'

Haya looked at Lander, and raised an eyebrow.

Lander took a deep breath. 'Elder Thea Haya of the Tribe of the Snake, we have thought and discussed among ourselves, man and woman, element to element. We wish to go with the lost ones to see them safe to their home, as guides and guardians.

I speak as a man of the Snake and as Earth, to offer my sword and my aid.'

Haya's gaze fell on Chell. 'Just your tribe and element.'

Chell spoke with her usual confidence. 'I speak as a woman of the Boar and as Water. I wish to escort the lost ones, and see them to their home.'

'I speak as a man of the Cat and as Water,' Arbon's voice rumbled out. 'For I wish to earn a place as a warlord someday, and the quest would add to my honor.'

'That's honest,' Seo growled.

'I speak as a man of the Hawk and as Fire,' El said. 'I wish to follow Gilla.'

Gilla blushed.

'I speak as a woman of the Snake and as Earth.' Cosana wiped her hands on her thighs. 'I, too, wish to restore the honor of this camp.'

'I speak as a woman of the Snake and as Air.' Tenna trembled as she spoke, her voice soft and meek. 'I, too, would restore our honor.'

'I speak as a man of the Fox and as Air,' Ouse said. 'I would learn my enemy, even as I aid them.'

Haya snorted. 'Children asking to quest. Next the sun will come down from the sky and heat my kavage.'

Quartis raised an eyebrow. 'There are already people falling out of the sky. Be careful what you call down upon us.'

Haya rolled her eyes.

Lander took a step forward. 'Elder Thea, I have made no secret that I wish to be a singer some day. What songs I may sing are yet to be determined. But these people offer a glimpse into other ways and lands. I would learn their language, of their towns and peoples.'

'Is this a good thing?' Quartis asked.

'Is any learning wasted?' Lander countered. 'If an enemy wields a weapon that is unfamiliar, do we hesitate to learn its arts?'

Seo coughed, giving Haya a sideways glance.

Gilla held her breath.

'You are still children, and will remain children until the ceremony takes place,' Haya growled. 'I will hear no more of this. Be about your chores, and swiftly.'

Gilla didn't wait to be told twice. She moved, grabbing as many mugs as she could, and headed out of the tent.

Haya watched them go, and shook her head. 'They're a bold group.'

Seo gave her a rare smile. 'Brave, to face down an ehat like you,' he said slyly.

Haya snorted.

'Change sweeps the Plains, like a grass fire at the height of summer. It destroys, but it brings new growth.' Quartis stood slowly. 'I wonder if Keir the Cat fully appreciates what he has started.'

'This cannot all be laid at his tent,' Haya said. 'He did not throw city dwellers through the sky at us.'

'They are so young, those children.' Seo sighed. 'They still seem as babies to my eyes.'

'But it is well thought out – this plan of theirs,' Quartis pointed out. 'And it speaks to your concerns. It offers your protection but removes them from your tents. You offer aid, but do not send your more experienced warriors.'

Seo nodded. 'We walk a fine line between the two sides and the warrior-priests, and protect ourselves. Who can challenge that?'

'But they sacrifice their first year of service under the warlord.' Haya protested.

'They can fight for a warlord later,' Seo said. 'If they go with the city dwellers, the warrior-priests may make them fight anyway.'

'I hate this,' Haya said suddenly. 'They are so young – their legs are barely sturdy enough to carry them past the horizon.'

'That is the pain we face each year: to send our young to war and battle,' Quartis agreed. 'Young warriors, young horses, we send them too soon.'

'The sun rises.' Haya stood again. 'Come, both of you, share my pallet. We will talk once we have slept.'

'I'd welcome that.' Quartis rose.

They'd taken only a few steps when one of the warriors entered the tent. 'Elder Seo, come quickly.'

'What?'

'It's another warrior-priest, Elder.'

ELEVEN

Ezren woke slowly, warm and comfortable on his pallet, the blankets wrapped around him.

Odd how those felt pads could almost be more comfortable than a feather bed. He drowsed for a while, enjoying the faint spicy smell of the blankets. Gurtle fur even stuffed the pillows.

With eyes still closed, he drew a deep breath, enjoying the warmth and comfort for just a moment longer. He felt rather odd. Tired, but restless. Starved, come to think of it. Part of him wanted to stay in bed for another few days.

The other part wanted to roast an ox and eat it whole.

Hunger won out. Ezren opened his eyes.

The warriors had rigged a top for the burnt-out portion of the tent. They'd managed to close the sides as well. The braziers were placed carefully, and they glowed with coals. Ezren wondered for a moment what the fuel was. There were no trees on the Plains that he had seen. Where did the wood come from? He would have to remember to ask.

Bethral was sitting up on her pallet, dressed in her armor, sword across her lap, facing the flap. His breath hitched in his throat to see her profile. A veritable Angel of Light. The living embodiment of tales of warrior women – tall, fierce, beaut—

'Good morning,' Bethral said softly as Ezren blinked his eyes clear. 'How do you feel?'

'Were you on guard all night?' Ezren demanded, rising up on his elbow.

'Yes.' Bethral gestured to one of the braziers. 'There's warm kavage, but I warn you it's strong.'

'Good.' Ezren sat up, the blankets falling away, and reached for the mug she handed him. 'Why did you—'

Bethral raised a finger. 'Best to keep your voice low. We've guards around the tent, and they could learn our language as fast as you're learning theirs.'

Ezren took a sip of kavage, and blinked at its strength. Bethral handed him a bowl of gurt, and he took a handful.

'As to why, well, what do you remember of yesterday, Story-teller?'

'I remember the attack, and . . .' Ezren thought for a bit. 'I killed someone, didn't I? With the wild magic?'

'You did,' Bethral responded. 'The warrior-priest had a lance in his hand, Storyteller. If you hadn't – if the magic hadn't – lashed out, you would have died. I could not protect you.'

'Your leg,' Ezren whispered.

Bethral smiled, and rubbed her hand on her thigh. 'Healed. As if it had never happened.'

'He kicked you.' Ezren growled at the memory. 'I saw bone and blood—'

'He took advantage of an enemy's weakness.' Bethral shrugged. 'I would have done the same.'

'I doubt that,' Ezren said. 'The wild magic healed it.'

'It's not the first time,' Bethral said slowly. 'That time . . . in the swamp . . .'

Ezren swallowed hard. He'd become conscious in a rush, on an altar in the swamp, where a blood mage had plunged a dagger into his chest. He'd turned his head, seen Bethral lying there, dead, her eyes glazed—

'Perhaps you have some control over it now?' Bethral asked.

Ezren shook his head. 'I would love to claim so, Lady, but the truth is that I don't remember much beyond the attack.'

Bethral gave him an odd, unsure look. 'Do you remember anything—'

There was a light cough outside their tent.

Bethral rose to her feet, her hand on the pommel of her sword. 'Come,' she called.

The flap opened, and Haya appeared. The older woman looked as if she hadn't slept all night, and her face was tight with anger. 'A warrior-priest has come,' she said abruptly. 'He would speak with you.'

'Talk?' Ezren asked in her language. 'Only talk?'

Haya nodded, then rattled off a phrase he didn't understand.

'She says he sits upon the bare earth,' Bethral explained. 'Only the most important of rituals is done upon the bare earth.'

'I do not understand that,' Ezren said. 'But I do understand ritual. We will come.'

They walked a fair distance from the camp, through the waist-high grass. As worried as she was, Bethral took pleasure in the simple act of taking a step on a healthy leg. Being able to move freely was something she would not take for granted again.

Healthy, whole, there was no longer a need to go to the snows. She could journey with Ezren Storyteller and keep him safe. Bethral felt lighter, somehow. Dangers there were, that was true. Still . . . her heart rejoiced.

Haya stopped as they topped a small rise. They looked down on a grassy depression, almost bowl-shaped. At the center was a circle of bare earth where the grass had been cut back to the roots and peeled away. Off to the side, Bethral could see a stack of sod pieces piled up, as if they'd be replaced once this meeting was over.

At the edge of the circle, facing them, was a warrior-priest sitting on the bare dirt. No stool, no blanket. His face and chest were covered in tattoos, brightly colored and vivid against what little skin could be seen. His only clothing was his trous. Bare-chested and barefoot, he sat on the dirt as if he would wait forever.

He had a staff adorned with what looked like feathers, skulls, and bells, all tied with strips of leather. It had been rammed into the earth by his side, and it swayed over him. The bells chimed faintly in the breeze.

The man was clearly old, and he had a gaunt look about him, as if he'd recently fasted. Bethral frowned.

There were two bowls before him. One held water, the other a small fire.

'Well, now,' Ezren muttered, 'there's a threshold guardian, if ever I saw one.'

'He is Wild Winds, Eldest Elder of the Warrior-Priests,' Haya said softly. 'One of my scouts spotted him on the morning sweep of the area.'

Bethral scanned the grasses around the man, looking for an ambush. 'Is he alone?'

'As far as we can tell, and that is not normal. An eldest elder travels with at least four, and usually more,' Haya said, frowning as she stared at the man in the circle.

'The grass could hold an army,' Bethral said.

'What does he want?' Ezren asked.

'I spoke to him.' Haya took her bow off her back and started to string it taut. 'He would not discuss what had happened, would offer no explanations. Would not speak to me, the Elder Thea of this camp. He will talk only to those who fell from the sky.'

'We do not have to talk to him, Elder Thea.' Ezren said. 'He offers you no honor. He deserves none from us.'

'I thank you for that, Singer.' Haya gave him a tight smile. 'But he invokes the four elements and he waited for us to find him. He may have truths to tell you, and I think you should hear those truths. So I will take you down. If he refuses to speak to me again, I will return here, bow at the ready. I will wait and watch. If he or any other offers you injury, I will kill them.'

'We cannot ask for more,' Bethral said.

Haya nodded, and started down. Ezren followed, and Bethral took the rear, still keeping a watchful eye out for others.

As they neared the seated man, he stood with the help of the staff. He faced them calmly, his expression unreadable under the tattoos.

'Here are those that you seek,' Haya said. 'Bethral of the Horse, and Ezren Silvertongue, Singer of Palins.'

'Leave us,' Wild Winds said.

Haya bristled.

The wind caught the bells in the feathers, and they chimed slightly.

Haya took a deep breath. 'I am the Elder Thea of the camp, and responsible for the safety and well-being of the children of the Snake. Yet you will not tell me what this is about?'

Wild Winds just stared at her.

'Do not wonder at the cause for the divisions among us, Warrior-Priest,' Haya spat.

She turned on her heel and marched back up the rise.

Wild Winds sat down, and gestured for Bethral and Ezren to join him. Ezren sat, but Bethral hesitated. She'd see more standing, and could react quicker if—

'You speak our language?' Wild Winds asked.

'I do,' Bethral said.

'You will give my exact words to the Singer?'

'Yes, she will,' the Storyteller interrupted. 'I have learned some, and she will explain what I don't already know.'

'Sit,' Wild Winds said. 'I give you my word that you and the Singer will not be attacked. You came freely. You will leave freely.'

Bethral studied him for a moment, then sat in the dirt just behind the Storyteller.

'I am Wild Winds, Eldest Elder of the Warrior-Priests of the Plains. I have come to speak with you. I sit here, on the bare earth and under the open sky. I ask the water and the fire to witness my words.'

'I am Ezren Silvertongue of Edenrich. The Tribe of the Snake has honored me with the title of Singer.' Ezren's voice was formal, and he was speaking slowly. Bethral had no trouble translating his words. 'Beside me is Bethral of the Horse, who is also my Token-Bearer. What do you wish to say?'

'The winds bear word that you fell from the sky,' Wild Winds

93

said. 'I wish to hear, with my own ears, how you came to the Plains.'

Ezren nodded, and started to speak. He kept the version to its barest form, but he gave a detailed description of the scarred black man who had traveled with Orrin Blackhart. Wild Winds didn't interrupt the flow of words. He just listened, his eyes half closed.

Ezren finished with the moment Bethral identified herself to Haya. There was a brief silence, then Wild Winds spoke. 'How did the power come to you?'

'How do you know——' Bethral demanded, but Ezren stopped her with a slight gesture and began to speak. Bethral watched the old man, watched his eyes as Ezren told him of the ambush in the swamp. Ezren's voice remained steady as he described the altar and the spider statue that loomed over it.

'I have shared my tale,' Ezren continued. 'Now I would ask, Eldest Elder, why did the other warrior-priest attack me?'

The breeze caught the bells, and they chimed again.

'Those other warrior-priests,' Ezren said, 'they tried to kill Bethral and to capture me. Why?'

'We can see it,' Wild Winds said. 'Within you.'

'What?' Ezren leaned forward. 'See what?'

'The magic,' Wild Winds said.

Ezren leaned back, and considered the man before him as he spoke in their own language to Bethral. 'Marlon could see it without a spell. Remember?'

All too well. The High Mage Marlon had tried to kill Ezren on sight, because of the rogue nature of his power. If his daughter had not stopped him, Bethral would have.

Bethral waited for Wild Winds to speak, but the man sat there, staring at them.

The Storyteller was unfazed. He stared back, as if waiting for answers. Bethral held her breath.

Wild Winds broke the silence first. 'Word came that you had been found. Word also came that the Token-Bearer took down two warrior-priests before she was injured, her leg broken so badly that the bone shone in the sun. And that when the Token-Bearer fell, you used the magic to kill Grass Fires. Is this so?'

'It is so,' Ezren said. 'Bethral killed two of your people, and I killed my attacker.'

'And healed your Token-Bearer. Is it true that your leg was broken?' Wild Winds asked, leaning forward slightly, his eyes intent on Ezren's face. Bethral nodded as she translated the words.

'The magic healed her, yes,' Ezren said.

'Can you heal someone with the power that is within you?' Wild Winds asked.

Ezren shook his head. 'No. I do not have control. The magic seems to . . .' Ezren glanced at Bethral. 'It seems to respond to my emotions.'

Wild Winds sagged back slightly. He looked out over the grasses for a moment, before looking back at the Storyteller. 'So, you do not control that which you bear?'

Bethral wasn't sure that she wanted Wild Winds to know the answer to that, but Ezren was speaking before she could stop him.

'No,' Ezren replied.

'Then it will control you,' Wild Winds said. 'And destroy you. The magic needs the land as the land needs the magic. If it doesn't feed from the land, it will feed from you, until you are consumed. I would ask you to travel with me to the Heart of the Plains.' Wild Winds looked at Ezren. 'Singer, what you bear may kill you, and then more than your life would be lost.'

'His life is worth more than—' Bethral interrupted, but Wild Winds held up his hand.

'You speak of a man. I speak of a people.'

Ezren tilted his head. 'Why should I trust your words?'

Bethral sucked in a breath. They didn't have the man's token. But the older warrior-priest just shook his head.

95

'You can trust my words, Storyteller. For one simple reason.'
Wild Winds had an odd look on his face.

'What is that?' Ezren asked.

'I am dying,' Wild Winds said.

TWELVE

Wild Winds sat silently looking out over the grasslands. The two before him sat in silence as well, waiting for him to continue. When word had come, he'd found it hard to believe, but here was the truth before his eyes.

Who could say that the winds did not have a sense of humor?

He looked back at the green-eyed man and the blonde woman just behind him. Two city dwellers, holding the fate of his world in their hands. All the wisdom of his elders told him what he should do. And yet . . .

'I am the Eldest Elder of the Warrior-Priests of the Plains,' Wild Winds began. 'I have led my people as I was taught – as my elders were in their turn taught. There was wisdom in the ways – our ways – or so I thought.'

The Storyteller sat, still and quiet, as if absorbing every word. Perhaps he was, but these city dwellers had such bad memories . . .

'Now – I am no longer certain. Change sweeps over the Plains as surely as a grass fire and with almost as much destruction in its wake.' Wild Winds could not keep the pain out of his voice. 'Now warrior-priest fights warrior-priest and the Council of Elders is sundered. I'd hoped to restore the Council, perhaps even talk more with young Xylara, the Warprize. Even find an understanding with Keir of the Cat, for he hates the warrior-priests more than most.' Wild Winds shook his head. 'I have little time left. Know you our ways?'

Ezren nodded as he listened to Bethral's translation. 'Your people seek the snows when ill or disabled.'

'I will lead my people to the best of my ability for as long as I may.' Wild Winds straightened his back, his decision made. 'I will speak to you as I would a young warrior-priest with his first tattoos.'

'I will remember your words, Elder,' the Storyteller said.

'We warrior-priests are the Strength of the Plains. Once we walked with the magic, and the magic and the land were one. We kept our people strong and proud. Magic was gifted to us by the elements themselves, and the land that nurtured us.' Wild Winds recited the old tale slowly, so that Bethral could translate.

'Warrior-priests have always sacrificed for the Plains and its people. We sacrifice our names, taking new ones. We sacrifice our blood, to create our blades. We sacrifice our bodies, to bear the ritual tattoos. We sacrifice our bones' – Wild Winds looked at the three skulls on his staff and could almost hear his mentors echo the words as he spoke – 'so that our knowledge is passed down to those that learn from us.

'But somehow, for some time, we no longer walk with the magic. The land and the magic were sundered in a time long past the living memory of any warrior-priest.' Wild Wind kept his voice low. 'But we know – we remember through the truths of those that came before, for their words have been passed from the old to the young, in an unbroken chain, to this moment.'

'How many?' the Storyteller whispered. 'How many old and young?'

Wild Winds held up a hand, his fingers spread wide. 'Ten generations. And each elder tells the young warrior-priest the same thing upon initiation: "Magic was taken from the Plains. Only the blood of the Plains can restore it, in a willing sacrifice. Willing blood, willingly spilled."'

Bethral stiffened. Ezren glanced at her and she translated for him, but her glare was only for Wild Winds.

'The magic was lost,' Wild Winds continued. 'Now we are but a shadow of our former selves, using what little magic remains within the earth. It is bare and thin, and used only with the greatest need. We no longer have the magics; therefore we maintain our status through silence. Thus it is, and thus it will be until the magic is returned to the Heart of the Plains.'

Ezren leaned forward. 'How did it happen? How was the magic lost?'

Wild Winds shook his head. 'The details are lost. All we know is that it will be found again, and returned to us—'

'Through willing sacrifice,' Ezren mused. He ran his fingers through his hair. 'And what magics do you still wield?'

Wild Winds shook his head again, his locks swaying back and forth. 'That I will not say.

'For years, we have sent wanderers out into the kingdoms that surround the Plains to search for the magic. To find it and return here – to be the willing sacrifice.' Wild Winds looked up at the sky. 'Yet here you sit. A city dweller. Not of the Plains, yes?' Wild Winds focused back on Ezren. 'Perhaps you are of the blood?'

Ezren shook his head. 'Not that I know of. I am a son of Edenrich as far back as my own history goes.'

'It was but a hope. You would bear tattoos, had any in your family been of the Plains.' Wild Winds shrugged. 'I can only assume that when Grass Fires saw you and what you bear, that he . . . was too swift in his actions.'

'He paid,' Bethral growled.

'So he did.' Wild Winds nodded. 'But others will try to bring you to the Heart of the Plains. There are those that would perform the ritual with or without your willingness.'

'What is the ritual?' Ezren demanded. 'What is the sacrifice?'

'We do not know,' Wild Winds said. 'All we know is that the sacrifice must be made at the center of the Heart of the Plains. Beyond that—' Wild Winds shrugged. 'We do not know.'

'Except that it involves blood,' Bethral said, trying to keep the anger out of her voice. 'You are going to ask him to go to his death.'

'I do not know what I ask.' Wild Winds stared at Ezren. 'But I do ask.'

'I don't believe—' Bethral growled.

Wild Winds raised his hand and cut her off. 'I ask this of you, Ezren of Edenrich, Singer of the City. Come with me to the Heart of the Plains under my protection. Once there, I will summon all of the warrior-priests, and we will try to resolve this with no further shedding of blood. What say you?'

'Can you promise his safety?' Bethral demanded. 'Here, before the elements, can you promise that if they can't restore the magic, they will allow him to go free?'

'I cannot,' Wild Winds responded. 'But if the magic does not leave him, he will die anyway, consumed from within.'

'So you want him to return the magic to arrogant bastards who think more of their—'

Ezren reached back and put his hand on her knee. The Token-Bearer cut her words, but her eyes still flashed with anger.

'The warrior-priests are no longer of one mind,' Wild Winds explained. 'There are those that will honor my pledge to you. Others will not. It matters not. The magic you bear cannot be sustained by any one man.'

'I am new to the Plains. New to your ways.' Ezren spoke slowly as Bethral translated. 'I am new to the power I bear. What has happened to me in the last few years, since I was enslaved, I understand very little of it.

'It seems to me that the warrior-priests of the Plains have cared too much for their own prestige and too little for the people they are supposed to serve. But how am I to judge the truth of that, being an outsider?'

Ezren paused, and Wild Winds waited. When Ezren continued, he did so in his own language. 'I hate bullies.'

Wild Winds looked at Bethral, who began to translate.

'I hate those that try to force my actions or words by threat of violence or injury. In my homeland, my voice was . . .' Ezren hesitated, then continued. 'My voice was silenced, so that I could not speak of my opposition to the actions of others in power. And violence was used to try to force me to speak words I did not believe, to force me to tell stories that had no truth to them.'

'Now, warrior-priests have tried to kill my Token-Bearer and

to take me by force. Their actions speak louder than your words.
I will not aid them.' Ezren stood, and inclined his head. 'I thank
you for your truths, Wild Winds. But I . . . we . . . are going
home.'

Ezren stepped out of the circle of earth and headed back up the
rise toward Haya. Bethral had to move fast to stay close. She'd
been caught up in Ezren's words, admiring his strength even as
she had translated.

Now her back was to the warrior-priest, and it itched. She
couldn't see them, but she was certain there were other warrior-
priests hidden in the tall grasses. It was all she could do not to
look back. Ezren was walking forward without a single backward glance, and Bethral could do no less. Haya was watching;
she would have to be satisfied with that.

'Your talk is done?' Haya growled once Ezren drew close.

Ezren nodded.

'Then let us return to the camp. Who knows what forces lurk
in the grass?' Haya started walking, but Bethral noticed she kept
her bow strung.

'My thought as well,' Bethral echoed.

'Arrogant fools,' Haya grumbled as she walked, scanning the
grasses around them. 'To refuse to talk to me, then to speak to
you and bind your tongues . . . it's a wonder the sundering did
not happen before this time.'

'Wild Winds did not bind my tongue,' Ezren said as he kept
walking.

Haya stopped in her tracks.

Bethral stopped even with her, keeping watch. 'Ezren,' she
called.

Ezren looked back and frowned. 'What?'

'Singer, I would ask for your token,' Haya said.

Ezren fumbled in his sleeve for the gold coin, then gave it to
her.

'We should keep moving,' Bethral said.

Haya ignored her. 'I would give voice to one truth.'

'I will speak to your truth,' Ezren responded.

'City dwellers forget things,' Haya said quickly. 'Is it possible that you have forgotten that Wild Winds sealed your mouths? Bound you not to speak of what was said?'

'No,' Ezren said firmly, then continued in his own tongue. 'Yes, it is true I do not have a memory such as yours. But I would never forget a promise to stay silent or to keep what is said to myself. If you did not hold my token, I would be insulted.'

Haya looked at Bethral, who translated for her, then added her own assurance. 'It is as he says, Elder Thea. I offer my own truth with his.'

Haya shook her head in disbelief.

Ezren reached out for his token, and Haya returned it. 'Crafty bastard, isn't he?' Ezren pointed out as he put the coin in his sleeve. 'Wild Winds can't bring himself to tell the tale to anyone of the Plains, so he uses us instead.'

'We need to keep moving,' Bethral insisted.

'Will you tell me what he told you?' Haya demanded.

'Yes,' Ezren said. 'But then we have to leave, Haya. More warrior-priests will come, and the children must be safe.'

'You will tell me what he said?' Haya repeated, as if she doubted his words.

'Everything,' Ezren said.

'But not here,' Bethral added.

'No.' Haya started to walk again, picking up her pace. 'No, tonight, after the Rite of Ascension begins. We will gather in your tent and we will talk.'

'Rite of Ascension? For the young ones?' Ezren asked. 'Can I watch?'

'No,' Haya said firmly. 'We will return to the camp. You will sleep, and I will summon those I trust to guard you. After the rite begins, we will talk, but we must speak swiftly. Because at dawn, you must flee.'

Wild Winds watched as the trio walked over the rise and out of his sight. With a sigh, he shifted to his knees and reached for the bowl of burning fat. 'Fire, receive my thanks for witnessing these truths.' He carefully tipped the fat onto the ground and covered the remaining flames with the bowl, smothering them.

He reached for the other bowl. 'Water, receive my thanks for witnessing these truths.' Just as carefully, he poured the water on the ground and covered the dampness with the bowl.

He lifted both hands, palms up, and tilted his head back. 'Air, receive my thanks for witnessing these truths.'

Finally, he bowed, setting both palms firmly on the soil. 'Earth, receive my thanks for witnessing these truths.'

Wild Winds rose to his knees, letting his hands rest on his thighs, and took a deep breath.

A rustle of leaves, and Snowfall rose from the tall grass, sheathing her dagger at her belt. Her soft brown shoulders were covered in tattoos that were not yet complete, as befitted one who had not yet made her final vows as a warrior-priest. 'You heard?' he asked.

She nodded as she moved toward the pile of sod and reached for a piece. 'What will happen, Elder? When he dies?'

'I wish I knew.' Wild Winds used his staff to lever himself to his feet. The skulls swung on their leather strips and clattered together. 'It is his choice, and we will abide by his decision.'

'The others will not, Elder.' Snowfall knelt and pressed the sod back into place.

'That is beyond my control,' Wild Winds said. 'We will conduct the rite of passage for the young of this tribe, and then I will seek out other warrior-priests who will still listen to my truths.'

'As you wish, Elder.' Snowfall took up another piece of sod.

'It is not as I wish, but it is as it is,' Wild Winds growled. 'And you should do as I bid.'

Snowfall said nothing as she pressed the grass back to the earth.

'Perhaps you have not heard my words?'

'I have, Elder.' Snowfall raised her lovely face and fixed her light gray eyes on him.

'You wish me to travel to the Heart of the Plains where the contests for warlord will be held. You wish me to find Simus of the Hawk and seek to serve as his token-bearer.'

'So,' Wild Winds said, 'you do listen. If Simus achieves the status of warlord, he will be able to support Keir of the Cat. And you—'

'Elder,' Snowfall interrupted, 'I do not see—'

'We cannot continue as we have,' Wild Winds repeated patiently. 'The sundering of the Council of Elders means that we must end our isolation and our silence. Simus will have the status of a warrior-priest as token-bearer, and you will have access to Simus and, through him, to Keir the Cat and the Warprize.'

'He will never accept—'

'He will. In time,' Wild Winds argued. 'It is what I ask of you.'

Snowfall looked up. 'I will not leave you, Elder. You have taught me all that I know of our ways, and I will—'

'Obey your elder. Your eldest elder,' Wild Winds said. 'As you honor me, you will do as I bid.'

Snowfall shrugged, and started to place the last piece of sod.

'I assume that silence is assent,' Wild Winds commented dryly.

'Silence is silence, unless the silence speaks to the listener,' Snowfall replied. 'Is that not what you taught me, Elder?'

'Bitter indeed, the retort of an ungrateful student who learns her lessons all too well.' Wild Winds sighed.

Snowfall shrugged. 'The contests for warlord are not for some time yet. The task can wait.'

'Summon the others,' Wild Winds said. 'We will perform the Rite of Ascension and then depart.'

Snowfall rose. 'After that, Elder?'

'The winds alone know.'

THIRTEEN

Haya was true to her word. She'd seen them to their tent and insisted that they finish their packing and rest until sunset, when the senel would begin.

As the sun began to set, they were escorted into her portion of the tent. 'The rite has begun,' she said softly as she settled in the chair beside Ezren. 'Tomorrow morning, when the children emerge as warriors, there will be feasting and pattern dancing until everyone drops with exhaustion.'

'Pattern dancing?' Ezren asked.

'Group dancing,' Bethral murmured. She was standing just behind his shoulder.

'Ah.' Ezren would ask for more details later, if he remembered. For the hundredth time, he wished he had paper and ink, so he could write down everything about these people. Might as well ask for a portal to Edenrich.

For now, he'd just have to trust to his storyteller's memory and remember what he heard and saw. But as he watched, more warriors entered the tent and settled down before them, and all he could think was how very different everything was here on the Plains.

'I've gathered the ones I trust.' Haya spoke for Ezren's benefit alone. 'Old and wise. We must hear, and we must consider.'

Ezren nodded and watched as a few more entered. Haya had seen to food and drink, with pitchers of kavage warming in braziers and bowls of gurt. Finally, Haya gestured, and the flap was sealed with what seemed to be a hundred bells. They chimed softly as people moved around the tent, settling down.

'So' – Haya raised her voice as the last one took his seat – 'we are guarded and private. I would have you hear the words of Ezren Storyteller, Singer of the City, words that even I have not yet heard. But before he speaks, let us make sure we all know of recent events.' She started with the arrival of Ezren and Bethral.

There were fifteen warriors all told – a few that Ezren recognised, a few he didn't. They listened in silence, their full attention on Haya. Some had their eyes half closed, looking down, absorbing the words.

She told of the fight with the warrior-priests, and the discovery of Wild Winds seated out on the Plains. Then she turned to Ezren, and all that attention focused directly on him.

Ezren glanced at Bethral before he started to talk, to make sure she was ready to translate. He didn't want to risk any misunderstanding with this information. And he didn't embellish, either – there was no need for dramatic pauses. The information was enough. He saw that in their eyes as he spoke of what Wild Winds had told him.

The warriors were silent, still, deep pools taking in every word. They reminded him of someone else, another warrior who had listened intently to the secret that he had shared. He frowned a bit, and forced himself to focus on the task at hand.

Finally, Ezren reached the point where he told Wild Winds that he would not go to the Heart of the Plains. There was silence after his last words, then Haya reached for a pitcher of kavage and poured him a mug. Everyone filled their cups and some took handfuls of gurt.

'This is the night of the Rite of Ascension, when our children emerge at dawn as warriors.' Haya spoke softly. 'This is a night normally spent in consideration of what is past and what is to come. Joy that our children have grown tall and strong. Pain that they now leave our tents for the freedoms and the dangers of the Plains.'

Seo grunted. 'But not this night.'

'No.' Haya drew a deep breath. 'Not this night. The Singer of the City has honored us with information withheld by the—'

'Bragnects,' Urte growled. The warriors around her nodded in response. 'Bragnects, all.'

That word. Bethral had used it when they'd first been challenged. Ezren turned his head slightly in her direction.

'A grave insult,' came a soft whisper. 'To be used with care.'

'Is that a hard "g" or a hard "c"?'

There was a pause, and a stifled cough. 'They have no written language, Storyteller.' Bethral's voice sounded a bit strangled. 'It can be as you wish.'

'Ah.' Ezren turned his attention back to the group.

'Their status and power are all they care for,' another warrior spat. 'May they wander in the snows forever.'

'Yet . . .' Seo waited until he had everyone's attention. 'Yet it is a warrior-priest that gives us the very information that has been withheld for so long.'

There was a murmur at that.

'Wild Winds is a clever fox,' Ezren said, then hesitated. 'You know foxes?'

There were many smiles at that. 'Aye, we know them well.'

'Seo is of the Fox Tribe, Storyteller,' Haya said with a smile.

'Oh.' Ezren flashed a nervous grin. 'Then you know what I mean.'

'We do,' Seo said. 'And I agree. I think Wild Winds is caught between rutting ehats and raging grass fires.'

'Pah. He does little enough, if what he says is true,' Urte said. 'Does he offer the Storyteller aid with what he bears? No. "Come with me or die" is all that he says.'

'He did not bind my words,' Ezren said. 'By speaking to me, he spoke to you, even if it was indirectly. Maybe' – Ezren hesitated – 'maybe he didn't offer more because he has no more information to offer. No protections to give.'

'A warrior-priest who is . . . dying . . . and who has not sought the snows . . . his truths may not be considered,' Quartis spoke up. 'For all their claim of magic, who has heard of a warrior-priest who cannot heal his own pains, eh?'

'What magics do they have?' Ezren looked intently at the faces around him. 'He said their magic was weak and thin now. Do you know?'

A warrior growled. 'For years, they have claimed much, and done little for the tribes. They have taken of the best of the raids, and claimed the prime meats of hunts. They swagger around as if the elements moved at their will and whim.'

'They are said to be able to heal,' Quartis said. 'But they heal only those they deem worthy. They withhold that power more often than not.'

'And now we know why,' Urte grumbled.

'They disappear with no warning, out in the grasses,' another warrior added. 'Seeming to disappear into the land itself.'

'And they seem to know things before any other, as if the messages ride the wind,' Seo said. 'How else did Wild Winds know what had happened so fast?'

'One thing I know for certain,' Haya said. 'I have never seen them throw fire at an enemy, Storyteller. Never once have I seen such a thing, in all the battles I have fought in. That I have heard of only in the oldest songs.'

'Songs so old, they are sung rarely. Songs of warrior-priests wielding magics in battle. Of calling fire from the skies, and freezing enemies with blasts of cold,' Quartis nodded. 'Had I time, I'd sing them for you.'

'But time is what we do not have. The night flows past us like a stream, and we must make decisions before the rite ends.' Haya poured herself more kavage. 'So—'

'We must leave,' Ezren said firmly. 'Wild Winds said that more warrior-priests will come, and I will not endanger your camp. The children—'

'Peace, Storyteller,' Seo said. 'I agree.'

There were nods all around.

'We are not comfortable with what you bear, Singer,' Haya said. 'Although I think you would burn yourself to a blackened husk before you would hurt a child.'

Ezren gave her a grateful look.

'But the real question is where?' Quartis mused. 'Where should you go?'

'I see three choices,' Haya said.

Ezren felt Bethral shift behind him.

'Three?' Seo looked at her. 'Name them.'

Haya held up a finger. 'They can return to their own land and seek out the wisdom of their own people in this matter.'

Ezren didn't react, but he knew full well that the most experienced mages in the Kingdom of Edenrich hadn't known how to deal with him and his rogue powers. But he kept silent.

Haya lifted another finger. 'They could seek out Keir of the Cat and the Warprize. Who knows, perhaps the appearance of the Warprize called these people here.' Haya snorted. 'If it is change Keir wants, here is change by the handful.'

'And the final choice, Haya?'

Haya hesitated, then lowered her hand. 'They could seek the snows.'

Ezren jerked.

'I do not demand this,' Haya said. 'But if you cannot control the magic, and you do not wish to see it used by the warrior-priests . . .' She let her voice trail off. 'I know that is not your way, but it is ours.'

'No,' Ezren said firmly. 'I understand your words, but we are going to return home. Wild Winds claims that the magic I bear is of the Plains, but I have no proof of that. We will go.'

'Then I will end this senel now,' Haya said.

'But there is more we need decide,' Seo protested. 'What will we do now that we—'

'True,' Haya said as she rose to her feet. 'But these two must prepare to leave, and I will not waste another moment of their time. Later, we can debate what to do with our knowledge. For now—'

'We must end this talk,' Quartis said. He rose to his feet as well. 'I wish you well, Storyteller.'

Ezren nodded as the others rose and left the tent.

Haya retied the flaps. 'There is much to say, and little time.' She knelt on the edge of the platform. 'Look here.'

She dipped her finger in a mug of kavage and drew a large circle on the rough wooden planks. 'These are the Plains.'

Ezren leaned over as Bethral knelt next to the circle.

'The Heart lies here, beside a large lake.' Haya wet her finger again and dotted the center of the circle.

'The Kingdom of Xy?' Ezren asked. 'Where is—'

Haya placed a dot almost due north of the Heart.

'Palins?' Bethral asked.

Haya placed a dot to the southeast of the Heart. 'And we are here.' Her finger pressed a point just below the Heart of the Plains. 'The mountains that circle the Plains are high and vast, but in certain places they are easily crossed.'

'That's how you raid the surrounding kingdoms,' Ezren said.

Haya nodded. 'As far as I know, there are but small trails into your land. But in a few places, like Xy, there are wide valleys that will take you to other lands and cities.'

'How far?' Ezren asked, pointing to the dot that was Palins. 'How many miles?'

'Eh?' Haya looked at Bethral.

'How long to get there?' Bethral said.

'I do not know for certain.' Haya shrugged. 'Almost a full round of the seasons.'

'A world away,' Ezren said slowly, studying the drying markings on the rough wood.

'To seek out the Warprize would take us past the Heart. I do not think that is wise. So we should head south,' Bethral said. 'The most direct path.'

'No. The warrior-priests will expect that,' Haya replied softly. 'Go northeast. There is a trade route through the mountains to the cities of Dellison. Those of the mountains will see you through.'

'Dellison shares a border with Soccia,' Bethral said.

'We don't have much coin,' Ezren pointed out.

'But we have my sword and your stories,' Bethral replied. 'We might not travel in the highest style, but we'd get you home.'

'Dellison, to Soccia, to Palins and home.' Ezren shook his head. 'Months of travel.'

'But once you are off the Plains, you are safe – or at least safer,' Haya said. 'Away from the warrior-priests and their schemes.' She looked at Bethral. 'Tell no one of your path. Head south from the camp, then circle to the east and north.'

Bethral reached for the mug of kavage and spilled it on the platform, erasing the crude map. 'Thank you for your wisdom, Elder.'

'There is more.' Haya looked at Ezren. 'Some of the children' – she paused with a rueful smile – 'some of the warriors have asked to quest, to travel with you and see you safely home. I have agreed to their request.'

'The young ones?' Ezren frowned. 'Haya, no. They are children—'

'Children that know more about survival then we do,' Bethral said. 'At least, under these conditions.'

'They are warriors now,' Haya said. 'They have a right to make their own decisions. Normally, the young ones go off to the Heart to join the armies of the warlords once they have been selected. But that is not always the way. They will restore the honor of our tribe by seeing you home. Once that is accomplished, they can seek out the service of a warlord or take some other path. That is their choice.' Haya sighed. 'I know you will take a great care for them, even as they care for you.' She stood. 'You need to prepare. Bethral, come with me and we will see to the horses.'

'The new warriors will be disappointed that they will miss the celebrations,' Ezren said.

'Little do you know, Storyteller.' Haya chuckled. 'They will think themselves in one of your stories, living a great adventure.'

*

Haya took Bethral with her to see to a selection of horses. Ezren went to their portion of the tent, to gather up the last of their things.

The cat was spread out on Bethral's pallet on its side, taking up every inch of space it could. When it spotted him, it half curled onto its back, purring roughly.

'Oh, no,' Ezren snorted, 'I reach down to scratch that fat stomach and you bite me. I am not fooled.'

The cat half closed its eyes and increased the intensity of its rumbling.

'We're going home. You had better stick close, because we are going to be moving fast.' Ezren rattled on, kneeling down to start rolling the bedding. Bethral had given him instructions, and it seemed easy enough.

'Although the Lady knows you are getting fat on the mice here.' He was babbling. He knew very well he was babbling, rattling along, talking to a cat, for the love of the Lady.

They will think themselves in one of your stories, living a great adventure.

Haya's words came back, haunting him as they echoed in his brain.

Living a great adventure was not a comfortable thing. People suffered in great adventures – died, even. He should know. He'd been in a few 'adventures', hadn't he? Some, like Bethral, came out unscarred and unchanged. Others . . . he looked at the scars on his wrists. Others were not so lucky.

Not that he wished anyone to be hurt, or to have to go through what he had endured. Still . . .

He chuckled ruefully. He had told those kinds of stories for years, watched his audience suffer with the heroes. But those were not just characters that he had made up in his head. At one time, they had been real people, flesh and blood, flesh that suffered and blood that spilled.

And true enough, heroes suffered in stories. Else of what interest would they be?

The cat lifted its head, as if spotting prey. With a graceful ease, it rose and stalked over by Bethral's packs, sniffing the area around them.

Ezren frowned as he continued to roll the bedding tight. With any luck, they would ride straight for the mountains with no trouble, no one hurt, no great adventure.

He sighed. Maybe he should go to the Heart.

The cat started pawing at Bethral's pack, worming its head under the flap, trying to climb inside.

Ezren paused, looking down at the bedroll without really seeing it. Haya and the other warriors had explained the warrior-priests and their arrogance. He'd seen it himself when his attacker had raised the lance against him. He knew of the abuses of power, he'd felt that firsthand when he had been taken and enslaved. The scars on his wrists were a constant reminder of men and women abusing their power.

There didn't seem to be any correct answer, and no sign from the Gods or the elements that those of the Plains worshipped. He had made a decision, and he'd abide by it. If the warrior-priests respected it as Wild Winds had, maybe their journey home would be a peaceful one.

Ezren finished the roll and looked about for the leather ties that Bethral had said were by her pallet. There was no sign of them. The cat had probably dragged them off someplace. Or perhaps there were more in her pack.

'Here, let's see if your prey is in here.' Ezren reached over and started to empty the pack, piling the contents on Bethral's pallet.

No mouse. The cat pawed around the various items as he worked, then pounced on a bundle of leather in the middle of the heap.

'Ah.' Ezren picked out the cluster of leather strips and started to return the other items to the pack. 'Not the neatest job, but everything will at least be in the bag.' He glanced at the cat. 'Now what is that you are playing with?'

The leather bundle lay open, and there, in the middle of a

ragged bit of cloth, lay a dagger with a horn handle and a blade of stone.

The sacrifice blade.

The blade used to sacrifice him.

FOURTEEN

A vision flashed before Ezren Storyteller's eyes.

They had him, five warriors, one holding each leg and arm and one gripping his collar. They dragged him, screaming, toward the altar and heaved him up as if he was nothing more than a pig to a slaughter table.

Another moved up, a robed figure with dark hair and eyes as cold as Ezren had ever seen during his slavery. The mage held a dagger with a blade as black as night.

The warriors stretched him out; his spine cracked as they pulled. Ezren's breath came fast as he gasped out every curse and insult he could think of, unable to stop this horror, unable to . . . he looked away—

—and saw Red Gloves, in tattered gambeson, her face filled with rage and a rusted, jagged shard of a sword in her hand. She was running toward them with deadly intent.

They hadn't seen her. Surprise was her only advantage. His captors were focused on him, and him alone, and he had to make sure—

Ezren jerked his head around, and stared into the eyes of the mage. The man had the dagger high, ready to strike.

'Damn you,' Ezren shouted. He spat in the man's face. 'Go ahead, foul monster, kill me. Kill me!'

The mage plunged the blade into Ezren's chest.

Something bumped Ezren's ankle, and he looked down; the cat was twining itself around his feet.

Ezren swallowed hard, his mouth as dry as dust. He felt flushed and chilled at the same time, and he sank to the ground and sat for a moment, trying to breathe.

The stone dagger lay there in the cloth and leather as if it had never plunged into his chest.

Red Gloves had told them the rest of the tale. How she'd killed the mage and then each of his men. How she'd pulled the dagger free from his chest and the magic had surged up and out, restoring his life and the lives of their friends.

Ezren remembered awakening to her wide eyes with a sense of heat and power, and looking over to see Bethral lying there, her body tossed aside like a rag doll. Remembered extending his hand, and asking . . . wanting . . .

Ezren swallowed hard.

Lord High Mage Marlon had said that he carried the wild magic within him, and that the dagger was not magical. But Ezren wasn't sure he believed that.

There was something else . . .

The cat was batting at the bundle of leather strips now, as if it were prey. Ezren closed his eyes and forced himself to remember, to see again what had happened.

They had him, five warriors, one holding each leg and arm and one gripping his collar. They dragged him, and heaved him up as if he was nothing more than a pig to a slaughter table.

No emotion in their eyes, as if they were doing a simple chore.

He saw Red Gloves, in tattered gambeson, her face filled with rage and a rusted, jagged shard of a sword in her hand. She was running toward them with deadly intent.

Too late. He had known she could not stop them, known she needed surprise . . .

'Damn you,' Ezren shouted. He spat in the man's face.

He could see the man's sharp face and his cold, dead eyes. So cruel, and yet it was as if the soul behind those eyes was frozen in pure ice.

'Go ahead, foul monster, kill me. Kill me!'

The mage plunged the blade into Ezren's chest.

Ezren opened his eyes, and stared at the leather walls of the tent.

He'd been willing. Willing to die to give her the chance to avenge them. Willing sacrifice, willingly made.

Wild Winds's voice echoed in Ezren's head. '*Magic was taken from the Plains. Only the blood of the Plains can restore it, in a willing sacrifice. Willing blood, willingly spilled.*'

Lord of Light and Lady of Laughter, what did it mean?

A rustle at the tent flap was the only warning he got. He looked up, and saw Bethral staring at the dagger.

Her blue eyes took him in with concern. 'Did you touch it?'

Ezren shook his head. 'No. The cat—'

Bethral knelt, and wrapped the dagger in the cloth and leather. She crammed it into the saddlebag with a sharp thrust. 'We'll talk about this later. Haya is just behind me.' She paused, looking at him. 'I . . .' She looked away. 'I didn't pack it. I wouldn't—'

Ezren drew a breath, caught by the fear now plain in her eyes. 'I think,' he whispered, 'I remembered—'

Footsteps outside brought them to their feet as Haya pushed aside the flap. 'Let's see if this fits you.'

'Who?' Ezren asked, confused at the sight of the leather armor in her hands. Bethral was already dressed in her plate.

'You, Storyteller.'

Dawn was well past when they gathered before the tent with horses, remounts, and gear.

The rite had ended, and the new warriors had emerged into the sun to be greeted by the tribe with loud rejoicing. Wild Winds and the other warrior-priests who had conducted the ceremony had left immediately, destination unknown.

In the distance, sounds of celebration came from the main camp. The drums were signaling the start of the dancing. Bethral looked for disappointment in the young faces around her, but all she saw was fascination.

Rare to have such an audience for horseshoe removal.

Bessie lifted her last hoof at Bethral's command, then leaned in on her. Bethral grunted, and dug an elbow into the horse's side. 'Not so much, lazy girl.'

Bessie snorted, but straightened a bit. She bore only her normal saddle and saddlebags. The barding had been packed away, distributed between the pack horses. Bethral had tried to gift it to Haya, but she had refused. 'Our horses would not tolerate it,' Haya had said. 'Besides, I suspect you'll need it at some point.'

Bethral was afraid she was right. But for now, for a full-out forced run, Bessie didn't need the weight.

Bethral worked the shoe loose and let it drop to the grass. Gilla picked it up, examining it. 'All the horses wear these?'

'Yes,' Bethral said shortly, checking Bessie's hoof for splits before she released it. 'It protects their feet in the cities.'

'But why remove them?' El asked, his brown eyes intent.

'Think,' Seo commanded.

El frowned. Arbon elbowed him in the side. 'Tracks.'

'Tracks,' Haya confirmed as Bethral put her tools in her saddlebags. 'Now, warriors, to me.'

Bethral watched as the young ones gathered close to Haya, surrounding her. They all wore newer armor and all had been given weapons. The tribe had equipped them with the basics they needed to start their new lives as warriors. Their horses were saddled and packed, and each warrior bore a bow with arrows and a quiver of lances. Anything else they would have to earn from their military service.

Haya lowered her voice, and they leaned in and listened intently, nodding.

Bethral gave the lances another look. They were about four feet in length, with deadly stone tips and feathered ends. The tips were designed to break off in the enemy's body, causing terrible wounds. She'd like to try her hand at using one, if she had the chance.

She'd thought of going without her plate and arming herself as one of the Plains. But the plate was her best defense . . . and a Plains warrior or a warrior-priest might think twice before attacking a warrior wrapped in metal.

Haya stepped back, away from the young warriors. 'So. The tribe has provided you with your needs. Honor the tribe with your deeds and your truths. Mount and away. Seo and I must return to the celebrations before we are missed.'

'Orient me,' Ezren said. 'Which way is the Heart?'

Everyone pointed north.

'So Palins is—'

Everyone pointed south.

Ezren muttered something under his breath that sounded like Elvish. Bethral suppressed a smile. Knowing him, it was probably something fairly rude.

Ezren reached for the reins and turned to mount his horse. Bethral took a moment to appreciate the view as he put his foot in the stirrup.

They'd found hardened leather armor for him to wear. It was an older set, and the brown showed signs of use. But the color suited him well, echoing the reddish tint of his hair. And the leathers . . .

Bethral swallowed as they tightened over his buttocks when the Storyteller swung into the saddle.

Haya had insisted that he be armored. Her concern had been more for arrows and lances than for sword fighting. 'The armor isn't as good as Bethral's,' she'd said, 'but it's better than plain cloth.'

Yes, Haya was right. The leathers had been a fine idea.

Bethral flushed a bit at the fact that she was ogling Ezren, but she could not tear her eyes away as he settled in the saddle. So she caught an odd look in Ezren's eyes when he gathered the reins and looked to the north.

'Storyteller?' She moved closer, and saw a haunted expression in his green eyes.

'You didn't tell me he couldn't ride,' Haya said.

'What?' As Ezren spoke, the odd look disappeared, to be replaced with indignation. 'I can ride.'

'The way you sit—' Seo frowned.

'Maybe he could ride double?' Haya asked.

'He'll be fine.' Bethral swung up in her saddle. 'All he has to do is stay in the saddle.'

All eyes turned to her, and Seo nodded in satisfaction. 'Now, she can ride a horse.'

'I can ride.' Ezren gave them all a glare. He gathered the reins, clicked his tongue, and urged the horse on.

Nothing happened.

Bethral had to bite her lip hard and look away at the outrage on the Storyteller's face.

'Double, I think.' Haya confirmed. 'With Gilla. She's the smallest.'

Now Bethral had to look away from Gilla's face before she laughed right out loud. 'Storyteller, lean forward and use your toes under the horses' front legs, instead of your heels.'

Bethral looked over at Haya. 'We use different signals with our animals, that's all.'

Ezren's horse moved a few steps, but Haya frowned just the same. 'His seat is pathetic.'

'Look here,' Seo asked, 'the last warrior to join the party, eh?'

Bethral looked down and saw the cat at Seo's feet. The cat thumped down on its side and curled up, showing its belly. 'Don't fall for—'

Too late. Seo had already bent down, reaching for the enticing softness. 'You've grown fat on our mice, Warrior.'

The cat bit his finger.

Seo jerked his hand back, and the cat leaped for the bedroll attached to Bessie's saddle. It kneaded the cloth for a moment, then sank its claws deep and settled down with a smug look.

'Ha!' Seo shook his head with a rueful look. 'I should have known a fierce warrior wouldn't show its belly that way.'

'Looks are deceiving,' Bethral agreed, relieved to note that the skin of his finger was unbroken. She looked around the group. 'Ready?'

The Storyteller was facing north, but he turned to her and nodded. The rest of the warriors gazed at her, their faces eager.

Bethral looked down at Haya, who also gave her a nod. 'Time, and past. Storyteller, when you tell this tale, speak of the honor of the Tribe of the Snake, and those who have dealt with you fairly.'

'I will,' Ezren promised.

'Bethral of the Horse' – Haya stepped close and lowered her voice – 'You ride with unblooded warriors. We have offered you one of our most precious resources, the lives of our young.'

'I am their warlord in all things,' Bethral said softly. 'Their flesh is my flesh, their blood is my blood.'

'Then ride.' Haya stepped back, and raised her voice for all to hear. 'May the elements guide and protect you all.'

Bethral started Bessie off at a trot, and the others followed.

The sun was high before Wild Winds signaled to the others to make camp in a thicket of alders by a wide stream.

He swung down from his horse and had to clutch at the saddle, willing his legs to support him. The rite had taken much of his strength. He closed his eyes against the weakness. He should have left it up to the younger warrior-priests, he supposed, but he'd always enjoyed bringing the young to adulthood. Something about their eager faces . . .

'Elder,' Snowfall said quietly behind him, 'I've set your stool in the shade. Take your rest while we set up the tents.'

Wild Winds nodded. He untied his staff from his saddle, and took a step away from the horse. His legs steadied beneath him.

Snowfall moved with him, and he gratefully placed a hand on her shoulder. Gone were the days when he tried to hide his weakness from his fellow warrior-priests. And as for the people of the Plains learning of his illness, well, that prey had fled now, and he'd been the one to spook it, hadn't he?

Using the staff for support, he eased onto his stool with a sigh.

'Do you wish food, or kavage?' Snowfall asked softly. 'There's none hot, but—'

'I'm well enough,' Wild Winds replied.

Snowfall hesitated. 'Your scrying bowl?'

'Not right now,' Wild Winds said. 'That can wait until the camp is set and we have eaten.'

'As you say,' Snowfall replied, the slightest of smiles on her lips. 'Night Clouds has decided to hunt, and a few of the others are going with him. They spotted a herd of red deer, and there's odan root along the stream.'

'Fresh meat is always welcome.' Wild Winds set his staff down, careful of the skulls. 'Leave me to my thoughts, Snowfall. I am not so far gone as to need a thea once again.'

'As you say,' she answered, and her tone made it clear that she wasn't pleased. But she did as he had bidden.

So. Wild Winds drew a breath of sweet air and let it out slowly.

There would be no healing at the hands of the Singer of the City. When he'd heard that the token-bearer's leg had been healed, he'd hoped. But it was not to be. And even if the young man . . . Ezren Storyteller . . . had been willing to release the magic with his death, still it would take time to relearn the old ways. Wild Winds wasn't such a fool as to think that the magic would instantly gift warrior-priests with powers.

But they were such fools, and they were not listening to an elder sickened and dying.

The sundering of the Council of Elders had torn the Plains in two. Between two camps, as it were. Keir of the Cat sat on the one side, firm in his belief in changes to come and his hatred of the warrior-priests. Antas of the Boar on the other side, firm in his refusal to change the way of the Plains, and his certainty of the rightness of his actions. Two strong warlords, stubborn and determined.

As Eldest Elder of the Warrior-Priests, Wild Winds was caught between the two, his fellows ranging on both sides. Add to that his . . . what was the Xyian word the Warprize had used?

He frowned. Eh, he was getting old.

Cancer. That was the word.

The coming of a Warprize. The sundering of the Council of

Elders. The appearance of the Sacrifice. And his cancer on top of everything else.

He could almost hear the winds laugh as they rustled the leaves in the alders about him.

Wild Winds wasn't sure he'd done the right thing by letting the Sacrifice – by letting Ezren Storyteller – return to his homeland. Certainly the others would not agree with his decision. But their belief had always been that a warrior-priest would return the magic to the Plains. The magic borne by a city dweller?

And if magic was restored in the midst of all this turmoil, what would that do?

Oh, yes, that was laughter on the wind, all right.

He watched as his warriors worked on the camp. Watched the ripple of their muscles under the colored tattoos they all bore. Tattoos they had earned as they had learned the ways of the warrior-priests and had shown that they had the ability to wield magic. What little remained in the land. He'd taught them well, and they were loyal to him. How best to ensure they survived the coming wars?

For there would be wars. Wars between warlords, between the tribes. Wild Winds wasn't certain there was any way to prevent that. Hadn't Gathering Storm attacked him at the Council of Elders? Hadn't Antas shouted orders for the death of the War-prize?

Wild Winds drew in another breath and tried to empty his mind as he released it, seeking guidance from the elements. He closed his eyes and listened, focusing on the now, on the essence of his life and breath, on the moment.

No easy answers flowed to mind. Such was not to be.

The only truth he knew at this moment was that he would not seek the snows. His death would come, that was sure. But as long as he drew breath, he'd try to do what he had sworn to do when he became the Eldest Elder of the Warrior-Priests of the Plains.

He would serve his people.

A slight creak of leathers. Wild Winds opened his eyes and

saw young Lightning Strike standing there, his tattoos not yet filled in all the way. The youngest of his band.

'Your tent is ready, Elder. Would you rest until the meal is ready?'

Wild Winds considered. There were those waiting for his report, for news of the Sacrifice. But who could blame a dying old man for needing a nap?

Make them wait. Serve them right. Maybe even wait until the morning.

'Elder?' Lightning Strike repeated.

Wild Winds nodded, and accepted his hand to rise. He'd let them stew in their own juices.

And give the Sacrifice time to flee.

FIFTEEN

'You did what?'

Wild Winds arched an eyebrow and said nothing.

Night Clouds had been successful in his hunt and had brought down a fat red deer, a young buck. The meat had been roasted well, and full of juices. Wild Winds had been offered the organs, as his rank required, but he'd declined, leaving first honors to the hunter. He'd managed to eat a few bites of meat and drink the rich broth. His belly was pleasantly full. The tent had been warmed with braziers, the kavage was hot and strong.

Life was good.

Four of the younger warrior-priests sat on the corners of a ceremonial blanket, a wide bowl of water in the center. They were casting their magics, working together to throw the spell that let him speak to the one whose image appeared in the bowl as if standing on the water. They were doing well enough to see him from the top of his head to the soles of his feet. They had learned well, and Wild Winds was proud of them.

Life was very good.

And, he admitted to himself, it was a pleasure to see the ethereal figure of Hail Storm before him, sputtering in rage.

Snowfall and some of the others sat back in the shadows of the tent, where they could see and hear but not be seen. They needed to listen, to learn and know what was said.

So far, all they had heard were some fairly colorful curses.

'I let him go,' Wild Winds said at last. 'He refused to accompany me to the Heart, and I accepted his decision.'

'He is the Sacrifice!' Hail Storm sputtered again. He was a tall man, strong and broad of chest, with colorful tattoos. A handsome man when his face was not twisted in frustration. Wild Winds tried not to smirk.

'He bears the magic,' Hail Storm said, bringing himself under control and acting as if he were instructing a child. 'You should have forced him.'

'Which worked so well for Grass Fires,' Wild Winds observed dryly. 'And how is taking him by force "willing"?'

'The words of the past can be changed to meet our needs,' Hail Storm said. 'It would be fitting that one city dweller brings a challenge to our powers and another restores them.'

'Even at the loss of our honor?' Wild Winds asked.

'Now we have lost time,' Hail Storm snarled. He looked about a tent at people Wild Winds could not see. 'We must hunt him down.'

'No,' Wild Winds said calmly.

Hail Storm jerked his head around to stare at him.

Wild Winds sat, serene. Waiting.

'I cry challenge, Wild Winds. I challenge you, before all, for the position of Eldest Elder.'

'A difficulty,' Wild Winds said. 'Since I am here, and you are miles away.'

'Do you accept the challenge?' Hail Storm asked politely.

'I do,' Wild Winds answered. 'And I will return to the Heart, there to face your challenge.'

'I will kill you,' Hail Storm said with calm assurance. 'Or the elements will.'

'But until you do or until the elements act,' Wild Winds replied mildly, 'I am the Eldest Elder and I will be obeyed.'

That made Hail Storm hesitate, conscious of his audience. Wild Winds remained still, listening to the murmurs behind the healthy, strong warrior-priest before him. Caught on the horns of an ehat, they were. If they clung to the old ways, as they said they did, then his word was to be obeyed until he lost his title through challenge.

But oh, how they hungered for the magic and the power it

would restore. He could almost feel it through the spell. Which would win? Their hunger? Or their honor?

The murmurs continued, yet Wild Winds stayed silent. He'd reported his meeting, he'd announced his decision. The next few minutes would tell which way the winds would blow.

He fancied he could see Snowfall's gray eyes glittering in the shadows. She felt as he did, and was willing to use her sword to prove it. Ah, the young . . .

'You are ill, Eldest Elder,' Hail Storm said slowly. 'Your mind is not what it was.'

Ah, so it was to be their hunger.

'We shall see. You have challenged, and I have answered. I will arrive in the Heart soon enough. Prepare your blade.' Wild Winds snapped his fingers, and the spell broke.

The four young ones blinked, and looked around them as if dazed.

'You did well,' Wild Winds said. 'I am very pleased. Were you able to hear and see as well?'

All but one nodded. Young Lightning Strike shook his head. 'I am sorry, Eldest, but I could hear very little. The spell took all my focus.'

'The skill will come, in time.' Wild Winds looked at them. They'd set protective wards around the area before the spell had begun, so that all could witness this exchange. 'We will tell you what you missed. Just know for now that they have chosen power over honor.'

'So they will pursue the Sacrifice?' Moon Waters asked.

'Let us hope that he and his token-bearer have already fled,' Snowfall said. 'It will be hard to find them in the Plains, if they are careful.'

'I am not so sure,' Night Clouds spoke up. 'One of them might reveal him. I was approached at the end of the ceremony by one of the young, one who wishes to join our ranks and is qualified. Some of the young have asked to quest, to go with the Sacrifice.'

Wild Winds sighed. 'Where is the honor in betrayal?'

'That was my response, Elder,' Night Clouds said. 'But the warrior was called away before we could talk more.'

'What now, Elder?' Snowfall asked.

'We go to the Heart of the Plains.' Wild Winds sighed. 'One way or another, my journey ends there.'

'He's gelded,' Lander said.

'Lander!' Gilla checked to make sure that neither Bethral nor the Storyteller was nearby. Bethral was carrying the Storyteller's packs, showing him a good place to bed down. Once Gilla knew it was safe, she rolled her eyes. 'He's not.'

'He is, else they'd be sharing. And there she is, setting up his tent for him to sleep in, alone,' Lander said firmly, as he took the saddlebags off his horse, 'So, he is gelded.'

'Fool.' Chell was nearby, unloading another horse. 'To speak so without a token in your hand.'

'More fool for worrying about sharing,' Tenna said. 'I'm so tired I can barely think. I'm sure the Storyteller is, too.'

There was that. Bethral had pushed them hard for two days straight. She'd made no apologies for it, and ignored even the Storyteller's discomfort. For two days they'd alternated between a fast trot and a gallop, staying low, off the rises, and with a cold camp in between. Frequent breaks, but only to water the horses and change mounts. Even Lander was sagging a bit as he worked to get this camp set up.

And it was to be another cold camp. No fire, and they'd eat only gurt and drink water. Gilla sighed ruefully.

On the other hand, they'd put quite a distance between themselves and the thea camp. And the farther they traveled, the less likely it was that the warrior-priests would find them, skies willing.

'Perhaps another day and she will relent,' Gilla said hopefully.

'Perhaps she shouldn't lead this party at all,' Arbon said, tossing back his black hair.

They all gaped at him.

'Have the winds taken your wits?' Lander said. 'I'm of her size, and I won't challenge.'

'She's not so tough. I can take her,' Arbon said, puffing out his chest. 'I should take charge, and see them safely off the Plains.'

'We came on this quest to aid them, not challenge them.' Lander threw his hands in the air. 'Why did you come, then?'

'Glory,' Cosana said sharply. 'He's going to be a warlord, now isn't he?'

'I will aid them' – Arbon lifted his chin – 'but I can do that better if I challenge her and take command.'

'We are warriors now, not children,' Chell reminded him sharply. 'She will kill you.'

'She's not of the Plains.' Arbon's jaw was set. 'And the skies favor the bold.'

'And the earth covers the stupid,' El said.

'She's coming,' Tenna hissed.

Gilla watched as Bethral strode up and reached to help Ouse with a pack he was struggling with. 'Cold camp again tonight. Five watches, two hours each. Each of you take one, I don't care what order. I'll take the last watch alone. I want you all sharp.'

'We will be, Warrior,' Arbon said, bold as could be.

Bethral gave him an appraising look. 'See that you are.' She looked around at the others. 'Tomorrow we will watch for a good camp, and stop early. Somewhere we can rest, and have a fire. Somewhere with water, and alders to shelter us, if possible. Keep an eye out as we ride.'

There was a chorus of agreement to that except from Arbon. Gilla held her breath, but Arbon did nothing else. Bethral noticed, though. But she just turned and walked away.

'Why didn't you challenge?' El prodded Arbon. 'You were insolent enough. If she'd been of the Plains—'

'But she's not,' Arbon said. 'And my time is coming.'

Ezren hurt.

He hurt in ways he wasn't about to confess. He'd ridden before, certainly, but not like this. Never like this. He'd taken abuse as a beaten slave, and this was nothing compared to that – it wasn't like he was going to collapse. But the muscle aches and twinges – Lord of Light, he ached.

Bethral was coming back, walking toward him easily, as if not a muscle ached. She had been riding just as hard, and encased in metal.

He needed to stop complaining and get some sleep. But even that held guilt, for he knew that the young ones were standing guard while he slept through the night.

And for the life of him, he couldn't figure out his leather sleeping tent. It had been set up for him the night before, and he'd crawled into it, grateful for its shelter. But now it lay spread out before him, limp and useless.

Bethral walked up. 'Problems?'

Ezren sighed. Yet another chance to look stupid in front of the Angel of Light. And she was speaking in the language of the Plains because he'd asked her to. The best way to learn the language was to immerse yourself in it in all ways. So now he had to think before he could say 'I can't quite—'

Bethral nodded. 'Lander had to show me twice before I got it.'

'Really?' Ezren asked.

'It's not what we think of as a tent.' Bethral lifted the circle of leather and spread it out carefully. Then she folded it over, so that the crazy quilt pattern of leather was on the outside. 'It's scraps of waxed leather sewn together with gut. Think of it more as a pocket of bread that you tuck yourself into.'

She reached for the alder branches that had been rolled in the leather. 'These go into the holes and keep the leather up off your body. Allows you some breathing space.' She thrust the branches in the special sleeves made for that purpose. 'Four of them are just enough. You are sheltered from the night and the elements, and can't be seen down in the grass. With the gurtle pads under you, you'll be as comfortable as you were in the main camp.' She looked up at him. 'Hand me your bedroll, and I'll see it right for you.'

'Thank you,' Ezren said, then stood and glanced over his shoulder at the horizon. 'Shouldn't I be standing watch? I feel—'

'The warriors are used to it – it was one of their duties in the camp. And I'm an old hand at watch.' Bethral stood. 'You need rest, Storyteller. Later, when your body has grown used to this, we will see.' She tilted her head, and gave him an odd look. 'What's back there?' she asked.

'What?' Ezren asked with a puzzled look.

'You keep looking back the way we came,' she said. 'Why?'

'I don't . . .' He looked over his shoulder again, the skin between his eyebrows wrinkling up. 'I don't know. I have this feeling. As if I've forgotten something. Something important.'

Bethral frowned. 'We didn't leave anything behind in Haya's tent.'

'It's nothing,' Ezren said, shaking his head.

'You're tired,' Bethral said. 'We all are. The horses, too. I've told the others that we'll stop early tomorrow once we find a good camp. Hot food, water to wash if we can manage it.' She leaned down and opened his sleep tent. 'Crawl in, Storyteller.'

'Armor and all.' Ezren took a final look to the north, then crawled in.

Bethral lowered the top, and he was encased in a moment, feeling the softness of his pallet beneath him. The gurtle pads beneath were also used as saddle pads, so there was a hint of horse in the spicy scent of the blankets. But right now it felt like the finest feather bed.

'Sleep well, Storyteller,' Bethral said. He heard the slight clank of her armor as she moved off. 'Tomorrow will be an interesting day.'

He frowned, not sure he liked the idea of 'interesting'.

It was a clever little tent. He was grateful for the warmth, but the best part was being off the horse.

His body was relaxing, and he took a moment to loosen his armor and get a bit more comfortable. Sleep wasn't far off, but he was going to try to stay awake for a while.

Ezren eased down, and settled beneath the blankets. The tent had warmed, but there was cooler air seeping through the opening. Bethral had been right, it was very comfortable. But Ezren didn't let himself relax too much. He needed to think. Because the ache in his chest was growing, and that meant only one thing.

The wild magic was back.

And growing stronger.

SIXTEEN

The ache in his chest was usually the signal that the wild magic was back – no, that was not the right way to think about it. More like the pressure was building within him to release . . . something. As if lying with a woman, and building toward . . .

Ezren snorted. Lord Mage Marlon had put it in less than elegant terms. He'd likened it to the need to piss.

'Your body knows – you know – and barring illness or extra-ordinary circumstances you are in control. The urge builds up, you delay, do a bit of a dance, but eventually you gotta go or pee in your pants.' Marlon focused on Ezren. *'He can't, because he's never learned. He doesn't recognise what his body and the magic are telling him.'*

Ezren flushed, and lifted his chin in defiance. 'I am certain I can learn.'

Marlon gave him the eye. 'Maybe. You can learn the feelings, what they mean. But can you learn control? Especially when you are angry, or startled, or—'

Ezren rolled over on his back and stared at the leather over his face. 'Or when I'm wandering on the Plains, where the only people who can help me deal with this want to kill me.'

'Mrowr.' There was a rustle down by his feet, and the edge of the tent lifted slightly as the cat thrust its head in and blinked at him.

Ezren eyed the cat. 'You're welcome to share, Cat. But no dead mice, if you please.'

The cat squirmed in, claiming the blankets over Ezren's feet. It pawed and kneaded for a moment, then curled into a ball.

'Next I suppose you will start talking,' Ezren grumbled.

The cat ignored him.

Ezren sighed. He could hear the others settling into their tents or starting their watches. He should be sleeping. Bethral would want to start early in the morning.

Except the ache was growing, the farther south they rode.

It was like a pull, a tug . . . No. It was a longing. Ezren frowned as he thought about that. It was an emotion, and it wasn't his. He'd asked Josiah about it, back when Josiah was trying to give him lessons. He'd lost control while trying to light a candle. It had felt like the magic had gotten excited. Overeager. But Josiah had shaken his head. *'Magic doesn't have a personality, Ezren. It doesn't have emotion. It's a tool.'*

Josiah had been a powerful mage in his time, and Ezren had no reason to think that he was wrong.

Except that Josiah had never used or wielded wild magic. Any mage that did was destroyed by the Mage Guild. Which had been why Marlon had tried to kill him the first time he had seen him.

Maybe they were wrong. Maybe wild magic had a personality, had emotions. Maybe it worked off his . . . feelings.

Which was why it had healed Bethral.

That brought a smile to his face, and a deep sense of relief. The wild magic might have caused this problem, but it had healed her. It eased some of his guilt, but not all. Bethral was determined to see him – both of them – safely back to Edenrich. Which meant that she stood between him and every warrior-priest on the Plains.

Ezren puffed out a breath. Enough worry. He shifted around a bit, getting comfortable, mindful of the cat at his feet.

Very well. He'd try to use some of this power. He'd try to light a fire, if there was time, when next they made camp. Not a candle – the memory of the burning tent and singed table were fresh in his mind. No, maybe a nice, large fire pit under an open sky. His eyes started to feel heavy.

In the morning . . .

*

'Change of plans,' Bethral said.

They had gathered together for gurt and water. The horses were all saddled, the gear ready to go for another day of hard riding.

Ezren had slept well, but the first few steps out of his tent had made him wish for magical healing powers for his inner thighs. Lord of Light, he hadn't known he had muscles in those places, but he knew now. Walking helped, and he assumed riding would help more, but what he wouldn't give for a hot mineral bath to soak in.

Odd. This little reality was rarely mentioned in the stories and tales of adventure that he knew.

He had a mouthful of gurt when Bethral made her announcement, so he raised his eyebrows, looking for more information.

'There's a large herd of horses off to the west,' Bethral said as she braided up her hair to stuff under her helmet. 'We're going to mingle with the herd and travel with it for a while.'

'Cover our tracks,' El said.

Bethral nodded as she tucked her braid up. 'We'll move with the herd, stay on the edges, and watch for a good campsite. We won't make any distance, but we will confuse our pursuers.'

Arbon stood there, his arms crossed. 'If we continue to ride hard, and make good time, we will outdistance them. That is a better course.'

'Warrior-priests have magic,' Ouse said. 'They will find us anyway.'

Bethral glanced at both of them. 'That may be true, or it may not. Either way, I say we join the herd.'

'No,' Arbon said.

Ezren looked at the lad in surprise, but noted quickly that the others didn't share his emotion. The young shifted about, and suddenly Arbon was facing Bethral across an open space. Bethral just stood there, pulling on her gauntlets, watching Arbon. 'What is this?' Ezren asked, conscious of the sudden tension.

'I challenge,' Arbon said. 'I challenge you for—'

Bethral took three fast steps, and punched him in the face.

Arbon staggered back. Blood streamed down his nose, and his eyes were wide.

Rage swept through Ezren, focused on Arbon. How dare he—

Bethral was already grabbing her two-handed sword and unsheathing it in one long move. Grim-faced, she positioned herself before Arbon, bringing the blade to bear on him. Arbon fumbled with his sword and shield, and Bethral turned her head just enough to catch Ezren's gaze.

She winked at him.

Ezren blinked, his anger draining away.

The young scattered, giving the two contestants room. Gilla grabbed Ezren's elbow, pulling him back.

Bethral waited, letting Arbon get his sword out and his shield in a guard position. He managed it, and stood there for a moment, breathing hard.

'Ready?' She asked, arching an eyebrow.

Arbon scowled, his lips parting to speak.

Bethral lunged.

Ezren watched in horror and fascination. Tales told of brave warriors using a two-handed sword to battle their foes. But those tales had led him to expect the wielder would slash and stab with the weapon, bringing it up over her head.

Bethral used it as a club, never raising it over her head. Her first blow smashed into Arbon's shield, forcing him to stagger back.

Gripping the second crosspiece, Bethral let the blade slide toward Arbon's head. Arbon blocked with his sword, forcing her blade out and down.

Bethral let him, only to smack his thigh hard with the flat of the blade, enough to make Arbon stagger again.

'Ah,' Gilla said softly. 'I best go keep watch.'

'Aye,' El said.

They both slipped off. Ezren couldn't understand how they could take their eyes off the two fighters still exchanging blows before them.

But after a few more moments, he realised what they already

knew. Arbon didn't really stand much of a chance against Bethral.

It wasn't that Arbon wasn't a good fighter. He was. But Bethral was better, and by quite a bit. She also had options with the great sword that he didn't have. She could use the reach of the weapon to keep him at bay, and slash with the sharp tip.

Even when Arbon tried to press in close, she used the cross-pieces to attempt to disarm him, or just smacked him with the flat of the blade.

That young man was going to hurt worse tomorrow than Ezren did today.

Ezren had to give the lad credit. He didn't give in easily; he kept at it even after Bethral scored the skin over his right eye, and blood poured down his face.

Bethral's braid had come undone, and her blonde hair swung with her blows. She wasn't fast; Ezren had seen her spar with other warriors and knew that others were faster. But she made every move count, waited for her best opportunities. He relaxed when he realised that she was enjoying herself.

He relaxed even more when her final blow cracked against Arbon's shield and sent him sprawling in the grass.

He lay there, breathing hard, as Bethral put the tip of her sword to his neck. He grinned at her. 'I yield, Warrior.'

'Really?' Bethral said. She didn't move her sword. 'On the Plains, the rules of challenge are clear. During the spring contests, but not once the army is in the field.'

Arbon's eyes went wide, and he licked his lips.

'You should have challenged before we left Haya's camp,' Bethral continued. 'I've every right to kill you now.'

'Warrior, I—'

Bethral pressed the blade into Arbon's skin. 'Do you think me less than a warrior of the Plains?'

'Warlord,' Arbon gasped, 'I yield.'

Bethral pulled the blade back, and turned and walked away. Her eyes flickered over the young warriors, and Ezren could tell that she had noted those on watch. 'Mount up,' she said. 'We're joining the herd.'

The herd was slowly moving south and east. The horses drifted for the most part, grazing and nursing the foals. It wasn't going to gain them a lot of ground, but Bethral was satisfied. Their tracks were well and truly covered, and there'd been no sign of pursuit. Still, she'd had the warriors spread out on the edges of the herd, scanning the rises around them. She was keeping to the center of the herd. Bessie was tall enough to stand out like an ehat. Not that Bethral had seen one yet, but she was sure she'd know one when she saw it.

She was checking off to the east when Ezren sidled his horse up to Bessie. 'Lady Bethral, I fear your idea of "interesting".'

Bethral chuckled. 'I knew it was coming. Arbon hadn't lowered his eyes to me, which is a sign of respect between warriors, and he'd been giving me that cocky smile for some time.'

'Damn bold of him, to try something like that,' Ezren said.

'He'd have gained quite a bit of status if he'd taken over the leadership of our journey. Even more if he could claim to have seen us safe off the Plains.' Bethral shrugged. 'I don't blame him for trying, but he won't do it again.'

'Why won't he?' Ezren asked.

'That's not done,' Bethral explained. 'You don't challenge a warlord while on campaign unless the circumstances are extraordinary. And you don't repeatedly try a challenge after you've lost, unless you have gained new skills or experience. The warlord will not spare you a second time.'

'Oh, how I wish I had paper,' Ezren said. 'I want to write this down, take notes, so that if we return—'

'When we return,' Bethral corrected him. 'Little chance you'll find paper and pen here, Storyteller.'

'I'm trying to remember everything I can. I could turn it into such a tale.' Ezren gave her a sly look, his green eyes bright. 'With young Arbon there the butt of my jokes.'

Bethral laughed as Gilla appeared among the horses and headed for them.

'Warlord,' she said, as respectfully as anyone could ask.

'My name is enough, Gilla,' Bethral said.

'Chell sends word that a pride of cats are following the herd on the western side. They're stalking right now, but she feels they will hunt soon.'

'Cats?' Ezren glanced at the cat perched on Bethral's bedroll. Its eyes were half closed, as if sleeping, but its claws were sunk deep into the bedroll.

'No.' Gilla shook her head. 'Cats of the Plains, Storyteller. Much bigger. Much, much bigger. Would you like to see?'

'Would I?' Ezren moved his horse forward. 'Show me.'

'Don't become prey yourselves,' Bethral called. She waited until they'd moved off before she started to wind her way through the horses to the eastern side of the herd. With any luck, the hunt would move the herd further east, which fitted her plans well enough.

But she couldn't help scanning the rises, looking for signs of pursuit. She knew well enough that she wasn't the only one making plans.

'Well?' demanded Hail Storm as he entered the tent.

'Nothing.' The young warrior-priest lowered his eyes. 'We have scryed, but have not found them in the area of the thea camp.' He hesitated, then continued. 'It hampers our efforts that we do not know what the Sacrifice looks like.'

'What of the one that brought us word?' Hail Storm growled as he settled in his chair. 'Did she not—'

'A fleeting glance, no more. Reddish hair, and outlined in magic.'

'Keep trying.'

'Elder, we have almost drained this place of its power.'

'Drain it dry, then we will move the camp.' Hail Storm paused. 'Have the summons gone out?'

'Yes, Elder. All of the warrior-priests have been summoned.

We have even sent out summons to those that wander, but it is doubtful that—'

'To the Heart?' Hail Storm demanded. 'You summoned them to the Heart?'

'Yes, Elder.'

Hail Storm paused, aware that he'd been a bit abrupt. 'You have done well, Gray Cloud.'

The warrior-priest bowed his head in quiet thanks, and left the tent.

If the magics had been drained, so be it. After years of conserving the power, there was now a need. And such a need. The source of magic, the source of the restoration of their power, was here. Hail Storm's heart beat faster at the idea of being the one who would lead the warrior-priests back to their glory.

Glory for the people of the Plains, certainly. But what heights of power could he rise to, with the magics returned to the Plains?

But he had to remain focused. The Sacrifice was wandering the Plains, and he must be found and brought to the Heart. Word of this must not reach the warlords or any of the eldest elders. This was a matter for the warrior-priests of the Plains, and them alone.

Hail Storm calmed himself. He'd wandered in his time, wandered the wide outer rim of the world. He'd ventured into the 'civilised' lands and learned what he needed to know of other paths to power that the weak feared to tread. When the time was right, he wouldn't hesitate.

He'd make any sacrifice necessary to achieve the powers of his ancestors.

SEVENTEEN

'They surely were not cats,' the Storyteller said. 'Closer to lions, I would think. The color is the same, but not the teeth. Theirs were huge.'

They were all gathered by the fire as the stars started to appear. All except Lander and Ouse, who'd drawn the first watch. The cat had climbed into Gilla's lap, and she carefully scratched the top of its head. It was rumbling fiercely, working its claws against her leather trous.

The warlord – Bethral – had warned her that the cat would bite, so she made sure to keep her fingers well away from its mouth. She wasn't sure of its sex, and she wasn't going to explore its nether regions to find out. Those claws were sharp.

'It's said that a pride of cats can pull down an ehat,' El told the Storyteller.

'What is "pull down"?'

Gilla giggled a bit at that. The Storyteller insisted that they all speak with him and force him to learn their language. Bethral was not allowed to translate for him unless he asked her to. So they had to try to use their own language to explain words. El was trying to mime a group of cats killing an ehat, and it was fun to see such a wise one try to figure out the meaning.

'Ah! To kill, to pull down,' Ezren crowed, his green eyes flashing with success. 'I want to see an ehat before we leave the Plains. That would be a grand tale.'

They'd found a good camp, one that already had a fire circle, by a pond. Farther east than anyone had planned, because the herd had run quite a way after the Plains cats had attacked. But the alders were heavy, and the water was sweet, so Bethral had ordered an early stop.

The herd had encircled them, to be near the water. Tenna and Chell had set snares for rabbits in the tall grasses, and gotten enough for their meal. Tenna had tried to tempt the cat with bits of raw meat, but it had sniffed at it in disdain and then disappeared into the grasses. It had returned apparently sated.

So, they'd taken turns watching, setting up their sleep tents, bathing, and preparing their meal. Although Bethral had said that the women must all bathe together, as would the men.

Gilla had stared at her. 'Why?'

'Is that the way of your people?' Chell asked, her eyebrows raised.

'Yes.' Bethral glared, her voice clipped. Although Gilla thought she saw a faint blush on her cheeks.

'Well,' Tenna said carefully, 'I think we should honor your customs as you honor ours.'

'That would be best.' Bethral said.

City dwellers were so strange. So very different, but still people. Gilla thought that surprised her the most. They ate and drank and laughed . . . but some of their ideas were very odd.

'So explain to me again,' the Storyteller asked. 'If we let the horses wander out into the herd, how do we get them back again in the morning?'

'We'll call, and horses will answer,' Ouse said.

'The same horses?' The Storyteller looked puzzled.

'No, not unless they want to,' El said.

'They want to be ridden?' The Storyteller looked over at Bethral as if sharing a joke.

'Of course,' Gilla said. 'Don't yours?'

'It's part of their training, both the horse and the human,' Bethral said. 'A Plains warrior who cannot summon a horse to ride is a dead Plains warrior.'

'It is said that to anger the Spirit of the Horse is to slay your own,' Ouse said.

The Storyteller nodded. 'Which is why "bragnect" is such an insult. To slay a baby horse would anger the Spirit of the Horse.'

'Regardless of one's tribe, all honor the Spirit of the Horse,' Bethral said softly.

'As your token honors Steel,' the Storyteller said. His voice was so soft, yet filled with admiration.

'Aye,' Bethral replied, just as softly.

'I—' Cosana broke the moment, her voice very hesitant. 'I have a question, if I may, Storyteller? Please?'

'How can I aid you?' the Storyteller asked.

'I have this—' Cosana pulled a small bag from behind her, and struggled with the knots at the top. Gilla was fairly certain she'd brought it with her after bathing, working up the courage to ask about it.

The bag spilled open, and small pieces of wood went flying. Cosana gasped, and started to pick them up. The others helped her, even rescuing one from the flames. The Storyteller was looking at the bag, which was really a large square piece of leather, marked with lines in an equal pattern. He held out his hand, and Cosana handed him one of the wooden pieces.

Ezren held it up to the light. 'I'm not sure, but it looks like a chess set.' There was an exclamation from both Tenna and Chell, but the Storyteller was looking at Cosana. 'Where did you get this?'

'Cosana' – Tenna gaped at her, holding one of the pieces – 'We're not allowed . . .'

'Children are not allowed,' Cosana said defiantly, jerking the piece from her hand. 'I am a warrior, and I can have—'

'Haya and Seo banned it from the camp,' El explained. 'It's from Xy.'

'The Warprize brought it with her,' Arbon said. He'd been quiet during the meal. Gilla wasn't surprised, given his black eyes and the bruises on his face and body. The cut had sealed, but she was certain it would scar.

'Do you know the rules?' Cosana asked the Storyteller. 'Will you teach me?'

'Sure,' the Storyteller said.

Cosana squealed with pleasure and dropped to her knees in front of him.

'Anyone wants to learn, gather round,' the Storyteller instructed. 'First thing you need to know . . .'

Gilla didn't move, she didn't want to disturb the cat that now slept in her lap. The others all surrounded Ezren Storyteller, listening to him explain the pieces and the moves. Bethral didn't stir, but something made Gilla look in her direction.

Her expression caught Gilla, who managed not to gasp out loud. Need, with desire . . . the pure want on her face. Gilla knew in that instant that Bethral of the Horse loved Ezren Storyteller.

But . . . She looked away and made as if petting the cat was her only concern. She was almost positive that they'd never shared bodies. True, they had been alone in Haya's tent, but on separate pallets. And Gilla was fairly sure that sharing was not on Bethral's mind when her leg had been broken. So how could they love each other and not know it?

She bit her lip, thinking.

'Yes, that's it.' The Storyteller's voice cut through her thoughts. 'The knight is on horseback, so he makes a very different move.'

'Agility.' El was looking over his shoulder. 'That makes sense.'

'And just think of the queen as a very powerful female war-lord.' The Storyteller flashed them all a smile. 'Like Bethral.'

'Or a Warprize,' Chell added.

'It's getting late.' Bethral's voice came out of the darkness. 'Time to relieve Lander and Ouse, and bed down for the night.'

Cosana gave her an anguished look. 'But can't we play just one game?'

'Tomorrow.' The Storyteller smiled, then stood and stretched. 'It will give us something to look forward to after the day.'

Cosana looked at him, and smiled back. 'Yes, Storyteller.' She paused, then reached for his hand. 'Would you share with me this night?'

*

Hail Storm stood before the warrior-priests that had gathered in his tent with calm assurance. 'When Wild Winds arrives, he will answer my challenge. But until then we must prepare for the Sacrifice to be brought to the Heart. Warriors have started to gather early for the spring contests. They must be moved off, far enough that they will not see or note our doings. It is not the first time we have claimed the Heart as our own for a space of time. This is no different.'

'It is different in that we interrupt the contests,' Sweet Grasses spoke up from the ranks, her braids filled with gray. 'We will be asked "For how long?" How will we answer?'

'As we have always answered. With a silent stare.' Morning Dew snorted. 'They need not know, and they will obey.'

'No doubt.' Sweet Grasses nodded. 'The early warriors will obey. But those who would contest for warlord? Those of the Council of Elders that may come? Not all will obey without question.'

'I have sent summons to all the warrior-priests to come to the Heart after they have conducted the Rites of Ascension.' Hail Storm held his temper.

There were grunts and nods of agreement.

'Morning Dew, if you would see to the clearing of the Heart. Once the warriors have been moved out of sight of the place, please begin the cleansing and blessing.'

Morning Dew nodded his head slowly, clearly pleased.

'And have you found the Sacrifice?' Sweet Grasses spoke again, her eyes sharp.

'No.' Hail Storm kept his expression neutral. 'And the groups that I have sent to do a physical search have not been able to pick up their tracks. The thea camp of the Tribe of the Snake has moved. We are looking for them as well.'

'Wild Winds said that the city dwellers were going to go home, and that home was the Kingdom of Palins.' The woman's voice from the back of the tent was dry and cruel. 'Have you tried to the south?'

Hail Storm's anger flashed, and he had to pause before he

could give a reasonable answer. 'Yes, Mist.' Old mare! But he must tread lightly, she was no fool. None of them were.

'You have also drained this place of its faint magics,' Mist continued. 'How do you propose to continue to scry when you have wasted—'

'I do not. The scrying will stop. Our people will be needed to clear the Heart and to patrol so that no one violates our privacy.' Hail Storm lowered his head, shaking it slowly. 'I regret the use of the magics, but our path is a clear one. Once the magic is restored to our land . . .'

He paused for emphasis.

'If . . .' Mist said, and there were nods of agreement.

'I believe that with your help,' Hail Storm continued, 'we can use the blessing spells on the land in such a way as to detect the magic the city dweller carries. We need only concentrate on the southern lands, since we believe the Sacrifice is headed in that direction.'

'How many groups are in the South?' Morning Dew asked.

'Enough,' Hail Storm replied.

'And how will you cast this spell of yours?' Mist pointed out. 'Without—'

'We will move the camp,' Hail Storms snapped. He drew a deep breath, furious at his loss of control.

Mist had a smug look on her wrinkled face as she rose from her seat. 'Then let us be about it, Hail Storm.' She turned and slipped through the tent flap, the others following.

Hail Storm stood still, trying to control himself. Damn her! Once he was eldest elder, he would . . . but he wasn't yet, and there were those here who would be willing to challenge him but wouldn't challenge Wild Winds.

Arching Colors, one of the youngest of the warrior-priests, slipped into the tent. Her tattoos barely covered her shoulders. Her eyes widened when she saw Hail Storm. 'Pardon, Elder.' She dropped her gaze. 'I thought to clear the tent, and didn't know—'

'No need.' Hail Storm gave her a hopeful look, and held out a hand. 'In fact, I'd ask you to help me with something. A spell I want to try. Would you?'

'Of course, Elder.' Her eyes were alive with curiosity. 'How may I help you?'

He lowered his voice and drew closer to her. 'We would have to prepare ourselves by fasting, lovely one. And the spell itself, it involves sharing our bodies.'

Her eyes melted as a shiver ran through her. 'I would be pleased to aid you, Hail Storm.'

'My thanks,' he whispered, as he pressed his lips to hers.

EIGHTEEN

'I can't believe you asked him that,' Gilla whispered.

'I can't believe he said no,' Cosana whispered back. 'I think Landers is right, else what's wrong with the man?'

Gilla rolled her eyes.

They had combined their tents with those of Landers and Ouse for the night. El and Tenna were on patrol, and Bethral and the Storyteller were asleep, each in their own tent. Chell and Arbon had squeezed in with them, and they were all folded in together, talking it out.

Landers was shaking his head. 'No, we checked as we were all bathing. He's whole, and normal, as far as we could see. Scarred, though. All over his back and chest. Wrists, too.'

'Did you get a good look at him?' Chell asked.

'Well, we didn't get to hold it, if that's what you mean,' Arbon said scathingly. His eyes peered out from the bruises around them. Cosana giggled as he continued. 'But he's fine.'

'Could you get him to talk about her?' Gilla asked. 'Did you—'

'Talk? Skies above, we could not get him to stop!' Landers laughed, and the others shushed him. He lowered his voice. 'I asked if all city women were as lovely as Bethral . . .'

'They are not,' El said in a dry voice. 'They in no way compare to her. "She is Light incarnate, a woman warrior of amazing skill. She represents all that is good and true in this life and the next."'

'Wow!' Gilla blinked.

'But he is not worthy,' Arbon said. 'For reasons that seem

important only to him. The fact that she is a skilled warrior, and he is not, seems to be the main obstacle.'

'But he is a singer!' Cosana protested. 'He's of a status above hers.'

'He also thinks he is too short,' Arbon added.

'Why would her height matter?' Gilla asked.

'Why would his?' Arbon shrugged. 'City dwellers!'

'Well, she's certainly made well. Her body is very defined and strong,' Chell said. 'Even for one of us. She said it was because of the armor. Carrying the weight of it.' Chell shrugged. 'I do not know for certain, but I was attracted enough to ask her to share.'

'You did?' El arched an eyebrow. 'And?'

'She thanked me, but declined. Said her taste ran to men.' Chell sighed. 'Pity. I bet she'd be good in bed.'

'She didn't want to talk about the Storyteller, that was clear,' Cosana said. 'I tried to ask her, but she cut me off.'

'I thought she was going to kill you, there by the fire, when you asked him to share.' Chell shook her head. 'The look on her face . . . they are bonded.'

'Bonded?' Ouse scoffed. 'They have never shared, that we know of.

'They have bonded without sharing bodies,' Chell repeated. 'Why else her feelings of jealousy? If they are not bonded, she would not feel that way. Bonded.'

'No,' Cosana gasped. 'How could they—'

'Each has bonded to the other but does not know that the other has bonded as well.'

'That is so . . . so . . .' Cosana sighed.

'Stupid,' Chell said firmly.

'Worthy of a song,' Landers declared. 'Or a story.'

'No, it is not,' Chell contradicted. 'What would you sing? That city dwellers share from a distance?'

'If that is so, I prefer our ways,' Lander said, reaching out to stroke Ouse's crotch.

'So do I,' Ouse said, covering Lander's hand with his and pressing it down. 'Maybe we should show them—'

'Maybe they do not share at all,' Cosana said.

'Please,' Ouse scoffed. 'Where would more city dwellers come from?'

'Maybe that's it.' Gilla said. 'Maybe they need to share under the bells.'

'Why bother with bells?' Cosana asked.

Ouse frowned. 'Gilla, I would offer no offense, but they are elders. Why do you worry yourself about this? They can solve their own problems.'

'No.' Gilla shook her head. 'In this, we are the wiser.'

'I think that you should have more concern for their lives than their hearts,' Chell pointed out. 'They are focused on getting home, not sharing.'

Ouse grimaced. 'All this thinking. My head hurts! Lander and I need to take our watches.'

'We will trade,' Gilla said. 'Cosana and I will take this watch.'

'We will?' Cosana asked. 'I want to sleep.'

'I need to think,' Gilla said, cracking open the tent. 'And if we don't, they will keep us up all night with the sounds of their sharing.'

'And sharing and sharing and sharing,' Ouse said proudly.

Lander stuffed a gurtle pad over his face.

It took the better part of two days for the warrior-priests to relocate the camp in an area where magic still could be found in the earth. Hail Storm would have raged in anger, except that every hour saw the arrival of more warrior-priests to listen to his position and to see Wild Winds face his challenge. He'd swilled many a cup of kavage beside fires over those days, using his smooth voice and reasonable arguments to bring them to his side.

But still the Sacrifice had not been spotted. He had no choice. It was time he used the other knowledge he'd gained in his wanderings.

It was late before he could see to his own project. His tent was set and warmed when he entered. Arching Colors was there, with a meal and hot kavage warming on one of the braziers. She was wearing a sheer, flowing tunic of green, and he could see her tight nipples thrusting against the fabric.

'I thought we would eat after the casting,' Arching Colors said softly.

Hail Storm nodded. 'It was well done.' He looked over at the private portion of his tent. 'Our pallet is prepared?'

'Yes.' Arching Colors shivered, her lips parted.

'We have fasted and purged,' Hail Storm said softly. 'I have cleansed myself.'

'I, as well, as you instructed.' Arching Colors moved closer, and ran her hands over his chest, along the tattoo lines. 'I hunger for you.'

'As do I.' Hail Storm swept her up in a kiss, pulling her close.

Arching Colors sighed, and responded, walking back toward his pallet, her hands falling to his trous. Breaking the kiss, she removed his belt, placing his sacrifice dagger off to the side. She gave him a sly smile, then went to her knees before him, her hands on his trous.

Hail Storm sighed at the wet heat of her mouth. He allowed himself to enjoy the sensation for moments. Arching Colors was well skilled.

With a sigh he pulled away from her and gathered her into his arms. 'No, sweet one,' he said as he eased her tunic off, and lowered her to the pallet. 'Your pleasure first, this night.'

'As you say,' she murmured.

She was so sweet, hot and wet and willing. So responsive. Writhing beneath him, Arching Colors dug her nails into him and urged him on as he eased slowly into her.

Hail Storm grunted with the effort, thrusting into her, concentrating on her pleasure.

Arching Colors moaned his name, her skin covered with a sheen of perspiration. He watched her face, using his skills to keep her on the very brink for as long as he could, until she screamed and reached her peak, crying out her joy.

A quick move, and his dagger was in his hand. Another instant to stab it between her ribs and into her heart.

Arching Colors gasped, her eyes wide.

Hail Storm continued to thrust, chanting softly under his breath, and concentrated on seizing the magic released by her dying. He kept the blade in her, holding it steady, letting it absorb her blood and her power.

Arching Colors gasped again, dying even as her pleasure faded. There was no struggle. Her breaths just grew slower and shallower. Her body grew lax, still warm under his.

It was well done. He was sure she hadn't even felt the blade. Continuing to chant, he strengthened his movements, riding the wave of his own pleasures.

After a time, he eased himself from the body, and then slowly drew out the dagger. Its magic almost pulsed in his hand, and he smiled in satisfaction.

Hail Storm wiped himself clean, and then treated the body as he would any lover, arranging it on the pallet to sleep and drawing the blankets over its shoulders. 'Sleep, little one.' He spoke just loud enough to be heard by anyone outside the tent. 'I've work yet to do. But I will return, and we shall share again, shall we?'

He gathered up his trous and his dagger, and went to the main room. With a sigh, he looked around at his tent as he dressed.

The large brazier in the center of the room was still glowing with coals. Hail Storm helped himself to the warm kavage, then added fuel slowly, until the flames jumped about eagerly.

'Elder,' a voice came from outside the tent flap. 'Sweet Grasses sends word that they are ready for you.'

'Very well.' Hail Storm swept up his cloak and let it cover his shoulders, then took up his staff. With a casual flip, he put the tip of the staff under the brazier, and tipped it over on the wooden platform. The coals made a gentle hiss as they tumbled out, the flames following playfully. A shame, really. This tent had served him well.

He stepped from the tent, letting the flap close all the way behind him.

Hail Storm had not anticipated that he'd have an audience for this casting. Mist was waiting with Sweet Grasses when he arrived, looking over the arrangements with a eagle's eye.

The center of the tent had been cleared, and the sod cut away. The earth beneath had been dug down for a hand's breadth in a circle as large as a man's height, and lined with leathers that had been oiled and sealed. At the very center sat a large tree trunk, cut so that the top just emerged from the water. Next to that was a large flat stone, also just above the surface of the water.

'So, it represents the Plains,' Mist said. 'And the wood is the Heart.'

Hail Storm nodded as he removed his cloak. 'The rock is the lake beside it.' He drew a deep breath. 'I think I can cast a blessing spell in such a way as to tell us where magic is in the Plains. When the Sacrifice loses control, as he will, there will be a flare of fire in that location. I have warrior-priests ready to sit and watch and wait.'

'A powerful spell, if you can manage it.' Mist eyed him closely. 'You think there is enough power here to do this?'

'With care.' Hail Storm moved to the northernmost corner, where a precious wood fire burned brightly. 'I would prefer to do this under the bells, Mist.'

'I am sure you would,' Mist replied. She planted her feet and crossed her arms, causing the two skulls on her staff to clatter together. 'But I would learn from you, Hail Storm.'

Damned old mare! She'd rattled her skulls on purpose. Hail Storm's temples pulsed with anger as he set his staff, empty of skulls, against the side of the tent. But there was little he could do. For now. He wondered briefly how much magic he could pull from her dying, but then he forced himself to focus on the task at hand.

He started with the fire element, then worked his way around to each corner and each element, chanting softly, pulling the magic from the land as he went, gathering it in his hand. He knew he'd have to move with care, so that the old mare wouldn't see the source of power at his belt.

Easily done.

Finally, he stood at the southern point and turned to face the center of the room. He knelt, and held out his arms, palms out, fingers wide. He softly chanted the traditional words of the blessing spell, with but the slightest of changes.

Blessing spells watched over the thea camps of each tribe, helping to keep their people strong and fit. In the old times, when the magic had been strong, the warrior-priests had been warned of any sickness or threat to the People.

So Hail Storm changed the words, changed his focus, seeking only to know when strong magic would flare anywhere on the Plains. The Sacrifice would lose control sooner or later, and with any luck it would happen before he could leave the Plains.

Hail Storm lowered his arms, letting his palm brush against the hilt of his sacrifice blade. He didn't even have to pull – the magic flared up within him. Hail Storm raised his arms again, this time to cross them before his chest and clench his fists. He wove this new power into the spell, and let it settle gently over the water. Only then did he let out a breath, allowing the tension to ease from his body.

'Well done,' Mist said grudgingly. She came to stand next to him.

'There will need to be watchers.' Hail Storm rubbed his face with both hands. 'At all times. I cannot—'

Mist nodded. 'I've young ones waiting. They will keep watch, and we will rotate them so their eyes stay sharp.' She hesitated, giving Hail Storm a careful look. 'It seemed to me that the magic surged while you were casting. It had an odd feel to it, a kind of—'

Shouts came from outside. 'Hail Storm!' Someone thrust the tent flap open. 'Your tent is afire!'

'Go,' Mist said. 'I will see to this.'

With a curse, Hail Storm ran from the tent, perfectly prepared to mourn the death of Arching Colors.

NINETEEN

'The Plains bathed in new life is lovely, Bethral.' Her mother's eyes were bright as she looked off to the west. 'I hope someday you can see it.'

'Horses, Mama? Lots of horses?' Bethral clung to her mother's trous, and bounced.

'Oh, yes,' her mother laughed. 'It's like a new world that comes to life after the snows. Horses, true enough. But oh, the flowers, little one. You would not believe . . .'

'I believe, Mama,' Bethral whispered to her mother as she looked about her.

It was amazing. The grasses were filled with color, so many different flowers it was hard to take in. Great swaths of blue and yellow, mixed with the white of the clover. Birds clung to the stems, eating the insects that buzzed about each blossom. The air was sweet with fragrance. The enormous blue sky stretched above it all, the sun warm and welcoming.

Her mother had told her that in the fall, all the grasses turned red and yellow so that the entire Plains seemed to be on fire. That would be a sight to see.

But after four days of travel, she'd had her fill of spring. If she saw one more mare mounted by the herd stallion, or yet another courtship display by hawks, or if the young ones didn't stop sharing at the top of their lungs every single hour of the night . . .

They had more energy and enthusiasm than Red Gloves.

Of course, Red Gloves would've laughed her head off by this time. 'Get that itch scratched, Bethral, or it will drive you crazy.'

That's how Red had always seen sex. As just a physical act, for the pleasure of the moment. Well, that was how she had treated it until she had met her goatherder. Bethral shook her head at the memory. Red had resisted, but Josiah had won her, that was certain.

That was what Bethral wanted. Not just the physical, but the other aspect. Someone who stood at your side, and not just in a fight, but in all those moments that made up life. She'd been close to Red, they'd been sisters in all ways. But Bethral wanted more than friendship. Someone who wasn't interested just in her body, or how she swung her sword.

Truth was, all this spring was making her itchy.

And it wasn't going to get scratched anytime soon, Bethral thought ruefully as she looked over at Ezren Storyteller.

He was riding along, surrounded by Cosana, El, Chell, and Arbon. The sunlight picked up the reddish tint in his hair, and with the brown of his leather armor, he looked . . . Bethral turned away.

'Pawn to queen's bishop five,' Arbon said.

There was a pause, then laughter. Bethral looked back and saw Ezren shake his head. 'No, I have lost it. Again.'

'You made it ten moves that time,' Cosana said kindly. 'That's better than before.'

'Not good enough for an entire game, I fear.'

'You truly cannot remember the board?' Arbon asked.

'I cannot,' Ezren said firmly. 'But that does not mean that all city dwellers cannot. We are not all the same.'

'But how do you track the details of your life,' El asked, 'without a memory?'

'We have memories,' Ezren said. 'And we have writing.' He paused. 'I may not be able to remember a chessboard, but I do not forget stories.'

They all perked up at that. 'Would you tell us a story?' Chell asked. 'Here? Now?'

'Why not?' Ezren glanced around as they brought their horses closer. 'I can repeat it later for those on watch.'

He thought for a bit as his horse moved on. 'Hear now a tale of the land of Palins, from long ago, when time and tide sat young upon the land,' Ezren started. 'This is the tale of the Lord of Light and the Lady of Laughter, and how the Lady brought Night to the Land.'

'We will remember,' the warriors chorused.

The Lord of Light, God of the Sun, was charged with the care of the lands and the people who were touched by his light. The Lord performed his duties well, bearing the responsibilities of his power and position until he bowed beneath the weight of his cares. Over and over he moved from horizon to horizon, spreading his sacred light and warmth over the lands. As soon as he dipped below the horizon, he rose again, bathing his creation in constant light.

Ezren looked about, making sure he had their attention. *But once, as he traveled the sky, his light happened upon a lady fair sleeping in her garden. The light and warmth touched her soft skin, and she awoke with laughter on her lips.* He paused for dramatic effect. *And the Lord of the Sun paused in his journey.*

Bethral listened with one ear as she scanned the rises around them, looking for signs of pursuit. So far, they'd had no evidence that anyone was searching for them, but it had been only a few days. They needed to stay alert, just in case.

Ezren's voice was husky and mesmerising. She wondered if he realised how different he sounded when he was telling tales.

The Lady rose from her bed, her skin warm, her nightclothes disheveled, her face alight with joy. She smiled, and held out her hand. 'Come down, Great Lord, and break your fast with me.' Ezren swept his hand up toward the sun. *Without a care, she sat at a table bright with berries and sweet cream, fresh bread and soft butter and kavage, dark and bitter.*

Ezren paused again and lowered his voice. *And the Lord of Light was tempted.*

But duty lay heavy on the shoulders of the God of the Sun. 'I cannot, Lady. The press of my responsibilities. You understand.'

'As you wish, Great Lord,' the Lady said with a smile. 'But do not waste the day your labors create.'

For just a moment, the God of the Sun felt that he'd appeared to be a pompous ass, instead of the hardworking God that he was. He hesitated, then continued on with his tasks. But even as he did, he thought on sweet cream and red lips . . . red berries. Red berries.

Tenna laughed as the others chuckled. Bethral saw the satisfaction in Ezren's face as he continued.

When next his rays touched her skin, the Lady was hunting alone in the forest, clad in leathers, bow in hand. She was hidden in a thicket, but his light betrayed her. The stag leaped away when her shadow appeared. The Lady cursed roundly, and with a sigh, unstrung her bow.

The Storyteller's horse had stopped, standing patiently as he waited for his rider to urge him on. But Ezren was lost in the tale, in the faces of his audience, who had stopped beside him. Bethral listened as well, but kept her awareness of their surroundings.

'Beg pardon, Lady.' The God of the Sun spoke softly. Ezren's voice changed slightly as he took the role of the God.

With a shrug, the Lady set off toward a nearby stream. 'It's a hunt. Were it a sure thing, it would be a slaughter.' She looked up and gave him a laughing glance. 'Next time your light may startle the prey toward me instead of away. It's a balance.'

'Still,' the Sun God pressed, 'I spoiled your shot.'

'Then make amends,' she replied lightly as she paused on the bank. 'Come, sit, and talk awhile.'

The Lord of Light, God of the Sun, paused, then spoke with regret. 'Lady, I cannot.'

'The press of duty,' she finished for him. 'As you will, Great Lord. I will sit in the cool shade, and splash the water with my bare toes. Be about your duty, Good Sire.'

The warriors were shaking their heads at that. Arbon looked up at the sun in the sky, as if to chide it.

The God of the Sun continued with his tasks, but not without a quick look at her lovely toes, Ezren continued. *His duties had never been so heavy, or so it seemed to him.*

'We need to keep moving.' Bethral hated to interrupt, but it had to be done. 'And the others need to be relieved.'

'You'll finish?' Cosana begged. 'Tonight by the fire?'

'I will,' Ezren promised. 'And I will repeat it until everyone has heard it.'

They all thanked him, and started to scatter. Cosana rode off, but not without a flirtatious look at the Storyteller over her shoulder.

Bethral looked away. Cosana was a lovely young woman. It had surprised her when the Storyteller had declined the offer of sharing. It had enraged her when Cosana had offered to share.

But if she wasn't brave enough to offer, what right did she have to jealousy?

None.

Yet she could not bring herself to approach him. The possibility of his rejection – the look of pity in his eyes – she couldn't do it. He'd avoided her in Edenrich, and now they were thrown together and she would not risk what friendship they had.

In the corner of her eye, she saw the herd stallion approaching one of the mares. Of course.

Another movement, and Ezren's horse was beside her. There was a strip of bells in Ezren's hand, and his expression was intent.

'We need to talk.'

Gilla rode at the edges of the herd, watching for signs of warrior-priests. But she was also stalking her prey. Only this time, the prey was information. No, that wasn't quite right. It was understanding that she sought.

She'd always been a good hunter. Not that she was the best shot with a bow, or quicker than any other. Her success lay in being patient. By stalking, watching, and waiting . . . that was how she'd brought down her quarry every time.

So now she stalked the Storyteller and his Token-Bearer.

Tenna smiled at her, and held out a fresh waterskin. 'It's still cold.'

Gilla took it gratefully, and drank eagerly. The fresh water tasted wonderful.

'How goes the hunt?' Tenna asked, knowing full well what she was up to. 'Learn anything more?'

Gilla rolled her eyes. 'It's an easy enough hunt,' she said. 'Bethral never lets the Storyteller out of her sight.'

'They are each aware of the other,' Tenna said.

'If longing looks counted as sharing, they'd both be sore and chafed.' Gilla shook her head.

'Maybe we could seal them in a tent, naked,' Tenna suggested.

Gilla arched an eyebrow. 'You did see what she did to Arbon, right?'

Tenna laughed. 'Oh, yes, which is why you go first.' She tilted her head at Gilla. 'Or do you want to contrive another way to get them together?'

'No.' Gilla handed Tenna her waterskin. 'I know what I am going to do.'

Bethral reached over the sleeping cat perched on her bedroll to dig out her own bells from her saddlebags. She tied them in Bessie's mane without looking at Ezren. 'What would you say?'

'The magic.' Ezren drew a deep breath and continued in his own tongue. 'It is growing again. And I feel . . . pulled is the best way to say it. Pulled back to the north.' He looked over his shoulder. 'It is a dull ache. As if I have forgotten something or someone important back there. I feel . . . a need to turn back.'

'Damn!' Bethral looked at him carefully. 'I think, too, that you are losing weight.'

'Eating like a horse,' Ezren said ruefully. 'More than I normally do. But that could be the riding. All this activity . . .' His voice trailed off, then he quirked his lips. 'I fear I am ignoring the truth.'

'When we were in Edenrich, the magic flared when you saw that warrior-priest,' Bethral said. 'It came roaring out, lashing out almost as if it were enraged.'

'Anger.' Ezren's eyes grew vague. 'Yes, I felt anger. Yet there was joy, too.' Those green eyes sharpened and focused on her. 'But Josiah said that magic has no emotion.'

'Josiah and Marlon deal with normal magic,' Bethral reminded him. 'And they both said that the power you carry is wild magic. I am not sure their rules apply.'

'They knew nothing of the altar and its surroundings,' Ezren said. 'Or of the knife.'

'I did not place it in my pack,' Bethral said firmly. 'Last I knew, it was in a chest in my sleeping chamber. I do not know how it came to be in my saddlebag.'

'Marlon said it contained no magic.' Ezren frowned, looking down at his hands. 'How did it get in your saddlebag?'

'Maybe it's like Josiah's goats,' Bethral said. 'Linked to you by the very magic that it released.'

'Come to think of it' – Ezren frowned – 'those goats do not really make much sense. I mean, if they are magic – and Josiah drains magic from the area around him, then how can they be magic? They never leave his side.'

Bethral blinked. 'I never thought of that.' She thought for a moment. 'Maybe that's part of the magic?'

'Circular logic.' Ezren shook his head. 'No, there has to be a better explanation than that.' He sighed. 'I wish we could ask Josiah or Marlon about this. Or even the warrior-priests. They might actually be able to help.'

'Except they think that you need to die,' Bethral reminded him.

'Yes.' Ezren's smiled flashed. 'That is a problem.' But then the grin faded. 'It is building up again, Lady Bethral.'

'You want to try to use it?' Bethral guessed, noting the seriousness of his expression.

'Both Marlon and Josiah talked about trying to bleed it off before it built up.' Ezren grimaced. 'And we saw what happened when I tried to suppress it using those bracelets that Evelyn gave to me. I thought maybe I could try to start a fire.'

Bethral looked down at her gauntlets and thought for a moment. 'Don't try just yet, Storyteller. We've been traveling more toward the east with this herd, and there are no signs of pursuit so far. But all we've been doing is drifting. I've been thinking of breaking out and making a run directly to the east. Once we are in the foothills, it will be easier to hide from pursuit as we try to find our way through the mountains.'

Ezren nodded. 'It is not bad yet. I can wait.'

Bethral frowned, and shook her head. 'Every time the magic has flared, you have had no control. I don't want to risk you or them, if I can help it.' She looked off to the west. 'That low line of clouds – see them? I am fairly sure that means rain for a time. I need to check with one of the others. If we can find a good camp and wait out the rains, then we can make our move.'

'If that is the case, I think we should also tell the young ones everything. About the magic, about the warrior-priests,' Ezren said firmly.

'Everything?' Bethral arched an eyebrow. 'Haya didn't—'

'Haya is not here, and they are risking their lives for us.' Ezren ran his fingers through his hair. 'It is only fair that they know it all. No secrecy, Bethral. That's how the warrior-priests act, and I will not have them as my guide.'

'Tonight, then.' Bethral leaned forward and removed the bells from Bessie's mane.

'Tonight.'

Gilla saw her opportunity when they all gathered at the center of the herd. Bethral had asked them about the line of clouds building to the north and west. She and the others confirmed that it meant rain, and probably a heavy one, from the looks of the clouds.

So Bethral rode off with Lander, Tenna, Arbon, and Chell in search of a camp where they could wait out the storm in some comfort.

That left Gilla and Ouse, Cosana and El to guard the Storyteller.

Cosana was content to bring up the rear, playing a game of chess with El. Gilla looked over at Ouse as she drew a strip of bells from her pack. He rolled his eyes, but urged his horse forward a polite distance. He might not approve of her efforts, but he wasn't going to try and stop her.

The Storyteller's eyebrows went up when he saw the bells in her hands. 'You want to talk?'

'Yes, please, Storyteller.' Gilla quickly braided the bells into her horse's mane. 'It has to do with your traditions. Concerning sharing.' Gilla drew a deep breath. 'I think I understand about your bonding ceremonies. But . . .' she let her voice trail off, suddenly uncertain.

'But?' Ezren asked her gently. His green eyes were curious.

'I would ask for your token,' Storyteller,' Gilla said.

'Ah, this sounds serious.' Ezren pulled his gold coin from his pouch, and gave it to her. 'I will speak to your truth.'

Gilla drew in a breath, and spoke in a rush. 'I do not understand why you are not sharing with your Token-Bearer, Bethral of the Horse. It is clear that she cares for you and you care for her, and I don't—'

'Ah.' A look of sorrow passed over Ezren's face. 'Gilla, our ways are very different from yours. Bethral is a warrior. What you see as interest is really just concern – pity, really – for a friend who is out of his depth, unable to—' He stopped and cleared his throat. 'Bethral wants – deserves – an equal as a partner. A man who is her equal in skill and . . .' His voice trailed off.

Then he frowned, and looked at her. 'Frankly, I do not really want to talk about this. If you did not hold my token, I would be offended. This is a very private matter, Gilla. I am sure that even among your people, you do not—'

'I do not wish to offend, Storyteller.' Gilla looked down at the gold coin in her hand. 'I just have one more question before I return your token.'

'Well?' Ezren snapped.

'So, when Bethral of the Horse kissed you, she was doing that out of pity?'

TWENTY

'Kissed?'

Gilla caught herself before she reached for her sword. The Storyteller's green eyes were hard as he stared at her.

'Kissed,' she said carefully. 'Putting your lips on another's. You know?' She held the gold coin where he could see it and remember that she held his token.

'I know "kiss",' Ezren snapped at her. 'When is this supposed to have happened?'

He turned his head, his body stiff in the saddle.

'After you killed the warrior-priest.' Gilla urged her horse closer to his. 'You collapsed. Elder Thea Haya moved to kill you—'

The Storyteller stopped his horse, staring straight ahead.

'Bethral met her blade,' Gilla continued. 'Then Haya backed away. Bethral threw herself down on the ground next to you. She looked frantic. Then she – her face filled with joy, and she kissed you.'

The Storyteller was still and silent.

'I've never seen a kiss like that,' Gilla said carefully. 'I just . . .' Her voice trailed off as she struggled for the right words. 'I want something like that, Storyteller. And for the two of you to have it and not share . . .' She drew a breath. 'I do not understand.'

'Neither do I,' the Storyteller said. 'But I intend to.'

Bethral was very pleased with the new camp. Even if the rains were heavy for days, they could wait it out tucked into this sheltered area.

Thick alders surrounded a small pond, and had spread out

around it and up a small rise. Their tents would be well hidden. They'd scattered them in the deep brush, and placed the fire at the pond's edge, where it was rocky.

El had a real gift for setting up the tents, and Bethral had taken the time to watch how he combined two for Lander and Ouse. He also showed her how to set each one so the rain would not seep into the edges.

Bethral looked around the heavy thicket. 'I want to make sure that the tents are fairly close together. If there is a disturbance in the night, I don't want our people thrashing about in these branches by themselves.'

El nodded. 'In the rains, it's normal to double up. Would you like me to combine the tents for you and the Storyteller?'

Bethral gave him a sharp look. El's face was bland and inquiring, but she was almost certain there was mirth lurking just below the surface. She shook her head. 'No. Just put his close to mine.'

'As you wish,' El said.

Bethral left him to his chore, shaking her head. It had been an odd day. The Storyteller had been so distracted, she'd finally had to take the reins of his horse. She'd never seen him so absent-minded.

The herd had stirred the pond up, so they'd taken their drinking water from the stream that fed it. Lander and Chell had set their snares, but no luck so far. They still had a haunch of red deer meat from the previous hunt, and the ever-present gurt, of course. They'd eat tonight.

She'd worry about tomorrow in the morning.

As the sun was setting, she walked down to the fire, where all the others had gathered. It would be a dark night, with thick clouds overhead. No moon, no stars, and a heavy rain on the way.

'No watches tonight,' Bethral said as she neared the fire. 'I think we are safe enough.'

Tenna was grinding kavage beans with two rocks. She looked up at the clouds. 'It will be an hour or two before the rain,' she pointed out. 'I don't mind watching until it really starts to pour.'

'I'll stand with you,' Arbon said.

Ezren yawned, and stretched. 'No stories tonight. I want food, and the shelter of my tent.'

Cosana looked disappointed, but Gilla nudged her hard.

Lander came up with a handful of long white roots. 'There are boar tracks by the pond.'

All the Plains warriors lifted their heads. 'A sow?' Gilla asked eagerly.

Lander smiled and nodded. 'At least four young ones with her.'

'Oh, now, suckling boar would taste wonderful.' Chell cast eager eyes at Bethral. 'If the weather is bad enough, could we delay here? Maybe hunt?'

'It's not a bad idea,' Bethral said. 'Let's see what the morning brings.'

Fed and watered, and all the necessaries taken care of, Bethral headed for her tent, following the Storyteller. There was still some light, but not much. It would be true dark soon enough.

Yawning, she stood before her tent and went through the business of removing her plate armor, slowly releasing all of the belts and straps. She didn't even notice the weight when it was on, but the task of getting in and out of it took some time. As did packing it in the saddlebags and wrapping them in a cloak. They'd stay as dry as they might there; she wasn't going to put them in her tent with her.

Bethral crawled into the tent and stripped off the gambeson, folding it and putting it to the side. She pulled on a tunic for sleeping.

She heard Ezren settle into his tent, and wondered if he was stripping down to skin or trous. Not that she could easily see. His tent was close, but she'd have to open her tent and look out. Not acceptable.

But in her mind's eye . . .

The sky was grumbling with thunder as she wrapped herself

in her blankets and settled down. The spicy scent of gurtle fur combined with the smell of the coming rain.

The cat had crawled in with the Storyteller, as usual. She could hear Ezren admonishing it to leave enough room for him.

Bethral lifted the edge of her tent and took a last look at the fire. Arbon and Tenna, their weapons in hand, were fading into the shadows. They had things well in hand; she could sleep.

Bethral lowered the tent edge and stretched under the blankets, then curled on her side. The blankets warmed quickly, and she was as comfortable as she could be. She took a deep breath and relaxed, waiting for sleep to claim her.

She was about to drift off when she heard her name spoken by a husky voice in a soft whisper.

'Bethral?'

She held her breath, certain she had imagined it, certain that it was part of a dream she'd soon be having. But the voice came again, soft yet clear.

'Bethral? Can you hear me?'

She lifted her head slightly. 'Yes. Is there a—'

'No,' the Storyteller responded. 'There is no danger. Well, yes, there is in a way, but it is not—' There was a pause, and she heard him shift in his tent. 'I need you to listen to me.'

She laid her head down, and waited.

'I need to tell you something,' the compelling voice continued. 'And coward that I am, I need the cover of darkness in which to say it. In the morning, the night will have flown, and we can act as if this was but a dream. But I have to speak, Lady.' Ezren Storyteller took a breath. 'I am afraid.'

'Of the warrior-priests?' Bethral asked.

'No,' came the rueful response. 'Of you.'

That took her aback.

'Why is it so hard to tell someone that you care for them?' Ezren said softly. 'Three small words that can change lives – whole worlds, if we let them. But we hold back – for fear of rejection, for fear of hurt – or worse, for fear of the look of pity in beloved eyes. So we take no chance and do not speak, and the opportunity passes us by.'

Bethral's heart lurched. She held her breath, listening.

'All the old tales make it sound so easy. To open your heart to someone, to expose your deepest feelings, to say "I love you" and wait for a long agonising breath for a response.'

There was a pause . . . a long pause.

Bethral's throat went dry. 'Ezren?' she whispered.

'I have reason to believe' – Ezren's voice was strained – 'that it might be possible that you would not spurn my . . . that is to say, that if I were to express . . . Damned if I can do this, even in the dark.'

Bethral heard him shift again in his tent, mere inches away. She could feel his stare through the leather.

'Lady Bethral, did you kiss me?'

Bethral went cold, then flushed hot, grateful for the darkness that surrounded them. She wanted the earth to open and let her slide into its depths, but the elements did not see fit to honor her thus. Instead, she opened her mouth and forced words past her dry lips. He deserved the truth.

'Yes.'

'When I was unconscious?' Ezren pressed. 'After I killed the warrior-priest?'

'Yes.' Bethral closed her eyes and whispered the truth. 'I feared you dead, and when you weren't . . . I was so relieved . . . that I took advantage of the situation. I regret—'

'Do you?' Ezren cut her off. 'Really?'

Bethral took a breath. 'No. Not really.'

'Is it possible that you are just as afraid to speak as I am?' Ezren asked.

'Yes,' Bethral whispered softly.

His heart was beating fast enough to leap from his chest, but Ezren could not stop himself now. 'I thought you pitied me,' he said quietly. 'That I was just another sorry creature that you had taken under your care.'

A murmur of protest came from the darkness.

'Then Gilla told me that she saw you kiss me,' Ezren whispered. 'I thought her wrong – or mistaken. But she assured me that she knew what she saw.'

'So I thought about that. And then I thought about other things. About why you bought me in that slave market for a copper. About why you would nurse a dying man. About why you didn't leave with your sword-sister when she left Edenrich. About why you took up a man cursed with wild magic and leapt through that portal.

'About how, ever since we've arrived here, you've been by my side, more than willing to do whatever it takes to get me home.'

Ezren paused to swallow hard. 'So difficult,' he said. 'And no way to cushion the blow if those three words are met with rejection.' He shifted so that he was facing Bethral's tent. 'And yet, if I do not speak, do not ask, I will never know.'

He waited. For a breath. And then another.

Then her voice came through the darkness, soft and low and sweet. 'I can handle the pain of a blow from a sword. Or the stab of a dagger. But this . . .' Ezren heard Bethral swallow hard. He was certain that she was facing him.

Another moment, and her voice floated over again. 'When I saw you there in the slaver's market, I was angered beyond reason at anyone who would treat a human that way. I flipped that copper coin to the slaver without a second thought,' Bethral said. 'But when I saw your green eyes open for just a moment, I started to wonder what secrets they held. And then, as you started to recover . . .'

Ezren waited, reminding himself to breathe.

'You bore hardships that would have destroyed many a hardened warrior, who would have fought the chains until he died. But you endured, and once free, you fought to free others.' Her voice grew warmer. 'Your ideas, your stories – they helped to summon an army for the Chosen, and she would never have taken the throne without your aid. Your stories . . . your mind – they amaze me.'

'I never—' Ezren shook his head. 'Bethral, you are so beautiful, so strong. You are a warrior. How can you . . .' He couldn't bring himself to say the words.

'I am a warrior, trained to fight. My body is as much a tool as my sword. But tools break, Ezren. A stray arrow, a quick slash of the blade, and my eye, my limbs, my life are gone. All that I am is my body, and even if I do not lose a fight, death will claim me as surely as any other,' Bethral said quietly. 'Age will claim the rest as well, given time.'

'Ah, you have me there,' Ezren said.

'But I want more than just a warm body,' Bethral added. 'I want your mind and heart as well. I want . . . more than just sharing.'

Ezren sucked in a breath as his body reacted to her words.

'It pleases me that my body pleases you.' Bethral shifted again in her blankets, and Ezren wondered if she was just as affected as he was by her words. 'I happen to think that you are very well made, too. Your eyes. Your hands. You have such strong hands. Thin, with long, powerful fingers. I wonder what they'd feel like on . . .' She stopped. 'This isn't a dream, is it?' Bethral asked, sounding so fearful.

'I doubt it,' Ezren said. 'The cat is in here with me, and taking up half the pallet.'

Bethral chuckled.

Ezren ran his fingers through his hair, and cleared his throat. 'I think it is two people, whispering in the dark, who might dare to take a chance. With their hearts.'

'Oh, please,' Bethral sighed. 'Let it be so.'

'But now we must decide. Do we face our fears? Or do we dismiss this moment as a mere wisp of a dream, roll over, and let sleep take us?' Ezren waited for just a moment. 'If I were to leave my tent, Bethral, and come to yours, would I be welcomed?'

'Yes.'

That was all he needed to hear.

TWENTY-ONE

Ezren's heart leapt in his throat as joy and no small amount of astonishment washed through him. He took a deliberate breath, lifted the edge of his tent, and felt the cool, misting night on his chest.

The cat grumbled. Its yellow eyes flashed, and it rose and headed out into the night. Ezren looked around, peering through the shadows. He'd stripped down to trous for sleeping, so he'd no worries there. But there was no need for everyone in camp to see him going to Bethral's tent. This was a private matter.

Harsh whispers broke the silence. It was Lander and Ouse, by the sound of it, arguing about something, their voices faint but urgent.

The darkness was almost complete. Ezren left the shelter of his tent. With a few steps he moved to Bethral's tent. The grass was cold under his feet, but the chill in the air felt good on his fevered skin. The alders rustled around him, promising rain soon.

A rustle of leather, and the top of her tent lifted. Warm air escaped, carrying a wisp of her scent. A flash of lightning through the sky, and he caught a glimpse of her long legs and hopeful face in an instant.

He slid in through the opening of the tent, and eased down to stretch out beside her. She lowered the top of the tent slowly, her breast brushing his shoulder. Ezren shuddered with the effort of controlling his body. She settled down, and he pressed close to her.

Bethral shivered. 'I—'

'No,' he whispered. 'Let me show you how I feel.'

He felt her barest of nods. With trembling fingers, he reached out and pressed his hand to her cheek. She sighed, and turned her head to kiss his palm.

The darkness was complete now, but he did not need to see. His thumb brushed over her soft lips, then he traced her brows with his fingertips. When his fingers stroked the soft skin behind her ear, she shivered again.

'Ezren.' It was a sigh, and he felt her joy and surprise.

He ran his fingers through her hair, along its entire silken length, working it from under their bodies. The long strands slid through his fingers. Pulling her closer, he nuzzled her, breathing in her warm scent.

He slid his free hand down her side, feeling the cloth of her tunic and then the softness of her thigh. He chuckled as he realised she wore nothing but the tunic, and started his hand back up, letting the cloth bunch as he slid his hand over the swell of her buttocks and up her spine.

Bethral arched against him with a breathless moan, and helped as he worked the tunic up and over her head. His hands were free to roam now, caressing her soft skin.

'Ezren,' she whispered, but he covered her mouth with his own, and kissed her. He had a thought to curse the darkness, but there was no need to see. Her breasts filled his hands, her nipples taut buds against his palm.

He could not resist the soft skin under her breast, and moved his mouth down to follow that curve, teasing her nipples with his forefinger and thumb.

She moaned, and reached for his trous, but he stopped her questing hands. 'Not yet,' he whispered against her skin.

He trailed a line of kisses up and back to her shoulder, grazing her collarbone lightly with his teeth. She drew a shuddering breath, bringing her hand up and winding it in his hair. He followed the course of her collarbone to the other shoulder, enjoying the taste of her skin and her soft urgings. He brought his hands to rest on her sides, avoiding her breasts deliberately now, just letting his thumb stroke the sides.

She moved, trying to urge him on.

Ezren chuckled, and bit at her neck, kissing the soft skin until he found his way back to her mouth. He claimed her lips hard, and groaned into her mouth as they parted beneath his. Ezren was grateful for his trous, or this would be over before it began, and he wanted this exploration to last.

The kisses were long, slow, and sweet. He was lost in her as she filled his senses. He didn't need any light to see her beauty. It was readily apparent in the warmth of her body and the gentleness of her touch. And she responded to him, to his hands, to his body, and that filled him with a sense of awe.

It was only when Bethral grabbed his hand and tried to bring it down to the core of her heat that he came to his senses. He murmured in her ear, keeping his voice soft. 'There's no rush, Angel.'

'Ezren,' her voice was in his ear, filled with yearning. 'We may not have tomorrow.'

Lord of Light, there was more truth to that then he wanted to think about. Ezren kissed her hard, and let her guide his hand within her wet folds.

One touch and she exploded against him, bringing her leg up over his, crying out something he didn't recognise but understood completely. He claimed her mouth again, stifling her cries, and stroked her hard. No more than that, and she was shuddering against him, taking deep gasps of air.

She melted down, her entire body relaxing beside him. He covered her face in kisses as her breathing returned to normal, enjoying the salty taste of her skin.

The rain started then, with a pounding of thunder. Rain poured down on the top of their small tent, but they stayed warm and dry.

Ezren thought he could stay like this for hours, listening to Bethral's soft sighs, feeling her body against his. His body ached, but that could wait. They had . . . well, they had this night. And truly, the Lord of Light and Lady of Laughter never promised more than that, now did they?

'Ezren,' Bethral murmured, rousing slightly.

'Angel,' he whispered.

'I could wish the rain never ends,' she said, her voice growing stronger. Her fingers found his lips, and traced them lightly before she kissed him.

Ezren nodded, pulling her in close as they lay in the soft darkness of the tent. The rain continued for a while, as he listened to Bethral breathe.

Finally, she stirred in his arms. 'My turn.'

She pushed Ezren to lie flat on the blankets as she explored his chest, circling his nipples first with fingers, then her tongue.

He tensed slightly as she touched one of the scars on his chest. Her hand paused, then slowly traced it up over his collarbone and over his shoulder.

'Bethral.' Ezren lifted his head, starting to apologise, but her fingers pressed on his lips as she pressed her mouth to his scar. Tracing it with open-mouth kisses, teasing his hot skin with her moist tongue. Groaning, he fell back, letting her do as she wished.

Bethral followed the scar along its length, past his nipples, down toward his navel. Ezren shifted as he hardened, his trous putting additional pressure on his sensitive skin.

Bethral shifted, careful to stay low, keeping the tent closed. She was above him now, her hair moving over his chest, the tips lightly brushing already sensitive skin. Her hands fumbled at his trous, to undo the bindings. Her struggles pressed his crotch, and the touch seared him through the cloth. His turn to gasp, then, as his body responded.

She almost had him free when his mind cleared for just a moment. He caught her hands in his, his breathing unsteady, his voice rough.

'Bethral,' he gasped out, trying to think. 'Your cycles. Is it safe?'

She tried to pull her hands free, then froze. For a moment, all he heard was their harsh breathing.

'No,' she admitted. 'I never thought . . . it didn't occur to me.'

Ezren groaned.

'We don't have to . . .' Bethral said as he eased her over on to her side. 'I could—'

Before he could really think about what he was doing, Ezren rolled out of the tent and into the cold rain, gasping as it hit his fevered skin.

'Ezren!' Bethral's voice came from the depths of the tent. He couldn't see in the darkness, but it sounded like she was peering out at him. 'You didn't need to do that!'

'Oh, yes, I did,' he muttered, rising to his knees. He pulled out the top of his trous and let the icy water flow down and kill his erection. 'Trust me, I did.'

'I am so sorry,' Bethral said. 'I never hoped that you . . . that we . . .'

Sane now, Ezren knelt and reached out, fumbling for her hand. 'I know.'

She tugged, trying to draw him back inside. 'I could have returned the favor, you know. You didn't have to douse yourself.'

Ezren sighed. 'I don't think anything else would have stopped me. I want you so damn bad.' He took a deep breath, released her hand, and stood. The rain had soaked him, and he pushed his wet hair back from his face. 'But I will not risk you, and I will not bring a child into this. Not here. Not now. But in other circumstances—' he paused. 'But I am presuming. I do not know how you feel about—'

'I'd love to bear your children,' Bethral whispered. 'I want to build a life with you, a hearth and home filled with joy and stories.'

'Lord of Light,' Ezren groaned. 'I am going back to my tent. Now.'

'It's pouring,' Bethral said. 'Crawl back in here. We can sleep warm and—'

'No,' Ezren growled. 'You are too great a temptation, Angel.'

'Really?' Bethral sounded quite pleased.

'Really,' Ezren said. Before he could change his mind, he stepped away, feeling for his own tent in the darkness. Two steps and he found it, and slid inside. With a sigh, he stripped down, and used one of the blankets to get himself as dry as possible. The gurtle fur blankets started to warm around him, and he settled down, resigned and alone.

'All's well?' Bethral's whisper came to him.

'Better than well,' Ezren said with a smile.

'And this isn't a dream?' Bethral said, her voice sounding tentative, and a bit fearful.

'No,' Ezren said. 'Sleep, Angel. In the morning, you will see the truth of it in my eyes. I promise.'

Gilla was already asleep when a cold nose pushed into her ear. She jerked her head up to find the cat trying to enter her tent.

'I thought you were sleeping with the Storyteller,' she grumbled as she shifted so that it had enough room.

The cat made its own grumbling noises, kneaded her blankets and curled into a tight ball beside her.

Gilla got comfortable and was starting to drift off when her eyes snapped open. If the cat was here . . . that must mean . . .

She closed her eyes and let sleep take her, a satisfied smile on her face.

Bethral woke to the sound of the rain and the smell of kavage brewing.

The rest of the camp was up and stirring. She'd overslept, which was rare for her. She yawned and stretched out her legs as far as she could within the tent. She felt good, warm, and relaxed, and—

Memory flooded back of the dark night and whispers in the night. Sweet kisses and his touch. Was it true? Had she dreamed it?

She was suddenly afraid. Afraid to learn the truth.

Only one way to know. Bethral dressed in the tent as best she could, pulling on her gambeson and reaching out to pull her armor inside. Somehow she felt in need of its protection. The day was cold and wet, and the rain dripped from the leaves of the alders as she emerged from the tent. They'd rigged a shelter by the fire with cloaks draped from the alders. Chell was cooking something on a low bed of coals, and the others had gathered to eat. Ezren was kneeling by the fire, filling a mug. Tenna said something to him, and he rose and turned as Bethral came up to the fire.

'Kavage?' Ezren asked.

Bethral met his gaze, looking for . . .

His green eyes were warm and steady, filled with something she'd never thought to see in this life. Confidence surged within her, and she knew that Ezren Storyteller loved her.

She returned his gaze, trying to put her heart in her eyes as she reached for the mug. The corners of his eyes crinkled, the confidence growing within him as well. 'Thank you,' she said, letting her fingers caress his in passing. Her skin tingled at his touch.

Chell started to hand out fried meat on pieces of flat bread. Ouse poured out kavage. Everyone ate either standing or kneeling by the fire, as if it was a perfectly normal day.

The meat tasted wonderful, but Bethral was certain that part of that was her quiet joy. The world seemed lighter, somehow. The kavage was hot and strong, and she savored it. Ezren was enjoying his meal as well, or so it appeared. He darted a few glances at Bethral, who looked away, trying not to blush. Which let her catch Gilla and Chell exchanging pointed glances. El and Cosana were in on the secret, too, whatever it was. They all were.

'Well?' Bethral asked. 'Something?'

They all looked at her, and then at each other. Finally Gilla puffed out a breath, clearly annoyed with the others. 'There is a matter, Warlord . . .' Gilla's voice trailed off.

Bethral raised an eyebrow.

'I would ask for your token,' Gilla finally said.

Bethral reached for the kavage. 'My token is in my tent. Let us take that as a given.'

Gilla's eyes went wide. 'There is no need for tokens between us?'

'No need, Gilla,' Ezren said warmly.

The others were all staring, then smiling, clearly pleased.

Gilla nodded to both of them, and her face grew serious. She reached toward one of the sacks by the cooking supplies, and pulled out two small leather pouches. 'You'll want to add this to your kavage.'

'Just two pinches, every morning.' Arbon added, as he started to eat. 'Don't forget.'

'What is it?' Ezren asked, but Bethral had a fair idea already. She opened the pouch to look at the dried leaves.

'Foalsbane,' El said calmly. 'It will start to work around sundown, if you take it now.'

Bethral started to laugh as Ezren sputtered.

'The cat slept with me last night,' Gilla said. 'So we assumed that you were both sharing . . .'

'And if you share, you have to be protected,' Lander said. 'All warriors take precautions when on campaign.'

'Wait.' Ezren managed to get his breath. 'Don't you mean just the women?'

'No,' Ouse said. 'Men and women.'

Cosana gave Ezren a puzzled look. 'You know it takes two to make a baby, right? A man and a woman?'

Bethral choked on her kavage.

'Yes,' Ezren replied, giving her an exasperated look. 'I do know that.'

'So both take precautions,' El pointed out. 'Especially on campaign. The penalties for getting pregnant while on campaign are severe, and the warlords are harsh.'

'The theas are even harsher,' Ouse added. 'Better that both take responsibility, rather than risk their wrath.'

'In the cities, don't they protect themselves?' Tenna asked.

Bethral arched an eyebrow at Ezren. She couldn't wait to hear his explanation of certain forms of protection. The one with dried sheep intestines came to mind.

But Ezren Storyteller wasn't stupid. 'We do,' he said and left it at that. 'Will it rain all day?' he said as he added the leaves to his kavage. Then he turned to Bethral and gave her a smile, his green eyes sparkling. Without a word, he held out the pouch.

Bethral extended her mug. Ezren let two pinches rain down into her mug with exaggerated gestures.

The young warriors all grinned, darting pleased glances at one another. 'It will rain,' Arbon said. 'It may not rain this hard all day, but there's no wind. The clouds aren't moving, and the herd is settled down around us.'

'Our horses could use a rest,' Tenna added. 'And I've a bridle that needs stitching.'

Lander looked around at the alders. 'Be nice if we can set some snares, and maybe find more ogdan roots to gather. If we can keep the fire going, we can bake them in the coals.'

'I can keep the fire going,' Ouse offered. 'I need to sharpen my blade.'

'I've a tunic needs mending,' Chell added.

'Enough,' Bethral said. 'We will spend the day here. No sense trying to travel in this weather, and the tents are sheltered well enough under the alders.' She took a sip of her kavage. The leaves didn't seem to affect the taste. 'Chell, I've needle and thread if you wish to sew up that tunic.'

'A metal needle?' Chell's eyes gleamed. 'I've only bone. Thank you, Warlord.'

'We could set a watch at the edge of the alders,' Arbon said. 'At least until the rains start again.'

Bethral nodded. 'I think so. It pays to be careful, even in this weather. We can choose our times after we eat.'

'After we eat and talk,' Ezren said firmly. 'It is time you all knew everything we know. This is not just about our leaving the Plains.'

'We've pieced together some of it, Storyteller,' Lander said. 'We know you throw fire, and that the warrior-priests tried to kill you.'

Ezren nodded. 'But I want you to know everything we know. That's only right. It seems to me that for too long the warrior-priests have used secrecy and mystery to hold power. No more secrets, not for us.'

It didn't take as long as Bethral had thought it would, even though Ezren started with the moment he encountered the magic by the swamp near the border of Athelbryght. The warriors' eyes went wide as he described being killed, then awakening to an explosion of power.

He explained how they had arrived on the Plains, and what had happened when the warrior-priests had appeared. Then the talk with Wild Winds, almost word for word. His audience remained silent and still, hanging on every word.

'There's one more thing you need to know,' Ezren said quietly. 'I can feel an odd sort of pressure, a kind of urge, that I need to turn around and head back to the north and west. As if I've left something behind me, and I need to turn back and get it.' He looked into his kavage mug. 'I fear that pressure is the magic building up in my body.'

'It is,' Ouse said softly. 'I can see it.'

TWENTY-TWO

Everyone froze.

Ouse was wide-eyed, as if shocked that he had spoken out loud. Lander nudged him. 'Go ahead, tell them,' he urged.

Ouse wet his lips. 'During the Rite of Ascension . . .' He swallowed hard. 'I—'

'We aren't supposed to talk about that.' Cosana bit her lip. 'It's not for—'

'That's what a warrior-priest said,' El pointed out.

'Rites and rituals are important,' Ezren said softly. 'Don't tell me everything. Only what I need to know.'

'There is a part . . . where they take us off alone and ask us to look at something,' Ouse blurted out. 'Then they whisper a question. I answered, and they said . . . they told me I could be a warrior-priest. That I had a gift.'

'I saw nothing,' Arbon frowned. 'What did you see?'

'A glow.' Ouse glanced at Arbon and then looked back at Ezren. 'The same kind of glow I see around you . . . around your chest.'

'Magic,' Bethral whispered.

Ezren nodded. 'I think so. It makes sense. You identify the gift when the children become adults.'

'The warrior-priest was a young one. He didn't have all of his tattoos yet,' Ouse said. 'He said that if I felt this was my path, I should approach a warrior-priest and ask whatever questions I had, whenever I was ready.'

'But you're not ready, right?' Lander said sharply.

Ouse looked hurt. 'Lander, all I said was that I was interested. You have to admit that they wield great power and that—'

'No,' Lander said. 'I can't believe you'd even think of joining their ranks. Don't you see that—'

'A singer and a warrior-priest,' Ouse pleaded. 'Think of the influence and power we'd—'

'Warrior-priests don't bond,' Lander said. 'And the years of separation. I don't want—'

'They haven't bonded in the past, but we could be the first.' Ouse folded his arms over his chest. 'And it takes years to become a singer. We could—'

'I refuse to listen to this,' Lander spat. 'I don't—'

'Stop!' Bethral commanded.

Both boys obeyed, each looking upset and angry.

'You refuse to hear a truth?' Ezren asked softly.

Lander looked away.

'What if the warrior-priests are right?' Chell asked softly. 'What if the magic you bear belongs here?'

'In the hands of those that tried to kill him?' Bethral asked.

Chell gave her a thoughtful look, then dropped her gaze.

Ezren Storyteller stood, and sighed. 'Ouse of the Fox, I cannot answer your truth. I do not know the answers. All I have are questions. What if magic was removed from this land for a very good reason? What if the stories are not true?'

'We have perfect memories, Ezren Storyteller. We wouldn't change a word,' Ouse argued.

'I do not believe that. I know of at least three versions of most stories from many lands, and there are always slight differences. And I know people.' Ezren was looking at all of them. 'People change stories. It is in the nature of stories to change over time.'

'Then if it's not the magic that was taken – what is it?' Ouse asked, gesturing toward Ezren's chest.

'I do not know. But I question the wisdom of trying to return this to the land. The warrior-priests are taking this for granted, and it makes me uncomfortable. Why did Wild Winds not recognise the altar where I – where this happened? And what about that spider statue – the one that disappeared?' Ezren shook his head. 'He did not react at all. What if when this happened, the warrior-priests changed the tale themselves – but did not tell the next generation?'

'How much of this is their own desperation to restore their lost powers?' Bethral asked.

'Are there any answers?' Cosana twirled her hair around her finger. 'All we seem to have are questions.'

'Welcome to the truth of being an adult.' Ezren gave her a sad smile. 'Sometimes there is no right answer. No clear trail.

'This much I do know.' Ezren stood. 'Long ago, someone did something that set a series of events in motion. Now here I am, like a chess piece on a board. Except I do not know all the pieces or all the rules, and I cannot see the entire board.'

'And you lose track of the moves after a while,' El said.

Even Ezren chuckled at that. 'So true,' he said. 'All I can do is make the best decision I can. The rest is in the hands of the Gods or the elements.'

The warriors nodded in agreement.

Ezren focused on Ouse. 'All I can ask is for your truths and that you deal with me with honor. Would you betray me to any warrior-priests we encounter?'

'No,' Ouse said. He lifted his chin and looked at Lander, who nodded. Ouse's shoulders relaxed. 'I can promise you honor, Storyteller. Honor and truth.'

'Well, then' – Ezren looked around – 'it seems the rain is letting up a bit. Shall we see to the day?'

'Do you two want help weaving your tents together?' Gilla asked.

Bethral blushed.

Bethral gave silent thanks that the rains began again as they finished combining their tents. Gilla and Tenna had left them with quiet smiles, each with their own plans for the day as the sheets of water poured out of the sky. Ezren held the tent flap open for Bethral as she crawled inside. There was plenty of room now. She started to remove her armor. 'All this rain,' she sighed. 'I'll have to oil this later.'

She pulled off her metal gauntlets and reached for the buckles that held the breastplate together.

'Let me,' Ezren said softly.

Bethral lifted her arm to give him access, watching his face as he worked. His eyes were intent, bright green with dark lashes. She looked away, and took a breath as he released the armor.

She caught the breastplate and held it in place as he moved to the other side, and the buckle under her other arm. With the pressure released, that one was easy, and she pulled the armor away from the gambeson as he caught the back piece.

'It is chafed here,' he said.

His warm breath touched the back of her neck. Bethral shivered. 'It feels fine . . .' she whispered.

'Just a bit of red,' Ezren whispered, and pressed his lips to her nape.

She sighed then, moving her head to let him trace her jaw with kisses. Putting on and taking off her armor was usually fairly tedious, something she did by rote. But not this time. Plate and chain seemed to melt away, each piece replaced with a caress and soft kisses.

Ezren eased the quilted tunic over her head, and Bethral pulled her head free. She knelt next to him, naked except for the curtain of her hair. 'Your turn.' She smiled, and reached for the clasp that secured his leather armor.

'Wait,' he breathed.

Bethral's face grew warm as his gaze wandered over her for the first time in the light of day. She didn't look away, and was rewarded by the warmth and desire she saw in his eyes. Her body responded as well, and that pleased him even more.

She reached for the clasp again. He held her hand for a moment, stopping her, and then with a rueful shrug, started to undress. 'There is no reason to hide it, is there? You have seen this all before, Angel. Scars and all.'

'Not like this,' she whispered.

It was her turn to stroke, and trace kisses over his skin. He flinched a bit as her lips brushed a scar on his back, then relaxed at her touch. Bethral noticed that his eyes never left her face, watching for any sign of disgust or pity.

He need not have worried. Bethral loved every inch, and in the light of day, his skin glowed. Ezren might not have the bulk that some warriors had, but he was all lean muscle. She hummed in appreciation for his arms and chest, although she hesitated over the definition in his stomach. The muscles there were pronounced, with almost no fat, narrowing down to . . .

She paused at the waist of his trous, and stroked his skin with her fingertips. 'You've lost weight here. Too much. Are you—?'

Ezren caught her hand, and then pressed his lips over hers, taking the time for a long, sweet kiss. When he pulled away, she was breathless.

'We are not going to worry about that right now. For a few precious hours, we are going to worry about only one thing . . .'

'What's that?' she asked softly.

'How to keep busy until sunset, Angel. When I know that the herbs have taken effect.' Ezren kissed her throat. 'Maybe I should tell you stories.'

'I love your stories,' Bethral said. 'But I think I owe you something, Ezren Storyteller. Seems I am in your debt, after last night.' She eased her fingers down into his trous. 'It's only fair . . .'

'No debts between us. Only pleasure.' Ezren freed her hands, letting them travel down to ease his trous over his hips. They were soon both sprawled on the bedding, the gurtle mats cushioning them beneath, the blankets folded as pillows. Bethral was taking her time exploring him, and he returned the favor, his hands everywhere.

Finally he lay back on the pillows and let her have her way. She kissed him as she covered his length with her hand, and watched his eyes close as he arched his back and gave in to the demands of his body.

Hot and sweaty, she cleaned him, then cuddled close, resting her head on his shoulder. His voice was rough when he raised his hand to stroke her hair. 'How I wish I had had the courage to say something sooner,' he said. 'Think of all the wasted time and energy.'

'No, Ezren,' Bethral said. 'We are the people we are now because of all those prior decisions. I refuse to regret any of my choices.' She lifted her head. 'But I won't waste one more moment.'

'All right, my love.' Ezren drew her in close. 'It may not yet be sundown, but we have this day. We can touch, and talk, and dream a little, if that is acceptable.'

'It is.' Bethral settled her head with a sigh. 'Tell me a story, Ezren.'

'Not the one of the Lord and the Lady,' Ezren said firmly. 'I promised the others. Besides, it ends in a tryst, and I will not torture us both with that.' He pulled one of the lighter blankets over their bodies. 'Tell me instead about your mother.'

'There is not much to tell,' Bethral said. 'Her name is Amastra, and she was born of the Tribe of the Horse. She had her required children, served in the armies, and then decided to see the world. Her wandering brought her to Soccia, where she met my father, Caden. Father said he pursued her until she caught his heart.' Bethral lifted her head a bit. 'Mother warned me that those of the Plains are prolific: I am the eldest of five children. Both Father and Mother taught me the way of the sword, and I set out to seek my way as a mercenary, which is how I linked up with Red Gloves.'

'Five?' Ezren asked. 'After she had five on the Plains?'

Bethral nodded. 'Two brothers and two sisters.'

'Would you have gone back to Soccia,' Ezren asked softly, 'if this had not happened?'

Bethral placed her hand over his heart. 'No. I'd thought to serve Gloriana for a few years, and then perhaps go to Athelbryght, and breed horses. I hoped that I might catch your eye, but I knew that in all likelihood you would be wed to one of the ladies of the Court within the year. Still, I dared to dream.'

Ezren snorted. 'Oh my angel, there was no fear of a noble marriage for me. I am of common merchant stock and no warrior. My parents were good people who despaired that their only son was a wastrel and a sloth. I had no interest in buying and selling, only in running with friends and causing havoc. I was the life of the party, and loved to regale my friends with tales of my misdeeds.'

'Until . . .' Bethral said.

'Until I chanced to go to a tavern of even less than my normal low standards.' Ezren chuckled. 'I and a few of my mates decided to go to the Crate of Diamonds, a tavern in the Wastesides of Edenrich. Its clientele was even more questionable than its beer.'

'I've been in a few of those in my day.' Bethral smiled.

'We grabbed a center table, demanded drinks, insulted the food, and began our usual drunken carousing.

'Until this tall, lean elf walked in, with a long braid of gray hair and a serious face. He sat on a stool by the fire, and the entire place went silent. Absolutely silent.' Ezren's voice was distant. 'We even shut up, if you can believe.'

'He opened his mouth and told the tale of Radaback Roc-Rider, adventurer extraordinare. His face was so serious, and yet the story was so funny . . . the entire place was laughing within moments, and he never once lost them.' Ezren darted a glance at Bethral. 'To tell a story that way – to hold your audience for that long . . . controlling everyone with his voice. It was like magic, the only kind of magic I ever wanted to wield. He was amazing.

'Once the tale was done, everyone pounded the tables and offered him drinks, but he shook his head, and waved them off with thanks. I could not believe it. He did not pass a hat, or have one at his feet.

'The next morning, I went to the Crate and found him, and asked him to teach me everything he knew.' Ezren gave her a grin. 'After a bit of persuading, he agreed. So I was apprenticed to Joseph Taleteller, to my parent's relief and my friends' dismay. I was very lucky. King Everead heard my tales and asked me to his Court, and I received royal patronage and access to the castle libraries. That is when I started developing my theories about stories and people and how we . . . and if you don't stop me, I can go on like this for days.'

Bethral propped herself up on her elbow, letting her hair fall on his chest. 'Wait until foaling season, when I won't leave the stables for any reason.' She ran her fingers through his hair. 'Are your parents still alive?'

'No,' Ezren said, 'and I thank the Lord of Light that they were gone before I was enslaved by the Usurper. Father died in his sleep. And Mother . . . well, the heart just went out of her. I lost her not six months later.'

Bethral leaned down and brushed her lips over his. Ezren cleared his throat. 'Yours?'

'Alive and well, when last I saw them.' Bethral pulled back to look at him. 'That was just before Red and I left Soccia to find work.' She rolled her eyes. 'Mother will gloat when she learns I've been to the Plains. All those afternoons making me learn her language when all I wanted to do was ride.'

'I am grateful to her' – Ezren lifted his hand and ran it through Bethral's hair – 'For her beautiful—'

'You think I'm beautiful?' Bethral asked.

'Yes.' Ezren frowned. 'Do you not think so?'

Bethral shrugged. 'I am not ugly. But I don't see where I am anything special, Ezren.'

'Let me show you,' Ezren said. He reached up to tug her mouth down to his.

'It's not yet sunset,' Bethral whispered against his mouth.

'No matter,' Ezren whispered back, 'there is still so much we can do . . .'

TWENTY-THREE

Bethral was sure she would perish, convinced that Ezren's strong fingers would take her breath at any moment.

If this was how it felt to be caressed, how would it be when he entered her? The very thought made every touch that much more maddening.

The man was so intense, so focused on her. Yet she couldn't get enough of him, wanting to learn so much. How the soft hairs of his nape lifted off his skin when she kissed the back of his ear. How he trembled as she stroked the soft skin of his inner elbow. The taste of his mouth, the scent of his body . . . it would take a lifetime.

One they didn't have.

They'd worked themselves to a fever-pitch, clinging and kissing and reaching for each other until the need to breathe drove them apart. The blanket was at their waists; Bethral reached down to push it off. Ezren lay gasping, a faint sheen of sweat on his chest.

Bethral's senses were swamped with their love play, but there was a silent part of her brain that kept watch. It listened to the birds in the alders and the rain dripping through the leaves. It kept track of her weapons, tucked next to her where she could get to them quickly. She was too well trained, too long a mercenary to let that portion of her mind drift off.

She knew the illusion for what it was; sooner or later they would have to stir from this shelter and set off again. But right now, she was in his arms and they had what was left of this day and this night.

Ezren sighed, and shifted so that he could open the tent flap. Cold air crept in, carrying the smell of the rain with it.

'Still raining,' he said, easing the edge back down.

'I love listening to it,' Bethral said, reaching for the blankets now that she was cooler. 'Being warm and snug while it beats on the roof.'

Ezren pulled her close and kissed her. 'Yes, but how will we know when the sun sets?'

Bethral used her free hand to guide his mouth to her breast. 'You'll think of something.'

At some point, they must have drifted off. Ezren awoke when Bethral tensed, lifting her head. There was a sound outside the tent and a polite cough. 'Warlord? Singer?'

'Cosana?' Bethral had a dagger in her hand. 'What—'

'All's well, Warlord,' Cosana said quickly. 'I wanted to know if you want food. The ogdan roots are done, and . . . well . . .' She giggled nervously. 'You've been in there most of the day.'

Bethral put her weapon away.

'We thought maybe you'd like the use of the pond to wash,' Cosana said brightly. 'So we're all set to give you some privacy. We'll retreat into our tents, and leave your food warming by the fire. It's going to rain on and off all night, at least that is what Arbon says.'

Ezren heard her shuffle her feet as she took a breath. 'I was wondering if you ever thought of three-souls sharing. Because I'd be will—'

'Cosana,' Bethral said, glaring right through the tent.

'I think it's a custom of our people that you should consider trying.' Cosana kept talking. The poor girl sounded so sincere. Ezren started to laugh, but Bethral put her fingers over his mouth.

'Our thanks,' Bethral growled. 'But no.'

'Oh,' there was silence for a moment. 'Well, if you are sure.'

'We are sure,' Bethral responded. 'Has the sun set yet?'

'Oh yes,' Cosana replied. 'Arbon and I will take watch until it gets too dark to see. The rains will start up again, probably around full dark.'

'Good,' Bethral said.

'Are you really sure?' Cosana asked quickly. 'About the sharing? Because I—'

'Yes,' Bethral growled. 'Very sure.'

Cosana sighed ever so sadly. 'Well, then, your food is by the fire.' She walked off quietly. After a moment Bethral took her hand from Ezren's mouth.

'Even her footsteps sound crushed.' Ezren gave Bethral a grin. 'How could you deprive her of a chance to teach us all the customs of the Plains?'

Bethral sat up, reaching for her tunic. 'I don't share the sharing, beloved.'

Ezren sat up. 'Say that again.'

She looked at him, her blue eyes startled, then warming. 'Beloved.'

He took the tunic from her hands. 'It is after sunset, Angel.'

'We should eat.' She looked at him from under her eyelashes. 'And bathe. Before the rains start again.'

Ezren caught his breath. She was so lovely, her long blonde hair spilling over her shoulders, hiding her breasts. How in the name of the Lord of Light could she love . . .

Yet it was there, in her bright blue eyes and calm face. His heart started to beat faster as he reached for her and pulled her down to their bed.

She came willingly, she who could kill with a single blow, his Angel of the Light. Her mouth opened to his as she welcomed him into her arms.

No more waiting, no more teasing. One move, and he was over her, nudging her legs apart with his. She opened to him and he slid into her wet heat. He froze, breathing hard as she moaned. 'Bethral?'

Her eyes opened, their blue depths clouded with a haze of pure desire. 'Ezren, please . . .'

He kissed her, thrusting as she arched her back and moved

under him. He fought back his own pleasure, trying to make the moment last forever, but he might as well try to hold back the sun. He'd just enough control left to make sure of Bethral's pleasure before he claimed his own shuddering climax.

Ezren collapsed on top of her, and felt her arms around him, stroking his back as he drifted off.

When he woke, she was sleeping next to him. He reached out, pulling a strand of hair away from her face. She opened sleepy eyes and smiled.

'I had planned to go slower, beloved,' he whispered.

'Any slower, any more waiting, and I'd have died.' Bethral bit his earlobe. 'There's time yet before the rains.'

Much later, after they'd loved and slept, they ate and bathed in the rain. The water of the pond was cold on their fevered skin. They returned to their tent, and dried off as best they could under the dripping branches.

Once they climbed into their nest, the blankets warmed their chilled skin. Bethral bound up her wet hair in a long braid, and they lay together and listened to the rain.

Ezren took her hand, weaving their fingers together. 'Marry me, Bethral,' he dared to ask. 'Be my wife.'

Bethral sucked in a breath, stunned into silence. She reached out with a trembling hand and stroked his face, her face luminous with quiet joy. 'Yes, Ezren Storyteller, I would be honored to be your wife.'

Laughing and crying, they kissed. 'Would you wear my ring? I wish we were in Edenrich. I would buy you the loveliest ring. I would not care how much gold it cost.'

'Oh, I don't know,' Bethral said, tears in her eyes. 'I'm more than satisfied with what a copper can buy.'

Bethral roused when Ezren stirred beside her.

She couldn't see much, for it was barely dawn. Ezren was on his back, shifting restlessly under the blankets. Dreaming, perhaps. She shifted to face him, and reached out to stroke his face.

He was moving his head back and forth, as if arguing with

someone. She whispered his name, and ran her fingers through his hair.

He settled then, with a sigh. She kept stroking him gently, easing him awake.

His voice was rough with sleep when he spoke. 'Bethral?'

'Here,' she whispered, leaning in to kiss his cheek. 'Bad dreams?'

She felt him nod. 'I need to go back,' he mumbled, and she knew he was only half awake.

'Go where, beloved?' she asked.

'There.' He lifted an arm and brushed her shoulder as he pointed. 'Need to go that way. It is important . . .'

Ezren went silent for a moment. Bethral put her head on his shoulder, and waited.

'Bethral?' His voice was clearer now.

'Ezren,' she answered. 'You were dreaming.'

'There was some place I had to be,' he said. His voice was taut. 'Some place important. Something I have to do.'

'You pointed toward the Heart of the Plains,' Bethral told him.

Ezren cursed in a language she didn't recognise. 'We need to keep moving, do we not?'

It wasn't a question. His voice was flat and determined. She nodded against his shoulder. 'I think so.'

'Bethral.' He shifted to face her. 'There is no way to know—'

She kissed him, opening her mouth and inviting him in. He returned the kiss with passion, wrapping her in his arms and pulling her close.

'There is still a while until dawn,' Bethral murmured against his mouth. 'That is all that is certain.'

Ezren rolled over, pulling her on top. 'Let us claim them for ourselves, then, Angel of Light.'

They loved long and slow, with a sweetness that brought them both joy and completion. Ezren yawned, and fell back into quiet slumber, but Bethral couldn't close her eyes. She lay there, watching the first hint of sun creep into their safe little tent and illuminate Ezren's face. Stolen moments of peace, watching her lover sleep. She let herself hope for a moment, for a future with him. Some land, a home, children, horses, and dogs. The boys would have his eyes, and the girls would have blonde hair. They'd have a big stone fireplace, and he'd sit and tell tales to his children by the fire in the winter months. Wild tales of their father and mother on the Plains, fleeing from the warrior-priests.

Bethral sighed then, and slowly started to ease into her tunic and trous, so as not to wake Ezren. The moment for hoping had passed.

Her armor could wait for later. Right now, she'd check the watches and start rousing the others. The sooner they were on their way, the better.

She was about to open the flap and step out when she heard a step outside the tent.

'Warlord?' Arbon's voice was soft.

Bethral emerged, closing the flap behind her. 'Report.'

'Trouble.' Arbon was calm, but his eyes were wide. 'Riders.'

TWENTY-FOUR

Gilla lay flat in the wet grass and watched for the riders she knew were out among the herds.

She'd crawled out of the hollow where they'd hidden in the alders, just enough so that she could see the herd. Lying flat, her sword on her back and her dagger in her hand.

Her heart raced, but she moved slowly and carefully.

The horses before her showed no signs of concern. They were grazing, a few with foals keeping close by. Nursing mares rarely responded to a summons call. It was doubtful that she would get a glimpse of the people calling for mounts, but she'd claimed this section. El and Lander might have better luck.

Were they warrior-priests? Or just warriors? Gilla bit her lip as she strained to see the edges of the herd.

A hand grasped her ankle. She lowered her head and wiggled backward. Bethral crawled up next to her.

'It's warriors, headed for the Heart.' Bethral had her mouth close to Gilla's ear. 'El got a good look. We are going to keep under cover and wait for them to move off.'

Gilla relaxed.

Bethral crawled back, and Gilla followed. They stayed flat until they reached the depths of the hollow. 'El and Lander are keeping watch, and will signal if they head for us,' Bethral said.

'There's cold kavage left from last night,' Gilla offered.

'Good,' Bethral said. 'We need to gather our gear and be ready to ride.'

'Warlord, I—' Gilla sheathed her dagger, and sighed. 'I don't know if . . .' She trailed off, unable to finish her thought. 'We are taught that fear is our enemy. That—'

'Fear holds you still when you need to move, and moves you when you need to be still.'

Gilla looked at Bethral in astonishment.

'Fear makes you silent when you need to be loud, and loud when you need silence,' Bethral continued, reciting the same learning wisdom that Gilla had been taught. 'Fear closes your throat, makes it hard to breathe. Fear weakens your hand and blinds your eyes. Fear is a danger. Know your fear. Face your fear.'

'I am afraid, Warlord,' Gilla admitted.

'When the time comes, you will be able to do what you have to do to stay alive and keep your people safe.' Bethral said.

Startled, Gilla looked at her. 'How do you know? What if I freeze up? What if I—'

'You won't.' Bethral walked through the alders toward her tent.

'How do you know that, city dweller?' Gilla hissed, her eyes filled with tears. 'You've known me for—'

'I will tell you after the battle.'

'And if you are wrong?' Gilla spat.

'It won't matter.' Bethral glanced back. 'Most likely we'll all be dead.'

Gilla stood there for a moment, drew a deep breath, and went to get the kavage.

Ezren was fumbling with the buckles on his armor when he heard Bethral call his name. He looked up as she entered the tent and knelt down. 'Warrior-priests?' he asked.

She shook her head, and pulled off her tunic and trous. Ezren caught his breath when she reached for her gambeson as she answered his question. 'Young warriors, probably on their way to the Heart for the challenges. They will move on soon, and then we can leave.'

'So there is no time to . . .' Ezren suggested.

'No.' Bethral paused, then shuddered slightly. 'Ezren, don't look at me that way.'

'I know,' Ezren said. 'We need to leave. But I will not apologise. You are just so very beautiful—'

Bethral was in his arms, her breasts pressed against his armor. Her hands went down to his trous and opened them. He pulled her closer with one arm, and cupped her breast. Suddenly he was flat and she was on top of him, wet and impaled, moaning softly.

He grabbed her hips. 'Beloved.'

Bethral leaned down, and her hair closed off the world and the dangers around them. She kissed him, cutting off any speech.

He didn't need words. Ezren gripped her hips hard, and thrust up as she moaned into his mouth. It didn't take long; it couldn't, after all. They both cried out and collapsed into a shuddering, sweating pile of arms and legs and love.

'Whatever happens,' Ezren whispered, 'we have had this.'

'We have.' Bethral raised her head to look into his eyes. 'But I want more, Ezren Storyteller. And I will kill anyone that stands between me and a lifetime with you.'

After the threat had moved on, they gathered by the cold fire pit, and shared dried meat and gurt. Gilla carefully poured out the cold kavage to each of them, then hurried to drink hers. It was dark, cold, and bitter, but it tasted good in her excitement.

She told herself that it was excitement she was feeling. Her heart racing, her senses afire. It was exhilaration, not fear.

The others seemed so calm, eating the cold food and drinking the cold kavage. Normally they'd have been hiding smiles and maybe gently teasing Bethral and Ezren. But the appearance of strange riders had brought the truth of their mission back to them.

'We will summon horses,' Bethral said. She stood and looked at all of them, her armor glittering in the sun that filtered through the alders. 'I want two remounts for everyone, and a few extra for packhorses. We are going to leave the herd, and ride hard for three days.'

'South?' Arbon asked.

'East,' Bethral said. 'Due east. We ride hard for three days, then find another herd we can hide in for a while. We'll rest then, and repeat the process until we reach the foothills.'

They all nodded. Gilla drained the last of her kavage, and put her mug in her pack. The others were doing the same.

'Ezren and I will stay with the packs while you summon horses,' Bethral said.

'One more thing,' Ezren Storyteller focused on Ouse. 'Ouse, if you see any change in me, in the glow, you need to tell everyone. Warn everyone.'

Gilla frowned. Those green eyes were filled with worry.

'I will,' Ouse said. 'I swear.' He hesitated. 'Storyteller, are you afraid that the magic will flare out of control?'

'It certainly reacts to seeing warrior-priests,' Ezren said. 'But I have a bigger concern.'

'We are afraid that the magic will try to control him.' Bethral looked at Ezren, her worry in her eyes.

Ezren drew a breath. 'If that happens—'

'We will deal with it,' Bethral cut him off firmly. 'For now, we need horses. Best to be moving as soon as we can.'

The stale air of the huge tent was disturbed when the tent flap opened. The fresh air was welcome, but Hail Storm didn't look away from the tiny image of the Plains before him.

'Anything?'

That would, of course, be Mist. The younger ones had seen his sorrow over the death of Arching Colors, and would honor his dedication to watch over the spell in the still of the night, to see if the Sacrifice used magic.

'Those that still scry have found nothing. And all of the warrior-priests that still travel have reported nothing,' Mist continued. She stepped forward with her staff so that the skulls rattled. 'When do we recognise this for the waste of power that it is?'

'We hunt prey,' Hail Storm said softly. 'Is not patience a virtue of the hunter?'

'True enough, but night falls and the hunt ends. And not

199

always in success.' Mist went silent for a moment. 'Wild Winds will arrive at the Heart soon. Will you be there to assert your challenge?'

Another entered, slipping in quietly. 'Hail Storm?'

Hail Storm sighed. 'Yes, Thunder Clouds?' Another of the older ones, who needed to be treated with respect.

'I had an idea,' Thunder Clouds said, coming to stand next to Mist. 'And I wish to try it with your permission.'

'How so?' Hail Storm raised an eyebrow. 'Mist is of the mind that we should abandon this hunt.'

Mist gave him a sharp look, but said nothing.

Thunder Clouds shook his head. 'When you find the Sacrifice, we must be able to send other warrior-priests after him. We need a way to see both the Sacrifice and those around him.'

Hail Storm nodded encouragement.

'Now, in each of the groups that conducted the rites there is an older warrior-priest, if not an elder. Each of us carries some magic within, for castings.' Thunder Clouds gestured at the display before them. 'I think I can make them appear here, for us to see.'

'You will disrupt his casting,' Mist objected.

'No.' Thunder Clouds moved to the northern point. 'Mine will lie over Hail Storm's casting. It's . . . well, let me try.' He raised his arms, preparing to cast the spell.

Mist moved back to the tent wall, out of the way. Hail Storm remained where he was, ready to protect his casting, if necessary.

Thunder Clouds raised his hands, as if he was gathering a net, preparing to cast it into the water for fish. He chanted under his breath, using a minimal amount of power as far as Hail Storm could see.

Thunder Clouds moved to each of the four points, standing and chanting and gathering his net. Hail Storm could almost see it, a fine weave of blue sparkles in his hand.

When Thunder Clouds returned to the northern point, he opened his hands, as if casting a net.

The surface of the Plains rippled ever so slightly. Then soft blue sparks started to appear. Hail Storm drew a breath as he realised that one of the large clusters of small blue points of light was their own camp.

Then, as if the net were falling over the Plains, blue sparkles appeared all over the map.

Mist stepped forward. 'Thunder Cloud, you amaze me.'

Thunder Cloud was breathing hard, and wiped sweat out of his eyes. 'That cost more than I thought it would, but it worked.'

'Can you see the Sacrifice?' Hail Storm asked urgently.

They all looked, but there was no sign of him. 'I was afraid that might happen,' Thunder Cloud said. 'What the Sacrifice bears is as slippery as ehat oil.'

Hail Storm frowned. 'The magic of our people is known to you. The magic of the Sacrifice is not. That may be a factor as well.'

'Look,' Mist breathed, 'you can see them moving.'

She was right. As Hail Storm watched, the sparkles were moving, all of them, heading for the Heart as he had directed. Satisfaction washed through him at the sight.

Hail Storm stood, taking his time, stretching muscles that had been still too long. 'This needs fresh eyes,' he said, keeping his tone soft and reasonable.

That was all he needed to say. The four warrior-priests waiting outside entered the tent, and took their places around the miniature Plains.

Thunder Cloud and Mist followed Hail Storm out into the dawn. He paused, staring at the bed of coals where his tent had once stood. The area had been turned into Arching Colors's pyre, and had been kept burning all night. Fragrant herbs had been added to the fire, to mask the scent of burning flesh. He paused, as if struck with new pain. 'It still burns?'

'The bone-crushing ceremony will be held as soon as the coals cool.' Mist was watching his face closely. 'You will wish to attend?'

Hail Storm nodded, as if unable to speak.

'My tent is close. Come,' Mist said, and so he turned to follow her, after a last lingering glance at the burnt grass.

Thunder Cloud fell in next to him, looking exhausted. Hail Storm gave him a quick look, but Thunder Cloud shook his head. 'I am fine. Just more magic than I had planned to use, that's all.'

Hail Storm risked a glance back then, as if to linger by the pyre. But Thunder Cloud took his elbow firmly. 'Come. We both need rest.'

Hail Storm submitted, but could not resist looking about as he walked, the pyre behind him forgotten in an instant. Many more warrior-priests had joined the encampment. Others would be coming, drawn by the summons and the news of the challenge. Each of those sparkles, headed for the Heart.

Hail Storm had no worries about the challenge. Wild Winds was old and weak. By all traditions he should have crushed the skulls on his staff and taken his own life by now. But if he failed to abide by the ways of the Plains, then Hail Storm would slay him. Maybe with the dagger at his belt.

He stumbled at the thought. One like Wild Winds . . . what kind of power would that death release? He caught his breath at the idea of the old man helpless before him, struggling as the blade pierced his—

'Hail Storm?' Mist stood holding open the flap of her tent, and looked at him with questioning eyes.

'Forgive me.' Hail Storm ducked within, and waited for her to be seated before he folded his legs and sat. Thunder Cloud sank down beside him.

'You seem distracted,' Mist said. One of her warrior-priests brought hot kavage, and served them.

'The events of the last few days,' Hail Storm murmured, and was rewarded with a brief flash of sympathy in the old mare's eyes.

'Understandable,' Mist responded. 'Others have asked to join us and speak with you. Morning Dew has reported that the Heart has been cleared, and that only warrior-priests remain within sight.'

'I must be there to challenge.' Hail Storm took a sip of his kavage. 'But the Sacrifice must be found, and brought to the Heart.'

Thunder Cloud took up his mug. 'It will happen, if we work together.'

Mist nodded. 'I am not sure of this path. Wild Winds may be correct. I do not support the challenge. But I will aid you in securing the Sacrifice.' She sighed. 'Our powers must be restored if our ways are to be preserved.'

A cough at the flap, and three others entered. Each was seated and served, and Hail Storm was pleased to see that they deferred to him during the talk. Here was the support he needed. Once Wild Winds was dead, he would claim the position of Eldest Elder. And if the Sacrifice died on his blade at the Heart, who knew what powers might be his?

He needed to be patient only a little while longer.

TWENTY-FIVE

The ride was brutal on all of them.

Bethral set a pace that demanded all they had, even the young ones. The horses were pushed to the edge of their endurance, but they loved to run, appearing in the morning to bear their riders willingly. Alternating trot and gallop, covering the ground as fast as the wind, the horses were in their element.

Ezren had feared for Bessie, who was larger than the Plains horses. But the big roan had more endurance than the others and more speed than he'd expected. Bethral would never let a beast founder under her charge, so Ezren decided to let that worry go.

There were other concerns. His endurance, for one.

It wasn't that he was weakening, exactly. More and more, he couldn't get enough to eat or drink, and when he rolled into the tent, he was asleep before Bethral had time to pull the blankets over them. He'd tried to apologise – he'd hoped to love his lady every night. Bethral had just pressed her fingers to his lips, and shaken her head with understanding.

He didn't have to tell her. He knew she saw it in his body, in the definition of the muscles, in the thinning of his wrists. Those old scars from the slave chains were more pronounced, at least to his eyes. The power within was consuming him, as Wild Winds had predicted.

So he concentrated on keeping in the saddle, and riding hard. Lander had given him a small bag of dried meat, and he ate as they rode, working it with his jaws. Gurt, too, although he was getting tired of its bitter taste. It wasn't that unpleasant, just not something he wanted to eat every day. Every hour of every day.

Interesting that adventure tales never seemed to mention trail rations.

'Third day.' Arbon was next to him as they saddled their horses and loaded the packs. Bethral had agreed to stop when they found a good-sized herd, and hide within it for a day or two to let them catch their breath. With any luck, maybe they could hunt. Fresh meat and greens would be more than welcome.

'Third day,' Ezren said with a smile. He swung into the saddle and turned his horse. 'Let us get started.'

'Ezren.' Bethral grabbed his horse's bridle. She was already mounted on Bessie, and her cloak covered her armor.

'What?' he asked crossly, suddenly irritated that she would get in his way.

'That's the wrong direction,' she said, her blue eyes pained. 'That's northwest.'

'Oh.' Ezren turned his head and looked at the rising sun. 'I thought—'

Bethral nodded. 'I know. Let's get moving.'

He nodded, and they headed out. Ezren noticed Bethral didn't release her grip on his horse's bridle until they were well on the way.

Gilla didn't see the horses until Cosana extended out her arm and pointed. They were riding at a gallop at that point. It was a smaller herd than the one before, but large enough to hide in.

Gilla looked over her shoulder. Bethral had seen the horses. She didn't say anything, but turned Bessie in that direction.

Gilla was grateful. It was early still, and the sun wasn't that close to the horizon. Sleep would come easily this night, even if the sun wasn't down. She was tired, and she wasn't the only one.

The Storyteller was exhausted.

You couldn't tell with just a casual glance, but the signs were there. A tremble in his hands and the strain around his eyes. Bethral was staying close, keeping an eye on him, trying to keep him in the center of the group. At the last rest break, while they had watered the horses and switched mounts, Ouse had said that the glow he saw seemed no different.

Gilla hoped it stayed that way.

Cosana had the lead. As they drew closer, she slowed her horse to a walk so as not to disturb the herd. She looked over her shoulder at Gilla with a smile.

So Cosana didn't see the warrior-priestess at the edge of the herd, flinging a saddle on the back of a horse. Gilla caught her breath. Usually warrior-priests ignored warriors, as if they did not exist. But this one was giving them a hard look.

'Cosana,' Gilla said sharply, but Cosana had turned and spotted the problem. She angled her horse away, as if to avoid the warrior-priestess, just as any warrior would do. Gilla held her breath as they rode past. She could see other warrior-priests within the herd, selecting mounts. Ezren was in the middle of their party, and Bethral was cloaked. If they could just get past them and ride farther on—

'SACRIFICE! THE SACRIFICE!'

Damn them to the snows, they'd seen the Storyteller. Gilla yanked her horse's head around and drew a lance.

She saw a flash of silver, and watched Bethral charge into the herd. Horses scattered, saddles falling off them and leaving warrior-priests standing there, drawing swords and bows. Bethral galloped past the first one, who was screaming and pulling a bow. She swung her mace at the woman's exposed head, connecting with a solid hit.

The warrior-priestess collapsed.

The other warrior-priests scattered, but another one had brought his bow to bear on—

Gilla didn't think. Her lance was in her hand, and she threw, aiming at his chest. She didn't wait to see the result. She pulled her sword and shield. Her horse surged forward at her urging, and they were in the midst of the enemy. A warrior-priest came at her, sword held high.

Gilla took the blow on her shield, and countered as she had

been trained. There was no thought other than to defend and strike, to dodge and parry, to protect . . . and kill.

Ezren pressed himself farther down in the grasses, and kept his eyes focused on the blades before him.

The first he'd known of an attack was the cry of 'sacrifice'. Chell had pulled him from his saddle and to the ground. They'd planned this – the two closest warriors were to keep him down and sheltered from arrows and warrior-priests. He was to control his emotions and keep the magic under control. El was kneeling beside him, shield up, watching the fight.

Ezren opened his mouth to ask, then closed it firmly. Bethral was – they all were – trained warriors. They were fine . . . would be fine. There was no reason to fear, no reason to get angry. The warmth in his chest was just warmth. *All's well,* he told himself, desperate to keep his emotions in check.

There were sounds, shouts, the clash of swords, the scream of a horse. Oh yes, this would be an epic tale when he told it back in Edenrich, with a glass of cold ale and a crowd's wide-eyed excitement. Him in the grass, that part he might just leave out, thank you kindly. No need to—

El shifted next to him, and Ezren looked over. The lad's eyes were fixed ahead, looking over his shield rim, his sword gripped tight in his hand.

Ezren could take no more. He eased up.

Chell pressed him down. 'No, Storyteller.'

Yes. He'd leave that bit out as well. Not that it wouldn't make for a decent comic tale, but one did have to think of one's reputation—

'Gilla,' El breathed, and was gone, running.

Ezren was on his feet next to Chell, both of them standing there. El was running toward a riderless horse and a warrior-priest with his sword high, about to strike at something on the ground. Bethral was fighting two of her own, and the others were too far away to aid.

Fear surged up, and then raw anger. Damn them! Lord of Light, damn them to the coldest hells!

Chell cried out, but Ezren ignored her. He raised his glowing hands and pointed at the warrior-priest.

The man went up in a pillar of fire.

'Elder!'

Hail Storm turned, and there on the tiny Plains was a small flame, burning bright for an instant, then snuffed out, disappearing from sight.

'Quickly, how many others close to that place?' he asked.

'Three,' Thunder Cloud said. 'And that one has to be Frost, coming from the south. He was performing the rites for the farthest tribe.'

'Prepare to send word,' Hail Storm ordered. The quick movements around him told him he was being obeyed.

He put his hand on the young warrior-priest who had alerted him. 'Excellent. But keep watch. We need to track him for as long as we can.'

Hail Storm exited the tent, holding his staff. Thunder Cloud was waiting for him. 'The others are preparing the casting in my tent. But the magics are failing – perhaps we should move—'

'No matter.' Hail Storm took his elbow and urged him on. 'I have sufficient power. We will get a message to Frost, and send him to that location as best we can. He can track from there.' Hail Storm stopped for a moment. 'We are so close, Thunder Cloud. I can feel it. Magics restored to the Plains.'

'And our powers restored as well,' Thunder Cloud finished for him. 'Come. There is much yet to be done.'

Gilla was on all fours, willing the heaving to stop and failing miserably. She'd already lost what had been within; now she just heaved and could not stop. All she could see was the warrior-priest's face as her lance pierced his chest. She'd never—

She threw up again, as the image flashed before her eyes.

A cup appeared before her face. 'Here.'

It was Arbon. If her face wasn't already burning red, it would be now. She turned her face away, gasping for air, blinking away the tears.

'Don't drink. Just rinse,' Arbon insisted.

She lifted a shaky hand, and took the cup. It did help, if only for a minute. She at least managed to stop heaving. Arbon took back the cup. Gilla crawled away from her mess and then sat, still trembling and shaking, trying to get her breathing under control.

Arbon knelt down next to her. 'Here. I found some crittney. It helps.'

She reached for the leaves and crammed them into her mouth, chewing as fast as she could. The familiar taste flooded her mouth, sweet and tingling. 'Thanks,' she whispered.

Arbon sat in the grass next to her. She dared a brief glance, and her eyes went wide.

His armor was covered with vomit. His face, red and tear-stained. And he was chewing crittney too.

'You, too?' she asked.

'Yeah.' Arbon's head hung down, his face averted. 'The warlord sent me over here, to get me out of the way. They're all dead. She gave mercy to the one that was still breathing. His head . . .' Arbon swallowed hard and looked away.

Gilla focused on chewing. Anything but—

'Killing isn't easy.' Bethral appeared and knelt in front of them, holding out wet cloths. 'It isn't supposed to be.'

'We're warriors.' Arbon's voice trembled.

Gilla took the cold cloth and pressed it to her face.

'You are,' Bethral said quietly. 'And you did well.'

'I've hunted and killed.' Gilla pulled the cloth away from her face. 'I've seen death before. The old die. Babies die in camp. There are accidents.'

Bethral nodded. 'But it's not the same, is it?'

'No,' Arbon whispered. 'It is not.'

'It never will be,' Bethral said. She rose to her feet. 'The warrior-priests have chosen to threaten us. You defended yourselves and each other. Do not forget that.' She looked toward where the others had gathered. 'We need to keep moving. The others are rolling the dead in their own cloaks. We will leave them here with their gear.'

'Some warriors we are.' Arbon looked down at his leather armor, and wiped at it with the cloth. 'The others aren't crying like a baby after a teat.'

'The others haven't killed,' Bethral said.

Gilla looked at Bethral, into blue eyes that seemed to understand exactly what she was feeling. She stood up on shaky legs, and looked at her warlord. 'I'm ready.'

Arbon stood, too. 'So am I.'

'Then let's be about it,' Bethral said. 'I want to be as far as we can get from this place before we rest for the night.'

'Can the Storyteller . . . is he well?' Gilla asked.

'He is unconscious,' Bethral said. Her face was calm, but her pain was in her eyes.

The others were gathered with their horses, reins in hand, waiting. Gilla expected some teasing, but Cosana just gave her a steady look as she handed her the reins.

Ezren Storyteller was already mounted behind El, slumped against his back and his hands tied around El's waist. His slack face was exhausted. For a moment, Gilla thought about the warrior-priest standing over her, about to kill her. He'd had a gloating look on his face until the moment his flesh had burst into flames.

El interrupted her thoughts. 'Are you well, Gilla?'

She nodded. 'I will be.'

'Mount up,' Bethral said. 'We need to go.'

TWENTY-SIX

Wild Winds looked over the Heart of the Plains, and raised an eyebrow. His horse shifted under him, as if sensing his displeasure.

'Hail Storm is not here?' he asked.

'No, Eldest Elder.' Morning Dew lowered his gaze respectfully enough. Just enough. 'The Elder Hail Storm has not yet arrived, although word was sent to clear the warriors away from the area and to delay the start of the spring challenges. That has been done. Our people are the only ones within sight of the Heart.'

Wild Winds grunted.

'When will Hail Storm arrive?' Snowfall asked.

'I do not know,' Morning Dew answered carefully. 'I was told that you were to make camp, and that he and those that travel with him will be here as soon as they are able.'

Wild Winds looked around. 'Where are your tents?'

'Hail Storm directed that the area around the Heart be kept clear of all tents. The camps are beyond the rises, Eldest Elder.'

Clearing the ground for a dramatic ceremony, no doubt. Wild Winds shook his head at the thought. 'Very well.' He turned to Lightning Strike and Snowfall. 'See to the camp. I've something I need to do. A private ceremony.'

Lightning Strike gave him a nod, and he and the others turned their horses, leading the pack animals away. Morning Dew offered to show them where best to camp, and they all set off at a trot.

Snowfall sat on her horse, and considered Wild Winds.

He raised the other eyebrow for her benefit. 'Yes?'

She just sat there, her calm, light gray eyes looking back at him.

'Very well. Come.' Wild Winds urged his horse forward and headed for the Heart.

In the spring and summer, this area was filled with tents as the tribes gathered around the Heart. But now it was bare, and Wild Winds let his horse walk at its own pace so that he could consider it well.

Before him lay the large circle of gray stone that was truly the Heart of the Plains. Large as it was, it was all one solid piece. It had been the gathering place of the tribes for as long as there had been tribes, yet its surface was unmarred and unstained.

When the Council of Elders was summoned, the entire platform was covered with a huge tent made of the skins of many ehats. The tent was so large, they used the trunks of enormous trees from far lands to support its weight. Those were stored for the winter in a special lodge, kept safe from weather and animals, waiting for the Council to convene.

Wild Winds wasn't sure that would ever happen.

They stopped their horses at the edge, and dismounted. Snowfall took up the reins of both horses as Wild Winds unstrapped his travel bag from the saddle. He pulled his staff free from its ties, cradled the travel bag in one arm, and stepped onto the huge stone.

The stone was the same as it always was, as never-changing as the Plains themselves. It was clear of debris. During the spring challenges it was swept almost hourly.

Wild Winds walked to the center, and paused. The last time he had been here had been for the Council of Elders that had erupted into violence, and he had seen the sundering of the Council and the Plains.

He turned a full circle, gazing over the wide grasslands beyond. The grasses were laced with flowers dancing in the slight breeze. That breeze brought the scent of water from the lake that lay to the east of the Heart, its shore but a short walk away. He turned again, and caught the scents of cooking fires and horses from the camps. He took a breath, faced north, then slowly lowered himself to the stone with the aid of his staff.

Wild Winds went to his knees, setting the staff gently to his right and the travel bag to his left. From the bag he drew a piece of red silk, one that he had used in many rituals in the past. He spread it on the stone, smoothing it carefully. Then he pulled out his sacrifice dagger, the one he had made under the watchful gaze of his elders when he had become a warrior-priest so long ago. Its stone blade was still as sharp as the day he made it, and the ehat bone handle was smooth in his hand.

He took up his staff, and with one stroke cut the leather thongs that bound the three skulls to it. Then he set the skulls on the silk, facing him.

'Well, old friends,' he said softly. 'It would seem that the final days are upon me. The time has come, I think.'

Snowfall approached from behind, bearing a small brazier with a fire of dry grasses and tinder burning in it. She placed it before him, then bowed. 'I will wait with the horses.' She bowed again, this time to the skulls on the red silk, and then retreated, leaving him alone on the stone.

Well, not completely alone. He felt the spirts of his friends gathering close.

'You have traveled with me for many seasons.' Wild Winds reached into his travel bag for a small cloth sack. He pulled out the pine cones and sprigs of balsam he'd acquired for this parting. 'I thank you for your wisdom and guidance.'

Hands held high, he straightened his back and started to chant. 'Birth of fire, death of air.'

Carefully, he added the fragrant cones to the tiny fire, letting the flames catch and strengthen.

'Birth of water, death of earth.'

Wild Winds dipped his fingers into water, letting it trickle into the bowl.

'Birth of earth, death of fire.'

He raised a lump of dirt, breaking it up to let the clods fall into the bowl.

'Birth of air, death of water.'

Now he blew on the coals, and the balsam he added caused a thin trail of smoke to rise.

'All life perishes,' Wild Winds said softly. 'This I know all too well. Our bodies arise from the elements, and return to them when we fall.

'But we are also more than our bodies. This I know. That which is within each of us lives on. Our dead travel with us until the snows.

'I honor you, my friends and mentors, you who offered me your wisdom and guidance, to travel with me. But my path is ended now, and I offer my thanks as I release you to journey on.'

Wild Winds paused, then continued. 'Skies above, earth below, hear my words. Let there be truth in what happens here, whatever it may be. Let us be guided by your wisdom and let all who come here act with honor.'

The only response was the popping of one of the cones in the fire.

Enough. He'd done what he could. He needed to finish this now.

He reached for the first skull, feeling the thin bone under his fingers. He ran his thumb over the dent over the brow ridge. 'Twisting Winds, my elder, you were the first to offer your head to me. Go free now.'

He set the skull down, took up his blade, and used the handle and a tiny bit of his own magic to crush the bone into shards.

'Summer Sky, I still see your beauty instead of bone.' Wild Winds smiled as he took up the next skull. 'I have no doubt the stars will be brighter for your dancing.' He crushed this skull on top of the other, breaking it into small pieces.

'Stalking Cat, if you were here, I've no doubt you'd slaughter Hail Storm and use his guts for tent ties.' Wild Winds chuckled. 'I suspect you are cursing me for a fool right this minute.' He settled back on his heels and stared at the last skull in his hands. 'You are no doubt right, and I am wrong. You can tell me so when I see you again. But for now, old friend, go free.' The small burst of his magic, a sharp tap with the hilt, and the third skull shattered into the pile.

'It won't be long, friends, and I will be with you.' Wild Winds gathered up the ends of the silk, and walked off the Heart, down to the shore of the lake. The pebbles shifted underfoot as he moved to the very edge of the water.

He twisted the silk about itself, then threw it as far as he could, putting the last of his magic into its flight. It arced high, then unfurled as it fell, dropping the shards deep into the lake.

Wild Winds returned to the center to retrieve his staff and travel bag. Snowfall had already cleared the bowls away for him. He staggered under the weight of the bag as he lifted it, but he drew a deep breath and walked slowly to where Snowfall waited for him.

He stopped then, breathing hard, unwilling to admit that he'd used up most of his strength with that simple ritual. But Snowfall merely took his bag from him and placed it on his horse.

'Done?' she asked.

'Done,' he confirmed as he mounted.

She mounted as well, and they both turned their horses toward the rise.

'When the time comes,' he said in a casual tone, 'I would give you my staff, and offer my head to you to adorn it. If you would have it, that is.' Wild Winds snorted. 'Perhaps you do not wish my spirit to travel with you.'

'You honor me.' Snowfall twisted in the saddle to look at him, and he could see that her eyes were glistening. 'But I prefer your head on your shoulders, and not on any staff of mine.'

'As do I,' Wild Winds responded. 'But that is not what is, as well you know.' He looked around. 'Where do you suppose Simus of the Hawk is camped?'

'I wonder if there is any fresh meat to be had,' Snowfall answered. 'I'm hungry.'

'It is to be hoped that you will obey me better after my death,' Wild Winds observed.

Snowfall raised an eyebrow, then urged her horse into a trot toward camp.

Bethral kept them moving until just after sunset. The skies were clear, and there would be no moon.

She dismounted first, and went to El's horse. 'How is he?'

'Still sleeping,' El assured her.

'There's very little glow,' Ouse added.

'Good.' Bethral put her hand on Ezren's knee, looking at his sleeping face. She'd have preferred to have him with her on Bessie, but if they'd been attacked, she would have been restricted.

Lander appeared, and the four of them got Ezren down without waking him.

There was little talk as the others dismounted. Everyone was too weary for anything other than setting up tents and watches. Soon enough, Bethral was tucked into their tent with Ezren by her side.

He'd roused during the ride, worried about all of them, but once he'd been reassured, he'd fallen asleep. He felt cold to her; his hands were clammy. Bethral stripped off her gambeson, then stripped Ezren as well.

She covered both of them in blankets, and snuggled with him, pulling him close, trying to warm him with her body heat. She tucked his cold hands under her arms to warm, and put her warm feet against his. The heat between them grew, and eventually, slowly, Ezren's body warmed.

She dozed fitfully, conscious of every noise outside and of Ezren's breathing. So she awoke the moment his breathing changed.

'Bethral?' he asked, his voice husky.

She kissed him softly.

It took him a moment, then he drew a sharp breath. 'The attack. Gilla?'

'Everyone is fine,' Bethral assured him.

'Thank the Lord and the Lady,' Ezren said, then went silent

216

for a moment. 'I used it, or more to the point, it used me, didn't it?'

'Yes,' Bethral said. 'There were six of them. If they were returning from a rite, that's the normal number that travel together.'

'We killed them all?' Ezren asked.

'As far as I know, yes,' Bethral said. 'But I didn't trust that someone didn't escape to take word. So we kept moving.' She paused. 'And I am assuming that they can sense the magic from a distance.'

There was a pause in the darkness as he thought. 'I agree. So they know where we are.'

'Sleep,' Bethral said. 'We will be up and moving at dawn.'

'More will die before we reach the mountains, Bethral.'

'With any luck, it will only be their blood spilled.'

She heard him about to protest, and covered his mouth with her fingers. 'They have a choice, Ezren.'

With a sigh, he nodded. He pulled her closer, and tucked her head under his chin. 'Here I am, naked with my lady and too damned tired to do anything about it.'

'We live.' Bethral choked, her throat closing on the words. 'That is all I can ask of this night.'

'Sleep, then,' Ezren said. He reached out and stroked her eyes closed.

Bethral kissed his fingers, closed her eyes, and listened to him breathe as she drifted off to sleep.

'We found their bodies rolled in cloaks and left with their tack and saddles.' Frost's image wavered in the scrying bowl. 'It was one of the groups traveling up from the south.' There was a pause, then she continued. 'One of them is burnt to a crisp.'

'Magic?' Mist leaned forward and asked.

'Obviously,' Thunder Cloud said.

Hail Storm grunted, but didn't smile as Mist leaned back, clearly offended.

Frost continued, 'Their tracks head in a straight line, due east, Elders. I can give chase, if that is what you wish.'

'How many are you?' Hail Storm asked.

'Myself and four others,' Frost replied.

'Dawn Breaking is close to your location, as is Sharp Sword,' Hail Storm said. 'Best if you link up before confronting them. That will give you enough.'

Frost considered. 'Yes. Even better if we can catch them between us.' She smiled, her teeth gleaming. 'We will secure the Sacrifice and bring him to you, Hail Storm.'

'No,' Hail Storm said, enjoying the mild shock that went around the tent.

'No?' Frost asked, her confusion clear.

Hail Storm leaned forward. 'He is too dangerous to confront. Besides, the Sacrifice must be willing, Frost.' Hail Storm leaned back, and gave her a slow smile. 'So attack, yes, but let your goal be to secure one of the others by any means possible. Bring us one of his companions, and he will follow you as night follows day.'

The other elders in the tent were nodding, murmuring their agreement.

'Ah.' Frost nodded. 'Easily done, Hail Storm.'

'Then see to it,' Hail Storm ordered. 'We will head for the Heart. I have business to attend to there. Send word only if you fail.'

'We'll not fail,' Frost assured him.

The casting broke, and the young ones who had held it sagged beside the brazier. Hail Storm rose, looking about. 'We must start to send everyone to the Heart.'

Mist rose as well. 'You've no tent, Hail Storm, so no reason to linger. Take an escort and go. We will follow as soon as we are able.'

Hail Storm gave her a deep nod. 'My thanks, Elder. But all need to witness the events at the Heart. I will continue to watch the scrying spell and see to the restoration of the earth. I should be one of the last to leave.'

He opened the tent flap and stepped out, giving her no chance to dispute him. The morning was crisp, the air sweet, and he took a deep breath as he strode off without a backward look. Now was not the time to rush. He needed one and all to witness his challenge and defeat of Wild Winds, needed witnesses to the Sacrifice.

And if the Sacrifice did not come? Well, there were many ways the old words could be translated. If he announced a new way to power, based on the willing sacrifice? Many willing sacrifices? There would be those that could be convinced that a few lives were worth the sacrifice. He'd be careful, of course. Go slow. But eventually . . .

Hail Storm nodded to himself with satisfaction. It was always good to have plans and alternatives. Who knew which way the winds would blow?

And when the time came, he'd take Wild Winds's tent for his own.

TWENTY-SEVEN

Ezren knew full well that the magic was draining him; every breath was an effort. The farther they rode to the east, the stronger the urging demanded he turn back.

He fought it and rode with grim determination, bent on not slowing them down. Bethral was watching him, he knew. He caught her worried gaze once again, and gave her a hard smile. She nodded with resignation and turned to survey the lands, on guard for further trouble.

Lord of Light, he loved her.

Lander brought his horse close, and held out what looked like a small ball of twisted grass. 'Crittney,' he offered.

Bethral was taking some from Ouse, so Ezren did the same. He bit down, and a sweet, almost spicy taste filled his mouth and nostrils. It was clear and crisp, and seemed to ease his head. Lander grinned. 'These taste very good,' he said in passable Elven.

'Yes. Thank you,' Ezren replied with a smile. They'd managed a few language lessons as they rode, and Lander learned quickly. Even faster than Ezren, probably thanks to his memory. 'Excuse me, but can you tell me where the necessary is?'

Lander laughed as he moved his horse back in position. Bethral had them riding in an oval with Ezren at the center. She was pushing them on, but had said they'd stop before sunset to sleep.

Cosana had looked back at the sound of Lander's laughter. She gave Ezren a flirty wink before she turned to face forward. As grim as their situation was, she'd probably offer another threesome this night. Ezren hoped Bethral's sense of humor held up under the strain. He wasn't sure that she found it quite so—

Five warrior-priests rose out of the grasses ahead of them, bows pulled taut.

'Arrows!' Bethral cried, and everyone raised their shields. Ezren hunched down, bringing his own shield up and urging his horse to a gallop. The others did as well.

Arrows whistled through the air. Ezren was relieved that no one had been hit, until he realised what they were doing.

They were shooting at the horses.

Tenna's horse went down. With a cry, Tenna left the saddle, falling, rolling, and coming to her feet, sword in hand. She screamed a battle cry and ran toward the closest archer.

Chell and El pulled their horses around, charging the archers. Ezren would have done the same, but Bethral grabbed his horse's bridle and kept them running forward.

No, they couldn't leave—

The whistling gave him some warning. The arrow caught his horse in the chest, and the animal staggered. Ezren tried to kick free of the saddle, but—

He saw the sky, and then the grass, and then nothing.

Ezren was down.

Fear washed over Bethral, but she clamped down on it and then thrust it away. Lander and Ouse pulled their horses to a stop, then maneuvered over the downed Storyteller, weapons and swords ready. Good enough.

Bessie's hooves tore up the grasses as she spun around at Bethral's command. Without hesitation, the big roan mare plunged into the midst of the fight.

The warrior-priests had dropped their bows and pulled swords. Tenna was on the ground, battering away at her opponent as she screamed insults. The others were doing well, but Cosana was fighting two, and they were trying to flank her. Bethral growled, and gave Bessie her target.

The warrior-priest's eyes went wide as Bessie charged him. He managed to dodge the big horse, but that only made it easier for Bethral to swing her heavy mace down on his head.

He crumpled to the ground. Bessie turned, trampling him.

Bethral used the moment to pick her next target in the confusion, but a cry drew her attention.

'Warlord!' Lander was pointing to the south. Three warrior-priests on horseback, coming fast.

Bethral sent Bessie toward them, guiding her with her knees. Fear was gone, replaced with exhilaration, and a grim determination.

Gilla parried the sword blow with her own blade, then bashed the warrior-priest in the face with her shield. He staggered back, nose dripping blood, then came at her again.

Her horse shifted and sidled, trying to knock the man to the ground. The warrior-priest ducked, and Gilla shifted in the saddle to keep him in sight, holding her shield high. But the warrior-priest rose on the other side, dagger in hand, and plunged it into the horse's neck.

Horrified, Gilla felt the animal shy and stagger. She swung her leg over and jumped free as it fell. She brought up her sword and shield, frantically looking for her opponent.

He came at her from the side, lunging with his sword raised. She brought her shield up, ready for the blow. But the man jerked to a stop.

El was behind him, on horseback, his sword buried in the warrior-priest's back. El's face was a mix of joy and horror as the body slid off his blade. She sympathised as she caught his gaze, and gave him a quick smile.

The point of a lance pierced his chest. El's face went slack as he slid limp off his horse, dead.

Gilla screamed, running toward the spot where he'd fallen. El's horse ran off, and there stood the warrior-priest that had killed him. She charged him, bringing her sword up, not thinking, only feeling. The warrior-priest watched her come, an odd look of satisfaction on his face.

A cloak blocked her vision, falling over her face. Gilla stumbled, then something hit her head. Pain and darkness claimed her before she could fall.

Bethral met her enemy head-on, charging for the one in the center. The other horse moved at the last minute, swerving to avoid the larger horse. Bessie continued on, ramming into its shoulder, sending it staggering to the side.

Bethral swung her mace, slamming it onto the shield, hearing the wood crack. From the way the warrior-priest flinched, the arm was probably broken. Good enough. Bethral brought the mace back in a wide arc, catching the woman on the chin. She fell from her saddle, and Bessie trampled her as they turned to face the other one.

This one wasn't stupid. He had his shield up, eyeing her with care, waiting for her charge. Behind him, Bethral spotted a few warrior-priests mounting up with their wounded and galloping off. She refocused on her opponent, snarled, and shifted her knees.

Bessie reared and lunged forward, her hooves flailing at the other horse. It shied away, forcing the warrior-priest to catch himself with one hand to the saddle.

Bessie dropped back on all four hooves, and Bethral swung, bringing the mace down on his sword arm with a satisfying crunch.

Ezren staggered to his feet, his head pounding with pain.

All around him raged sounds of the combat. He lifted his gaze and saw all his friends fighting the warrior-priests. Bethral was in the thick of it, her armor awash with light as she swung her mace.

A cry, and Cosana collapsed. Ezren growled, the magic flared, and the warrior-priests almost as one turned to look at him—

And they vanished.

'Oh no,' Ezren snarled. 'Let me see them. LET ME SEE.'

A blue light flashed around him, and he could see them all, running through the grass or trying to mount their horses.

Bethral, Lander, and Ouse were still mounted, and they went after the closest targets on foot. The others were his. Ezren clenched his fists and focused his rage.

But the power wasn't there.

Ezren watched as the remaining warrior-priests galloped over the rise. He closed his eyes and forced himself to breathe as weakness swept over him. What little magic he'd had was drained again, down to the dregs. He locked his knees, and looked around.

Bethral was finishing her opponent, and Lander and Ouse had dismounted to check theirs. Gilla's and El's horses were standing together, waiting for their riders, but he couldn't see them.

Tenna and Chell were kneeling on the ground. Tenna looked up and around wildly, her face filled with terror. She called out something, and Arbon came at a run, throwing himself down by them.

Ezren staggered toward them.

Cosana lay on the ground, her head in Tenna's lap, her hands pressed to her stomach, blood seeping between the fingers.

Ezren knelt by her side. 'Cosana . . .'

'We drove them off?' she asked, her eyes bright.

'Gone,' Arbon said. 'Fleeing like the cowardly bragnects that they are.'

Cosana laughed, but it turned into a gasp. She focused on Ezren. 'I wish we'd had three-souls-shared, Storyteller. It would have been a night you'd have always remembered.'

Ezren nodded, unable to speak. He put his hand on her shoulder, and desperately willed the magic to heal her. To do something. Anything.

The magic didn't respond.

'I'd have melted your bones. I'd have ridden . . .' she stopped, and coughed. The blood flowed faster from the wound.

'We will have to see to that,' Bethral said as she knelt by

Cosana's side. 'But I think you should close your eyes and sleep a while before we do. Save your energy.'

Ezren looked up, and he read the truth in Bethral's eyes.

Cosana frowned at Bethral. 'I am a warrior of the Plains, Warlord. Do not deny this truth to me.'

'You are right,' Bethral said. 'I thank you for your service, Cosana of the Snake, and I wish you well.'

'Finish your tale, Storyteller.' Cosana's eyes were bright, her words slightly slurred. 'The one about the Lord and the Lady.'

For a moment, Ezren's throat tightened, but then he managed to speak. 'I stopped at the hunt, did I not?'

Cosana nodded. 'I want to hear the ending.'

Tenna stifled a soft sob as she rested her hand on Cosana's head. Arbon touched his cheek to the top of her head, tears streaming down his face. Chell sat back on her heels, silent, her face a mask.

The blood was still soaking through Cosana's fingers.

Ezren cleared his throat. *The next time, the Lord of Light found the Lady sitting in her garden, sprawled in her chair, her leg over one arm, kicking idly as she read. She was frowning at the book, and he paused for just a moment. 'No hunt this day, Lady?' he asked as he passed overhead.*

She squinted at the page and looked up. 'Could you move just a little? Your light is making a glare on the page.'

'Er . . .' He shifted to the side. 'Better?'

'Not really.' She sighed as she closed the book. 'I'd thought this tale would help, but it has not. I guess I will make some kavage.' She set the book aside and rose to her feet. Her hair was braided, a long fat braid that fell past her waist.

Cosana smiled slightly, her eyes half closed. Her hands relaxed, falling away from the wound.

'Is something wrong?' the Lord asked, curious. Usually the Lady seemed to sparkle. But this day, she seemed flat, somehow. Sad.

'I am just bored,' the Lady said, pulling open the door to her home.

'But the day is a fine one,' the Lord pointed out. 'Warm and sunny and fair.'

'I know,' she said. 'Like the day before, and the day before that.' She glanced at him with sad eyes, and disappeared into her cottage, pulling the door closed behind her.

The Lord moved on, as was his responsibility. But his thoughts kept returning to the Lady. He frowned, puzzled as to why he felt so odd. She had been polite enough, but . . .

Did she mean he was boring?

Lander and Ouse arrived, walking slowly, taking in the scene. They stood together, Ouse's shoulder pressed to Lander's. Lander's face was covered in blood from a cut across his forehead.

There was no need for words. They knew.

Ezren continued. 'For the first time ever, in the years – in centuries – he turned and strode back along his path. He went right up to the Lady's door, and knocked.

'Yes?' Her voice came from within.

He opened his mouth, and then closed it. What if she did think he was boring? He was not quite sure what to say, when the door opened, and the Lady was standing there with one arched eyebrow.

He stared at her. At her lovely eyes and quirky lips, and skin as soft as the wing of a dove.

'Uh,' was all he could manage.

'Would you like some kavage?' the Lady asked very seriously. 'Or perhaps you need to use the necessary?'

He opened his mouth to deny it, but then he saw the laughter in her eyes. How they sparkled and danced.

'I would have kavage, Lady,' he answered. 'And talk. I am concerned about your happiness, as I am concerned for all my people.'

'Ah,' she replied. 'A duty, then.'

'No, Lady.' He shook his head. 'I believe it more a pleasure.'

One corner of her mouth quirked up. She tilted her head to look up at the sky, a deeper blue now without his presence. 'And how will your people bear your absence?'

'Shall we find out?' the Lord asked.

The Lady laughed, and so did he as she pulled him within her *bower, and closed the door behind them. As the door closed, night spread out from the cottage, bringing soft pleasure and sweet rest to the Lord's people and all his creatures. Duty and responsibility slipped away, to be replaced with the warmth and light of a fire, and the joys of the table and bed. All reveled in the night, and rejoiced at the comfort it brought their souls and bodies. Thus do we owe the Lord our thanks for our days and our duties, and the Lady our thanks for our joys and our rest.*

Cosana sighed, and stopped breathing.

'May the Lord and the Lady welcome you with open arms,' Ezren whispered.

Arbon put his head back and howled with wordless rage. The others stood silent, weeping. Lander wiped his face, and reached out to grasp Cosana's left hand. 'Cosana of the Snake!' he called in a loud voice.

He then took her right hand in his, squeezing it hard. 'Cosana, my friend, answer me.'

Silence was the only reply.

Ezren started to speak, but Bethral put her hand on his shoulder.

Lander moved to kneel at Cosana's feet. He squeezed each, one at a time, calling Cosana's name.

There was no response.

Lander bowed his head. 'Safe journey to the snows, Cosana. And beyond.'

Ezren rose to his feet and looked over the grasslands, then back at Bethral.

Rage burned in her blue eyes, but her face was calm. 'I found El. He is dead.'

The warriors stared at her, stunned, too numbed to react.

'They have taken Gilla,' Bethral continued. 'I saw some of them fleeing combat with a cloaked body over the front of a horse. I thought it was one of their wounded.'

'What now?' Ouse asked, still holding his sword in a tight grip.

'We see to our dead,' Bethral said. 'We see to Lander's and Tenna's injuries.'

'And then?' Arbon demanded.

Bethral looked at Ezren.

'We go after the bastards,' Ezren said.

TWENTY-EIGHT

'What?' Chell said in surprise, tears running silently down her face. 'Why? Gilla is dear to us all, but the mission is more important than any one member. We must go on, to the mountains.'

'I fear we lose either way,' Ezren said. The words were hard to say, harder to hear, but it was time he acknowledged the truth.

'Gilla is a pawn.' Arbon still held Cosana in his arms. 'The king and queen are still in play. We should go on.'

Bethral shook her head. 'It's check, Arbon.'

Arbon frowned, and lifted his tear-stained face toward her. 'How so?'

'Check for the taking of one of our warriors hostage, and the killing of Cosana and El,' Bethral said. 'We will not allow that to go unavenged.'

'Check for the magic, that might force me to the Heart anyway, even if we made our way to the mountains in peace,' Ezren added.

'Check for the fact that they will not be satisfied until they have Ezren one way or the other. If we continue on, they will continue their attacks. We cannot win that game,' Bethral added.

The warriors all stood, thinking it through.

'I'm going with you,' Lander growled. He wiped the blood from his face.

'But—' Ouse protested.

'No,' Ezren commanded. Both of them gave him startled looks. 'He comes, if he is able. Someone must sing the truth of this.'

Ouse closed his mouth and looked away, then nodded.

'You are another matter.' Ezren turned to Tenna. Her ankle had been badly sprained in the fall from her horse. It couldn't support her weight.

'I'll take our dead back to Haya,' Tenna said. 'I will tell her what has happened, and what you are going to do.' She looked at Arbon. 'Avenge them for me.'

'No,' Arbon said. He started to lay Cosana's body down carefully. 'I will go with you. We must take word to Haya and the Tribe. If this goes badly, they will need to prepare.' He looked at Tenna. 'With one, word might not get there. With two, we know that it will.' Arbon gave Bethral a rueful look. 'The safety of our people is more important than anything else.'

'What if the ankle does not heal?' Ezren asked.

'No worries, Storyteller. We have no healing, true enough, but sprains happen in practice. I'll take every care, I swear it to you.' Tenna struggled to her feet with Arbon's aid. 'Just get me to a mount.' She lifted her tear-stained face to look around at them. 'I can't believe they killed the horses.'

'I doubt they will pursue Tenna,' Bethral said. 'We are the targets.'

Ouse and Chell were seeing to Cosana's body, wrapping it in a cloak. Ezren stood, stifling a groan at his own bruises. 'Any chance we can catch them?'

Bethral shook her head. 'Unlikely. They will have aid and fresh horses along the way, I suspect. We can get remounts, so we can keep up. But catch them?'

'At least we know which direction to take,' Ezren said.

'We'll get El,' Lander said.

'I'll gather the horses,' Chell said.

The young ones scattered. Bethral pulled a waterskin from Bessie's packs. 'Drink.'

Ezren took the skin, and drank deeply. He wiped his mouth and looked at his lovely lady. She was examining Bessie, making sure she hadn't been injured.

He opened his mouth to tell her his regrets, to urge her to flee by herself, to apologise. But then she looked at him with those lovely blue eyes, and read the same intent in hers.

Bethral gave him a gentle smile. 'If we are for each other, then we are one in the darkness as well as the light. For good or ill, I am yours, Ezren Storyteller. I will not walk away from you.'

She'd taken off her helmet, and her braid had come undone. He reached out and claimed a strand, feeling its silkiness between his fingers. He tugged, and she stepped closer to him. 'As I am yours, Bethral of the Horse.' Ezren kissed her, her mouth warm against his cold lips. His hand moved to cup her neck and he demanded more. She opened her mouth, responding to him.

They broke it off for air, breathing hard, their heads still together.

Ezren chuckled softly. 'And they call me Silvertongue,' he whispered in her ear.

Bethral flushed.

Then he took a deliberate step back, and handed her the waterskin. She took it just as deliberately, and slung it on the saddle. 'I'm worried that the magic is taking more and more of you,' Bethral said. 'Will you be able to make it?'

'Watch me,' Ezren said.

Chell brought up a horse, and Ezren mounted. The others were mounting as well.

Tenna was on her horse, and had the leads for the animals bearing the bodies of El and Cosana. Arbon was mounted next to her.

Tenna stared at all of them, and gave them a weak smile. 'I don't know if I will ever see you all again.'

'If not in this life, then beyond the snows,' Lander said.

Arbon cleared his throat. 'The elements go with you all.'

Chell brought her horse in close and hugged the smaller woman. Tenna returned the hug fiercely.

She and Arbon gave them all another look, turned their horses, and rode away.

Ezren looked at the bodies of the warrior-priests left where they fell, and at Cosana's drying blood. In silence, he faced the northwest, and started his horse off at a trot.

The others followed.

When Gilla awoke, she found herself bound and gagged, riding in front of one of her captors. The horse was galloping, something it couldn't do for long carrying two people.

It took a few minutes to remember and understand what had happened. She'd been taken, and that could only be to lure Ezren Storyteller to the Heart of the Plains.

She had the sense to keep her head down and her body loose. The rider had one arm around her waist, her head against his chest. With half-open eyes, rolling her head, she could just make out that they were surrounded by other riders. It was light, the sun high in the sky. But how many days had it been? Her head ached, though not as hard as one would think after being hit to unconsciousness. A full day? Two?

She'd been stripped of her armor and was clothed in simple tunic and trous, her feet bare. She wondered who had stripped her, then how else they had used her body. Rape was rare on the Plains, but then again, they'd killed horses, hadn't they?

There were too many to try anything on horseback. She fought down a surge of fear, and concentrated on what she could do. Her hands were bound in front, and her legs were hanging loose. If she could get free, and get a weapon . . . they all wore those sacrifice daggers at their waists.

If she couldn't escape, she would kill herself.

She tried to stay limp, but the riding was too uncomfortable if she was flopping about. She straightened a bit, and put her bare feet on her captor's boots to steady her legs.

He noticed, of course, but said nothing. The arm around her waist tightened; that was the only response.

A bit more comfortable, she strained to remember. They'd been ambushed, there's been a fight . . . El.

She gasped, trying hard not to weep but crying anyway. The lance, the way he had fallen. He was dead, no doubt of that.

She'd run toward him, and now she kicked herself for it. If she'd gone for his horse, been focused on the battle, they'd never have been able to take her.

And the others? What about the others? What if they were all dead and—

Enough. She stopped her wild thoughts. Thinking that way did nothing but waste her strength.

She looked around openly now, and saw a small group of horses and warrior-priests waiting ahead. The horse started to slow. Remounts, most likely.

She was lowered to the ground and held by two warrior-priests, one on each arm. They took care of her needs with a callousness that frightened her. Almost as if she was a gurtle to be cared for until the slaughter. The two dealt with her quickly as a third kept watch just a few paces away.

The necessary details handled, the gag was removed and she was offered water. After she'd drunk her fill, she looked at the warrior-priest who bore his full tattoos. 'What are you—'

Another gag was flipped over her head, and tied tight.

Before she could struggle, she was on another horse, another arm around her waist. And the horses tore off at high speed, heading northwest.

Gilla swallowed hard, fighting her terror. A chance would come, eventually. They would make a mistake, and she would take advantage of it.

She closed her eyes, suddenly aware of a hard truth. Even if she managed to deprive them of their hostage, they already had what they wanted. The Warlord and the Storyteller would give chase, and wouldn't know of her death. They'd ride to their deaths regardless.

Enough of that. Her hands were in front of her, and they hadn't checked the ropes. She'd work at getting free, moving her arms with the rhythm of the horse so her captor didn't know what she was doing. Her chance would come, for either death or freedom.

She'd take either one.

Hail Storm watched over the scrying pool in the dark silence of the tent.

The camp around him was buzzing with the comings and goings of the others. They were taking down the tents and making the preparations to move to the Heart of the Plains. Some had already left. He watched the stone that represented the Heart, and the little sparkles clustered around it.

The largest gathering of warrior-priests the Plains had ever seen. Every warrior-priest would be there, except those that wandered the rest of the world, seeking that which had now been found. He had summoned every warrior-priest, and they had obeyed. He would guide them through the restoration of all that they had lost.

The large swirl of sparkles was smaller than it should have been. They'd lost many good men and women over the Sacrifice; they would need to be replaced. But that would be easier with a true source of power. Hail Storm had no doubt of his ability to deal with that issue in the future.

But for now, he had to consider the matter of timing.

He focused his gaze on two other sparkles, one behind the other, heading for the Heart in a straight line. It was almost possible to see them move if you sat still long enough. Not long now, and the hostage and the Sacrifice would be where he wanted them to be. And the Sacrifice would be more than willing, eh? At least once he saw the hostage kneeling at Hail Storm's feet, his dagger pressed to his or her neck. For a moment, he could see it in his mind's eye.

He'd surround the stone with archers. The woman that traveled with the Sacrifice was supposedly encased in metal. Hail Storm didn't see that as a problem. One swift arrow could pierce the metal easily, or kill the horse. Either one would deal with that problem.

The Sacrifice would approach the stone alone, unaided, and offer himself to Hail Storm's blade.

And after the Sacrifice had willingly shed his blood, the

hostage could die, too. That one would know too much of these events, and his or her truths would die with them. A demonstration of a new power source would be done, and swiftly.

Oh, there might be an uproar about the killing, but they'd settle down once they'd seen the benefits. It was really just expanding the language of the prophecy. Blood of the Plains, willingly shed, in willing sacrifice.

No, the question now was the timing. How should he deal with Wild Winds?

Hail Storm had issued challenge, and in order to control the arrival of the Sacrifice, he had to be the eldest elder before the man arrived.

Wild Winds still had support among the warrior-priests. It would be good to silence the old man with his death.

On the other hand, there might be more sympathy gained for him if he allowed the old sick man to live, rather than killing him outright. It also brought home that Wild Winds was failing to follow the traditions of the Plains, by going to the snows before his body failed completely.

A slight cough at the flap, and a server entered with kavage. Hail Storm acknowledged the service with a nod but remained silent, not taking up the mug until he was alone again.

It was best to bend with the winds on this. He'd wait and see what condition Wild Winds was in when he confronted him. If the old man was able to raise his sword, well, then death would be his fate.

If the old man only had words, then Hail Storm would respond in kind, dealing with the confrontation with mercy and compassion. He'd claim the authority, and let the title rest with Wild Winds until the man breathed his last.

With any luck, Wild Winds would seek the snows before he ever arrived at the Heart.

He'd arrange it so that he appeared at Wild Winds's tent at dawn. Once he was dealt with, Hail Storm would go to stand at the center of the stone circle, await the coming of the hostage, and prepare for the arrival of the Sacrifice. By day's end, he'd have all the position and power he'd need to deal with the warlords and singers.

He took a sip of kavage, and smiled as he watched the sparkles move, as if by his will, and his will alone.

Another cough. Hail Storm waited.

'A visitor, Elder. He claims that you sent for him.'

Ah. Hail Storm rose to his feet. 'Send him in.'

The man entered. He stood in silence, wrapped in a cloak, his face hidden by the hood. Hail Storm moved to the flap, and tied a set of bells to the outside. 'Welcome, Antas of the Boar.'

Antas pulled back his hood just enough to reveal his brown, deeply wrinkled face. He wore his customary glare. 'There's been no word, Hail Storm. Other than the order to pull back from the Heart. If you support me in holding to our traditional ways, why have you delayed the spring challenges?'

'I will tell you as much as I can, but we must be swift,' Hail Storm said. 'It would be best if you were not seen.'

'Granted,' Antas agreed. 'I do not wish to cause problems for your quest to be the Eldest Elder. I will need your support when I march to destroy Xy and Keir of the Cat. But what has happened?'

'Sit,' Hail Storm said. 'I will share my truths and my news.'

TWENTY-NINE

Wild Winds spent the last of his waning strength fighting a losing battle.

He fought with words, meeting with other warrior-priests, talking for hours, debating, discussing, and trying to convince them to see their error. The wrongness of this decision.

But the lure of power and magic was a brighter beacon than honor and truth. As much as Wild Winds wished to blame Hail Storm and Hail Storm alone, he could not. It was arrogance and pride that had brought them to this moment and this choice.

'After all, what is the life of a city dweller to us?' one had said as heads had nodded all around. 'City dwellers die at our hands when we raid for what we need to survive. How is this different?'

Now the day dawned, and word had been brought that Hail Storm was finally approaching. Clever, to delay his arrival and challenge. Wild Winds suspected that he was hoping the elements would remove Wild Winds before he arrived.

Pity he'd be disappointed. Wild Winds was still breathing.

But the truth needed to be faced. He had exhausted his strength in an effort to bring the others around, and now he wasn't certain he could draw a weapon, much less wield it. And his supporters numbered slightly more than he could count on two hands twice. Not enough. Not nearly enough.

Wild Winds sighed. Perhaps this was what the elements intended, although he found that hard to believe. Perhaps Hail Storm was right.

Perhaps rain would fall from the ground up.

Snowfall and Lightning Strike were seeing to the evening meal, although it had been days since he'd kept anything down but broth. The pain grew daily, and the snows called. But he had this itch of curiosity to see how events would unfold, and he wanted to view them first hand, not as a spirit.

It was warm in the tent, the braziers glowing. He closed his eyes and started a meditation to relax the stiffness in his muscles and ease his pains. He'd open his mind and heart to the elements, as he'd been taught, and see what came of it.

Snowfall's voice was raised outside, in protest. He felt the air stir as the tent flap was lifted.

'What, not dead yet?'

He smiled as he turned to look at his visitor. 'Mist. I see your breasts have not yet fallen to your waist.'

She stood before him, as lovely as always, his old friend. She snorted, shedding her cloak in the warmth of the tent and taking the pallet opposite his. She set her staff carefully to the side, the skulls rattling together. 'It's hot as summer in here.'

'I feel the need,' Wild Winds replied.

Snowfall entered the tent with a pitcher of kavage and two mugs. She appeared calm, but Wild Winds could see she was not pleased with Mist for barging in. She served him first.

Mist was giving him a good hard look, her sharp eyes taking in his lost strength, no doubt. She accepted kavage from Snowfall, then waved her off.

Snowfall raised both eyebrows and looked to him.

'Thank you, Snowfall. Please leave us now.'

Snowfall went, but not willingly, and probably not much farther than the tent flap. Wild Winds hid his smile in his mug.

'Hail Storm comes. He will arrive when the sun is overhead,' Mist said.

'So.' Wild Winds looked at her. 'You are in his confidence now?'

Mist looked at him over the rim of her mug. 'He comes, and the Sacrifice follows.'

'Ah.' Wild Winds set his kavage down. 'Willingly?'

'Hail Storm has taken a hostage. One of the young warriors that was part of the escort.'

Wild Winds pressed his lips together. 'I performed the rites for those young people. All strong young warriors, eager to serve the Plains. And in his hostage taking were any killed? Injured?'

'I do not know,' Mist said.

'You did not ask.' Wild Winds narrowed his eyes. 'Power is worth any price, eh? Even the very lives we take oaths to protect?'

Mist set her mug down, her face stubborn. 'What are a few lives to restore our powers? To possibly restore your health? Have you thought of that?'

'I notice that your life is not the one being offered,' Wild Winds said dryly. 'Your opinion might change.' He rested his hands on his knees. 'So you will support him.'

Mist took another sip of her kavage.

'I will say to you as I have said to others.' Wild Winds reached for his kavage. 'Each of us will have to make a decision, and each of us must live with the consequences of that choice.' He paused, and smiled at her. 'I wish you well, old friend. Regardless.'

'Wild Winds,' Mist started to speak.

He shook his head, and let his voice take on a formal tone. 'My thanks for your news, Elder, and your truths.'

Mist stiffened. 'There's—'

'I weary,' Wild Winds cut her off. 'I would prepare for the challenge with quiet thought and communion with the elements. Again, my thanks.'

Mist rose, taking up her staff and cloak, her lips pressed tight together. Her glance fell on his staff, and then flickered back to his face.

Wild Winds gave her a steady look, then a nod of dismissal.

Mist left.

Snowfall popped in the moment she was gone. She picked up the mug of kavage and looked at him questioningly.

239

He handed her his mug. 'You heard?'

She nodded.

'I wish to pray for a while,' Wild Winds said. 'The broth will keep?'

'Yes,' Snowfall said. 'I traded for a bit of ehat meat and fat.'

'I'll call when I am ready.' Wild Winds shifted on his mat, then arranged his mind for quiet thoughts and prayers. He heard Snowfall check the braziers, then slip out the flap without letting in much cold air.

This hunt was not yet done. If one was not careful, the prey could slip away, or even better, turn into something far more dangerous than the hunter.

Gilla got her hands free just as they were stopping for what seemed the hundredth time.

She'd been quiet and obedient, taking what rest she could in the saddle. They'd fallen for it, their watch growing lax. Now they were meeting up with another group, and it was time.

She'd brought her leg up and over the horse's head, and had slid to the ground before her handlers had reached her. Her captor still had the reins in his hand as she drew his dagger from his belt.

No one had reacted. As much as she wanted vengeance, as much as she wanted to lash out and take at least one with her, she brought the blade up to her neck as quickly as she could. One slash, and then, if there was time before she bled out, she'd cause as much damage as she could.

The stone blade was cold on her skin. She started to slash at her neck, just below her ear and . . . froze.

Unable to move, unable even to breathe. Her muscles trembled, but nothing. Skies, what was happening to her?

A warrior-priest appeared before her, his eyes blazing with pure rage, his hand on his own dagger. 'Secure her,' he snapped.

Hands caught her then, pulling the blade from her hands. The hold on her broke and she gasped as she drew in precious air.

There was no time to struggle. Her hands were bound again, behind her this time.

That warrior-priest stood before her, looking at her as if she was a piece of meat. His eyes were cold and dead in a strange way that made her shiver. He was in charge, that was certain.

'Don't bother,' he said as her handlers approached. 'Let the piss run down her legs. We need to be at the Heart by noon.'

Her captor grimaced, but obeyed. She was placed back in the saddle, and they were off, galloping like the wind.

The cold-eyed one was ahead of them, leading the way.

Hail Storm allowed a brief stop as they drew close to the Heart of the Plains. This gave him time to make sure he appeared at his best for the coming confrontation. It also allowed them to summon fresh horses and keep their pace.

The hostage was a bit the worse for wear. Hail Storm permitted them to dismount for a fresh horse but nothing else. The fool that had let her get to his knife looked miserable; his saddle was no doubt ruined. Punishment enough.

A clever girl, though. He'd been blessed by the elements that he'd seen her little suicide attempt and acted before she could do damage to herself. What a thrill, to see his will worked so fast on another person. He looked forward to more of that in the future. But it had taken a lot of power to freeze her like that, more than he cared to admit.

Ah, well. She was a pretty morsel. He'd get that back and more with her death.

Hail Storm cast an eye to the weather. The day was a fine one, flowers bobbing in the slight breeze, the sky clear. The sweet-scented air filled his lungs, as long as he was upwind of the hostage.

He'd be sure to arrive as the sun reached its peak. No doubt Wild Winds was in his tent, awaiting the challenge. Probably grateful for release. But it would not do to take that for granted.

He cast an eye back as well, but there was no sign of the

Sacrifice. Still, he was coming. Hail Storm had seen his movement before the scrying pool had been dismantled. He would come.

All was well. Hail Storm mounted, and started off at a gallop.

Soon, now. Very soon.

THIRTY

The gallop of a horse had a certain rhythm to it, Ezren realised; one that mesmerised you as you rode. Ezren got lost in the feel of the animal as it moved beneath him, lost track of the days as they passed in quick succession. There was only the horse, the ride, and the constant pull toward the Heart of the Plains. Ezren Storyteller had one goal, and one goal alone. Vengeance.

The others were with him, but there was little talk. They ate and slept and rode, following Ezren on a straight path across the vast grasslands. Whenever they came across a herd, Lander, Ouse, and Chell would summon fresh horses, and they'd shift the saddles and start to run again. Over and over, as the days and hours flew.

Night brought a quick meal, and sleep. Ezren would pull Bethral into his arms, and wrap the blankets around them. They sought comfort more than anything else, in their tiredness. But just having her head on his shoulder, her scent on every breath he took, provided the strength to face the next day.

They were close now. Ezren looked at the lowering sun as the others summoned horses for the final push.

He heard a soft sound, and glanced at where Bethral was saddling a fresh mount. Bessie was close by, grazing while she could.

He stepped closer to Bethral, and saw wetness on her cheeks. The others couldn't see her because she was concealed by the horse.

She glanced at him, then away.

He went to her side, and wiped her tears with his hand. 'Oh, my Lady,' he said softly.

She looked at him, and choked back a sob. 'It's just that . . . there's so much more I wanted with you. I just—' She cut herself off, and wiped her tears. 'I'm so afraid of losing you.'

'Do you want to turn back?' He asked the question, but he already knew the answer.

She brought her head up, her face fierce and determined. 'No.'

'Good. Because I am not sure I could, even if I wanted to,' Ezren admitted as he looked to the northeast. 'We are so close. Another few hours should see the end of this.'

Bethral nodded, wiping her face. She tightened the girth of her saddle. 'Give us some warning; we'll need to stop and prepare before we come into view.' She glanced at Bessie. 'I'll want to be on Bessie when the time comes.'

Ezren pulled her face around and kissed her softly. 'I wanted more as well, Angel.'

Bethral leaned in, seeking comfort. For just a moment, he breathed in her scent, lost in their private world.

'We're ready.' Ouse said, riding up with packhorses in tow.

Hail Storm hadn't quite known what to expect as they topped the last rise.

It wasn't this.

Every warrior-priest was there, standing around the great stone that marked the Heart of the Plains. Every single one.

Wild Winds stood alone at the center of the stone, leaning on his staff.

Hail Storm had a moment to frown, and then Wild Winds looked at him, and every head turned his way.

He straightened in his saddle. If the old fool wanted a public confrontation, so much the better. A kick, and his horse started down the rise, followed by the others.

The only sounds were the wind in the grass and his horse's hooves as he approached. The gathered warrior-priests melted away before him, leaving a clear path. Hail Storm dismounted and pulled his staff from its ties. The others did the same. Two of them pulled the hostage from the saddle. She kicked out, apparently not completely cowed. They threw her down, securing her at the knees and feet. She'd keep, until he was ready.

Hail Storm turned, and strode across the stone to stand some paces away from Wild Winds.

The old man did not look good. Ashen, with a white-knuckled grip on his staff. A staff with no skulls, Hail Storm noted immediately. Ah, he'd released his spirit mentors. A concession of defeat, if ever there was one.

Yet Wild Winds did not act defeated. He stared at Hail Storm with hooded eyes, and said nothing.

'Greetings, Wild Winds.' Hail Storm looked around at those gathered. 'I have come to challenge, in the name of the—'

'In your own name,' Wild Winds said. 'And in the name of your personal glory.' The old man's voice carried well over the stone.

'Not so,' Hail Storm replied, calmly. 'That which had been lost has been found, and the time of—'

'Spare me,' Wild Winds said. 'Spare us all the speeches you prepared in the darkness of your tent.' He extended a hand, and gestured to the two who held the hostage. 'Bring her here.'

Before Hail Storm could even speak, the two warrior-priests picked the girl up and brought her to stand before Wild Winds. As if the habit of obeying the old man was too ingrained to break.

'So.' Wild Winds looked at the gagged and bound girl, her hair in disarray, her trous stained and damp. Her face was stained with tears, but her eyes held frustration and rage. A low murmur swept through the crowd of witnesses as they noted her condition.

'This is how you treat the very people we are pledged to serve and protect.' Wild Winds let his anger show in his voice.

'Some must sacrifice, so that the magic can be restored to the

Plains,' Hail Storm said, realising that he had been put on the defensive.

'Willing sacrifice, willingly made,' Wild Winds said. 'The very words of our tradition distorted and shifted, as if they were no more than sand in the wind.' He looked about their audience. 'And those of you who stand here, the warrior-priests of the Plains, those that are supposed to be the very protectors of our land and our people, you agree with this? Sanction this?'

There were mutterings then, and some heads nodding as if agreeing with Wild Winds. But Hail Storm saw support for himself in the majority of those faces.

He drew his sacrifice dagger. 'Wild Winds, answer my challenge. I claim the position of Eldest Elder Warrior-Priest. It is I that will lead our people to—'

'Pah,' Wild Winds said. 'You are welcome to it.'

Hail Storm stood there, taken aback. What was the old man doing?

'I renounce my position as Eldest Elder.'

'You can't reject—'

'Ah, but I do. I reject this path.' Wild Winds's voice rolled over the crowd like thunder. 'There is no honor, no truth in this, none whatsoever.'

'You would not return the magic?' Mist spoke from the edge of the stone.

'If this is what magic requires,' Wild Winds said pointing at the girl, 'I want none of it. The Plains would be better off without its return.' He lifted his head, and looked around. 'Who will turn from this path with me?' With that, he started to walk off the stone, away from Hail Storm.

Hail Storm frowned, uncertain. He could kill the old man . . . but that might cost him support. He stared about, as others started to thread through the crowd, following Wild Winds. He held his breath, then let it out slowly when only twenty or so left the crowd. All young, none with full tattoos.

As Wild Winds left the stone platform, he staggered; a female warrior-priest ran up, and tucked herself under his arm to offer support. That decided Hail Storm. No need to kill a man already dead.

Mist watched Wild Winds leave, and for a moment it seemed as if she, too, would go. But then she turned her head and looked at Hail Storm, and seemed to make her decision.

Good. Hail Storm sheathed his dagger, and gestured for them to remove the hostage from the stone. Better if she was not so obvious. He turned, and smiled at those that remained. 'I claim the position of Eldest Elder of the Warrior-Priests of the Plains. Will any say me nay?'

For a moment, there was only silence. Then, to Hail Storm's delight, Mist started the chant to confirm his claim. With a deep sense of joy, he stood at the Heart of the Plains and received his due.

As the chant ended, he bowed his head, then began to speak. 'The Sacrifice approaches, and is only a few hours away. There is much to be done. Let the elders gather here with me, and we will make our plans.'

He'd failed.

Wild Winds was having trouble breathing as he leaned hard on Snowfall. There were only about twenty that had followed him. None with skulls on their staffs. None with their full tattoos. He licked his lips. Perhaps he should release them to return to the ceremony. The chant had just started.

An image flashed in his mind, one of a short woman with long, curly brown hair, looking at him with wide eyes of the lightest blue. Ah, of a certain the winds were laughing. He'd fought the change a Warprize represented, and now here was even worse, from his own people.

'Let us take you to your tent.' Lightning Strike came on his other side, and put his arm on his shoulders.

'No,' Wild Winds gasped. 'Take me to that rise. I want to see what happens. There's one last thing . . .' He lost his breath, and his legs failed.

'Let us do the work, Eldest Elder.' Snowfall handed his staff to another, and she and Lightning Strike formed a chair with their arms.

'I am no longer Eldest Elder,' he wheezed.

'You are,' she said. 'To us. Now, there's ehat broth left, and I can—'

'Send someone else,' Wild Winds tried to command, but it came out as a strangled whisper. 'I've another task for you, if you will. Take a message—'

'Breathe,' she ordered. 'I will do whatever you ask, once we are at the top of the rise.'

'Bossy,' Wild Winds muttered, then decided to do the wise thing and do as she said.

'Another hour,' Lander said, looking at the setting sun. 'From what I remember, the Heart is another hour away.'

Chell nodded. 'That's what I think, too.'

Bethral pulled her horse to a stop. 'Then we'll get ready here.'

'Rider,' Ouse said, pulling his bow up and taut.

They all turned and saw a rider coming at a gallop from the direction of the Heart. It was a warrior-priestess, heading right for them. When she saw that she'd been spotted, she raised both hands, to show that she carried no weapon.

'Steady,' Bethral said. They waited.

Chell squinted. 'Isn't that the female who was at the rites?'

'She was with Wild Winds?' Ezren craned to look.

The warrior-priestess pulled her horse up while still at a distance, then dismounted, and started to run toward them, her hands empty and no sword at her waist. She slowed as she neared, then stopped within calling distance. 'Ezren Storyteller. I bring word from Eldest Elder Wild Winds.'

Ezren urged his horse forward. 'What word?'

The woman walked slowly toward him, her hands held out to the sides. 'I am Snowfall, in training with Wild Winds.'

'She offers her name,' Chell whispered, her eyes wide with astonishment.

'He asks that you hear his truths before you confront the one that has caused your warrior to be kidnapped.' Snowfall stood by Ezren's horse, her face turned toward his. 'He has sent me as his living token, your hostage to his honor. Will you come?'

THIRTY-ONE

'I have failed them, and you.' Wild Winds whispered his regret, every word an effort. 'I am sorry, Ezren Storyteller.'

Ezren Storyteller knelt by his side as Wild Winds struggled to breathe. 'It was not your doing, Wild Winds. I understand that.'

They were just below the rise, on the far side from the Heart. The stars had come out by the time Snowfall had brought them to his side, but there wasn't much time to talk. They'd dismounted and gathered around where he sat in the grass, his followers surrounding them, keeping watch.

The Storyteller's chest glowed with magic, and it pulsed to the beat of his heart. The warrior-priests that had followed him were trying hard not to stare at the auburn-haired man.

Wild Winds drew another breath, trying to explain to this city dweller how bad the situation really was.

'I've sundered the warrior-priests as surely as Antas the Boar sundered the Council. But the few that followed me, the ones you see here, have not the rank or status to do much, if anything.' Wild Winds stopped to breathe again, and the Storyteller waited patiently. 'Snowfall will have my skull for her staff, for what it is worth. But will that be enough?' Wild Winds shook his head.

Ezren Storyteller was looking at Snowfall, who was shaking her head. They clearly thought Wild Winds was rambling, his wits taken by the wind. He still had so much to tell them. And there was no time.

'We could not rescue your warrior. She lies at Hail Storm's feet.'

That got the Token-Bearer's attention. She frowned. 'Describe the situation to me.'

Wild Winds gestured, and Snowfall gave them the description of the stone, of all the sources of light. The warrior-priests were surrounding it. 'We think they will let you in,' she added, 'but the archers will make sure that you do not leave. Hail Storm stands at the center, ready to place his blade at the hostage's—'

'Gilla,' Ezren said. 'Her name is Gilla.'

Snowfall nodded. 'Gilla's throat. The area is circled with torches, and the fire pits are all burning. The place is lit as bright as day.'

'We thank you for your truths, Wild Winds.' Ezren looked at Bethral, who nodded and moved toward the horses. Their young warriors were unloading their pack animals, pulling metal pieces from their bags that seemed to match the armor Bethral wore.

'Can you foresee how this will end, Wild Winds?' Ezren asked.

'I cannot,' Wild Winds said. 'I only know that Hail Storm is wrong.'

Ezren looked over his shoulder, to where they were working around Bessie. 'I will command Chell, Ouse, and Lander to stay here. We don't need to give them any more hostages. They are to witness the truth of this, and tell the tale.'

Wild Winds nodded. 'I've commanded my followers to head to Xy. There may be nothing here for them when Hail Storm restores the magics. Whatever happens, their lives will be endangered. Keir of the Cat may not listen, but Xylara—' He stopped, and started to cough. 'There . . . there isn't much time. They will suspect—' Snowfall supported him as he coughed helplessly.

'If I get a chance . . . or a choice . . . I will try to heal—' Ezren started.

Wild Winds shook his head, and reached out to grasp Ezren's scarred wrist. 'No. Heal the Plains, Ezren Storyteller. My time is almost done.'

'As you say,' Ezren stood. 'I need to prepare.'

Wild Winds looked at him. 'May your Gods walk with you, Ezren Storyteller.'

'Thank you, Eldest Elder.' With that Ezren rose and went to where Bethral was working. The younger warriors had completed their work on Bessie. Wild Winds blinked to see a horse covered in such metal. He'd heard of such a thing, but never had seen armor such as Bethral and her horse wore.

The young warriors were offering Bethral a quiver full of lances; their own, he suspected. She secured them to her saddle, reaching out to take each of their hands.

Bethral of the Horse mounted, and she and her horse glowed in the light of the torches. It was a light different from that carried by the Storyteller. Bethral was all silver, glittering like a star, while Ezren Storyteller glowed like the midday sun.

Ezren's horse was a fresh one, and they'd strapped a shield to Ezren's back as well as his arm. He took up a helmet, and gave a nod and a command to the young ones. There was a protest, but then Bethral spoke a command, and the three young ones bowed their heads and stepped back.

The Storyteller stepped to his token-bearer. He said something quietly, then kissed her gently. Wild Winds grunted to himself in approval. At least that much had been accomplished.

Bethral took his helmet from his arm and settled it on his head, securing the strap. They both mounted, and Bethral took her shield from the young man with the broken nose.

Wild Winds narrowed his eyes, trying to get a clearer view. Odd, it looked as if some small animal had leaped to the back of Bethral's horse, clinging to the bedroll. But Bethral didn't react.

Wild Winds blinked rapidly, trying to clear his gummy eyes. He had to have imagined that.

Bethral turned Bessie to face the cluster of their friends and allies, and Ezren moved his horse beside her. 'You don't have to do this,' he said softly. 'You are of the Plains. You could stay here, and live and help—'

Bethral shook her head, her face serene under her helmet. 'Ezren Storyteller, I want to live with you forever. How can you not think I wouldn't die with you as well?'

His throat closed as she graced him with her loving smile.

'Stay close,' Bethral said. 'They will let us pass, thinking we will offer ourselves up. But we're charging through, onto the stone. I'll hold them off, you free Gilla. Then we fight our way free. If the magic flares within you . . .'

'I'll burn them all,' Ezren said.

Lander, Ouse, and Chell knelt before them, and bowed their heads.

'We release you from our service,' Ezren said. 'The quest is completed.'

'We thank you for your service, warriors of the Plains,' Bethral said.

Ezren raised his voice. 'May the Lord of Light and the Lady of Laughter grace your days and nights.'

Lander looked up. 'May the elements protect you both.'

Bethral raised her mace over her head. 'HEYLA!' she shouted, a battle cry and farewell in one.

'HEYLA!' was the response.

Bethral turned Bessie's head, and the horse leapt forward, up and over the rise, Ezren close behind.

'HEYLA,' the response tore from Wild Winds's throat. Everyone around him cried out as well, and surged after Bethral and Ezren, running to the crest of the rise, wanting to watch.

Snowfall and Lightning Strike stayed by his side, but Wild Winds wasn't satisfied. He tugged at Snowfall's trous.

Snowfall knelt by his side. 'Eldest Elder, do you wish mercy?'

'No,' he managed to croak. 'Want to see.'

Snowfall frowned. 'You wish to see the end of this?'

Wild Winds laughed weakly as he tried to catch his breath. Snowfall took his arm, and heaved him up as Lightning Strike helped. They each took an arm, and helped him walk to the top of the rise.

'Ah, you are so young,' Wild Winds gasped as he struggled to take a step.

'Save your breath, Eldest Elder,' Lightning Strike said.

'You have so much to learn,' Wild Winds said. 'Haven't you realised yet? All endings are beginnings. And in turn, all beginnings mark the end of something.'

'Just a few more steps,' Snowfall said, ignoring his words.

Ah well, they'd learn. Eventually. Wild Winds smiled to himself as they crested the rise. He lifted his head, and strained to see what was happening at the Heart of the Plains.

Bethral led the charge, plunging up and over the rise, screaming the battle cry of the Plains. Ezren was keeping pace, his horse just a head behind.

Heads turned among the warrior-priests. As predicted, the crowd parted, making a narrow path for them to proceed to the Heart. Clearly, they'd planned that she and Ezren would dismount, and surrender themselves.

Bethral let her lips curl in a snarl. Not likely.

Bessie surged under her, charging forward, unconcerned about the humans between her and the goal. Bethral knew full well that few warriors could face a charging horse easily; and a fully armored warhorse was a fearful sight.

Bethral nodded in satisfaction as the eyes of the warrior-priests went wide. They dodged to the sides, scrambling to avoid the charge. The path became wider, and wider still as Bethral swung her mace.

Then Bessie's hooves rang on the stone, and they were headed straight for the man who had to be Hail Storm.

He'd pulled Gilla up, keeping her before him, his blade at her throat. But his eyes grew wide as Bessie covered the distance between them, headed straight for her target. Bethral almost laughed out loud at the look on his face. She swung her mace high, with every intent of crushing his skull.

Hail Storm jerked back, dodging the charge, dragging Gilla with him. Bethral had her mace ready as she passed, but Gilla was thrust toward her as a shield. Hail Storm ducked his head, his arms wrapped around Gilla as Bessie charged past. Bethral hesitated, checking her blow, cursing.

A yowl cut the air, and the cat launched itself off the bedroll, and straight for Hail Storm's arms. Claws and teeth bit deep, raking long scores down his tattooed arms.

Hail Storm cried out, releasing his hostage. He flailed with his dagger, fending off the enraged animal.

Gilla dropped and rolled clear as the big roan horse leaped over her, pivoting on its hind legs.

The cat fell to the stone, its fur puffed out. It streaked off, disappearing into the grasses at the stone's edge.

Bethral clung to Bessie's back, her mace swinging up in preparation. But Hail Storm was fleeing, running for the far edge of the stone, clutching his bleeding arm to his chest.

Bethral cursed, and made to follow. But the warrior-priests around the stone allowed Hail Storm to disappear into their ranks, and brought their bows to bear on her. She could hear the bastard shouting behind their ranks, and some of the others were drawing swords and coming toward her. They wore nothing but their tattoos and their trous. Fools!

'Ezren, free Gilla,' Bethral said as she tried to guard them from all sides at the same time. Hopeless, perhaps. Eventually, they could overwhelm her. But a few broken heads and arms might keep the others at bay. One of them was more foolhardy, rushing toward her with sword and shield high.

Bessie pivoted again and kicked out, striking him in the chest. Everyone heard the ribs break as he was tossed back into the crowd.

Screaming her battle cry, Bethral fell to with a will, trying to be everywhere at once.

Gilla rolled free, avoiding flying hooves as best she could, struggling against her bonds.

'Gilla,' came a voice. She looked up and saw Ezren Storyteller swinging his leg over the horse, preparing to dismount. Bethral was holding off the warrior-priests, but they didn't have much time. She watched as his boot touched the stone, relaxing at the thought of rescue.

The stone rang with a bell-like tone.

Gilla gasped through her gag. The warrior-priests at the edge of the stone all exclaimed as they backed away, looking around for the source of the sound.

Ezren Storyteller spread his arms, hands out, as if afraid of losing his balance. Gilla half expected him to sink into the stone as if it had turned to water beneath his feet.

Instead, the stone began to glow.

Gilla struggled to sit up, and saw the entire stone under and around her lit up with a white light. It wasn't on fire, thank the elements, there was no heat. The stone was still hard and rough under her, but the glow was getting brighter and bigger.

The warrior-priests had seen it, too, and they backed away as the glow expanded to the edge of the stone.

Ezren stood there, as if frozen.

Gilla's struggles drew Bethral's attention. She maneuvered Bessie close, and reached down. Gilla strained up, and found herself hauled to her feet by the collar. A cold blade slid against her wrists, and then the bonds gave as it sliced through them.

Gilla rubbed her wrists and took the offered blade to cut her legs free. Bethral stayed close, watching all around them for attack. 'Up,' she commanded as soon as Gilla was free to move. 'Get to Ezren's horse.'

Gilla yanked her gag free and scrambled to the free horse, calling it to her side. It came willingly, although its eyes were rolling with fear.

'What's happening?' she asked.

Bethral grabbed her collar and heaved her, sprawling, over the saddle. Instinct made Gilla seat herself and take the reins.

'Go.' Bethral pointed. 'Head for that rise. The others are there.'

'You'll be killed,' Gilla cried, wanting to deny the truth. She jerked her head around, looking at the warrior-priests, who were recovering from their shock. Their eyes were focused on Ezren; it was only a matter of time before—

Bethral smacked the horse, which leaped forward with no

other urging. Gilla sobbed, then leaned forward and let the horse run through the warrior-priests. She'd no weapon, no way to fight. She'd be more obligation than aid. Tears in her eyes, she risked a glance back. No hand was lifted against her; they were all focused on the glowing stone. And the man and the woman at the very center of the Heart of the Plains.

The world changed when Ezren stepped onto the Heart of the Plains.

A tone sounded, like the deepest bell he'd ever heard, resounding in his chest. The magic leapt within his chest, washing Ezren with joy. Home. It was home.

The mages he had talked to were wrong. Magic – this wild magic – had emotions. It was powerful, strong, and flared within him, bringing with it knowledge and power. And an offer . . .

Of power, beyond his understanding. His for the taking. At a price.

And for a moment he hesitated.

But he'd never wanted this kind of power. And that thought was enough. Regret flowed through him, but it was the magic's sorrow, not his.

Joy, then, and anticipation. Eagerness for home and freedom. Images flashed before Ezren's eyes, and he knew what needed to be done.

'Ezren.' Bethral's voice broke through, and Ezren looked up. She was down from Bessie's back, extending her hand.

'Ezren.' Bethral moved Bessie alongside Ezren and extended her hand. 'Mount. If we charge—'

'No.' Ezren looked up at her. His voice sounded odd, echoing ever so slightly. 'You are so lovely, my Angel of Light.'

'Ezren.' She tried very hard not to let her impatience show. 'Come up. If we are to—'

'You would take them all on, would you not?' Ezren asked.

Bessie shifted, her hooves chiming on the stone. Bethral

frowned at Ezren. With all the light, it was hard to tell, but she thought that he was glowing now. 'Ezren?'

He looked at those around them. Bethral looked as well. The one they'd driven off, who had to be Hail Storm, was in the second rank, screaming commands. So far, not one had the courage to step on the stone, but it wouldn't hold them back long. 'Ezren,' she repeated, trying to get his attention.

Ezren looked at her, his green eyes bright. She could see it now, the glow under his skin. But there was more. As if he understood everything that was happening. That would happen.

'Willing sacrifice, willingly made,' he recited. 'Are you willing, my Angel?'

Her heart full of the inevitable, Bethral dismounted with a smooth move, and stood next to him. 'Yes.'

THIRTY-TWO

Ezren's heart soared at Bethral's acceptance. He watched as she slid from the saddle without hesitation.

'I am sorry, Bethral,' Ezren said regretfully as she stepped to his side, 'for what we will not have.'

Bethral took off her helmet, shaking out her long hair. 'I'm grateful for what we have had. And who can say what comes after this life?' She hung her helmet on Bessie's saddle, and her mace from her belt. 'So, if you aren't going to let me kill them all, and I'm not going to let them kill us, what are we going to do?'

Bessie snorted and shook her head, jingling her harness as if asking the same question.

Ezren laughed. The warmth in his chest grew as the wild magic laughed with him. He turned to face the crowd. 'Bragnect!'

His voice rolled over the heads of the warrior-priests. That got their attention, and they all went silent. Even Hail Storm, the one that had held Gilla; he now stood at the edge of the stone, glaring with hate. Glaring with cold, dead eyes. Ezren knew that look all too well. Hail Storm's eyes were the same as those of the blood mage. The one that had driven the stone knife into Ezren's chest.

'Bragnect, all of you!' Ezren raised his voice, letting it carry above the crowd. He had a sense that his voice was carrying over the land, clear to all, even to those on the rise. 'Horse killers! Slayers of young warriors! Arrogant, self-righteous fools, filled with your own importance and pride! What else have you done over the years in order to protect your rank and standing?'

Those around the stone raised their weapons, their faces filled with rage. But not one of them stepped on the glowing stone.

'I do not know the answer,' Ezren said, 'but the Plains know. The Magic knows.'

Ezren focused on Hail Storm. 'You want power and magic, and you are willing to do anything to make it happen. Even distort the words of your own tales and history to make it work for you.' Ezren could hear his voice – it has never sounded so powerful before, so strong. It was still not the voice he'd had before, but it was his, and it resonated as he spoke.

'Yes!' Hail Storm drew his sword with one hand, and held his sacrifice dagger with the other. He stepped past the cowering fools and put his foot onto the stone. 'That which was lost is now found, and it is up to us, the warrior-priests of the Plains, to restore it.'

Bethral stepped forward, her mace back in her hand. But Ezren caught her elbow, and stopped her.

Bethral paused, watching the angry warrior-priests that surrounded the platform. It was only a matter of time before they gathered their courage to charge the two of them. Why was Ezren holding her back?

'Call them, Bethral.'

She tilted her head. 'Who?' she asked in a whisper.

'Summon them,' Ezren said. His eyes glowed in the light. But there was something else. Something more in his green eyes. 'Summon them here to witness and judge, Bethral of the Horse, Avatar and Warrior.'

Like that, Bethral knew exactly what he meant. She'd done this before, opened herself to that power; embodied all of the Spirit that was within her.

She whispered a prayer, put her hand on Bessie's neck, threw her head back, and cried the call to summon horses of the Plains.

Bessie reared, neighing, adding the call of the lead mare.

A trembling started underfoot. Hail Storm jerked his foot off the stone.

Bethral felt it under her feet, and shared a delighted glance with Ezren. She called again, and the thundering grew, now clearly heard. All of the warrior-priests started to look around.

'There is an old saying in my land, Hail Storm.' Ezren's voice rang with satisfaction. 'Be careful what you wish for. You just might get it.'

Gilla sobbed with relief as she saw Lander running forward when she topped the rise. She leapt from her horse and into his arms, hugging him. Chell and Ouse were there as well, laughing and hugging her.

They dragged her over to the crowd of warrior-priests at the top of the rise who were watching the Heart. Gilla jerked back, but Ouse shook his head. 'We'll explain, after.'

So they were standing close to the oldest of the warrior-priests, who was being supported by two younger ones. It was the one who had conducted the rites, the one who had spurned Hail Storm in the center of the Heart. Gilla gave him an uncertain glance, but the others were ignoring him.

'Look,' Ouse said.

Gilla's eyes were drawn to where Ezren and Bethral were standing, just standing, in the glow, next to the roan horse. Why didn't they . . .

'Bragnect!'

Gilla gasped as she heard every word, as clear as if the Storyteller was standing before her. Then the ground below their feet started to shake.

A group of horses came over the far rise, glowing with their own light. Horses like the ones on the Longest Night, when the dead appeared to bid farewell to the living. Spirit horses, too, ridden by . . .

Was that El?

Gilla's grief spilled over. El was there, riding hard. Her tears fell as she recognised Cosana at his side. There was another as well, a young warrior-priestess, and from the gasps around them, she was known to the others.

The spirit horses plunged down off the rise, galloping straight for the Heart. Behind them streamed real horses, hundreds, thousands. Gilla had never seen so many horses in one herd at one time. They ran, tossing their heads, neighing, following the spirit horses as they charged the warrior-priests.

The warrior-priests reacted in various ways, some running away from the stone, some standing and waving their arms so that the horses would dodge around them. But the spirit horses made it their business to cut between the Heart and the warrior-priests, forcing them away.

Ezren and Bethral stood at the center as the horses swirled around the edge of the stone, pushing the warrior-priests farther and farther back. The thunder of their hooves seemed to fade as Ezren's voice cut through the noise.

Hail Storm watched in horror as the spirit horses charged through the crowd, aiming for him.

He scrambled back, barely dodging the cold, glowing hand of Arching Colors as she reached for him. Then she swept past, and the real horses followed, forcing him back and away from the stone. They continued to swirl around, thundering past, but Hail Storm's attention was caught by the figures in the center of the glowing stone.

'You Warrior-Priests have wanted it all, and all for yourselves.'

The man, Ezren Storyteller, was digging in the roan horse's saddlebags, and he pulled forth a bundle of rags. He stripped them away, revealing a sacrifice knife with stone blade and horn handle. Skies above, where had he gotten that?

The Storyteller held it up for all to see, and his voice echoed over the horses. 'I bear the wild magic, by no choice of my own. But this was never the kind of power that I wished to possess. All I ever wanted was the power to tell stories, moving the hearts and minds of those that heard them, and learning the truths that are found in all tales.'

The Storyteller paused, and glanced at the woman at his side.

'That, and the magic of Bethral's love are all I need in this life, and the next.'

Once again he brandished the sacrifice knife, holding it high. 'We will give you what you want . . .'

The blade in the Storyteller's hands seemed to grow blacker somehow, as if the stone was absorbing the light.

The Storyteller continued, his green eyes glowing with light. '. . . but may all the Gods, and all the elements, grant that you get exactly what you deserve.'

Ezren turned to Bethral. 'Give me your hand, beloved.'

Bethral took off her gauntlet and tucked it into her belt. She looked beyond the horses that protected them, at the rise where they'd left the others. She smiled, extending her hand to Ezren, then took a deep breath, at peace with this decision.

'Blood of the Plains,' she announced, hearing the echo of her words. 'Willing sacrifice, willingly made.'

Ezren sliced her palm, and blood swelled from the cut.

He held his own hand up, and cut his palm. 'Willing sacrifice,' he repeated, his words echoing as well. 'Willingly made.'

He grasped the knife hilt with his bloody hand, and reached out. Bethral put her hand over his, also touching the hilt. Their mingled blood dripped to the stone below.

Bethral felt it then, felt the joy and anticipation of the wild magic. It danced over their hands, little sparks of light. It tingled, and left her breathless with its power and its promise.

But when she looked in Ezren's eyes, there was no regret. He was at peace with this choice. He meant what he had said about their love. This life, and the next.

She smiled and nodded, willing to follow his lead.

There was a shriek, and Hail Storm was visible for a moment, his face filled with horror. He was trying to dodge through the ring of horses, trying to prevent—

'You want power?' Ezren asked. 'Well, we want justice. For us.' He knelt, and Bethral knelt with him.

'For the land.' Ezren lifted the knife high as their blood flowed down the blade and added to the pool below.

'FOR THE PEOPLE OF THE PLAINS!' Ezren and Bethral shouted together, and their joined hands plunged downward and shattered the stone blade against the Heart of the Plains.

The world around them disappeared as the light flared bright, white, and forever.

THIRTY-THREE

Gilla cried out as the glowing Heart exploded with light. Ezren and Bethral disappeared from sight.

The power flared straight up from the stone, like a needle piercing the night sky. It towered over them, swirling around and around, like one of the deadly windstorms she'd heard about but never seen.

The horses were still circling, and the warrior-priests that surrounded the Heart were staggering back, covering their eyes.

The bright needle swirled, linking the land and the stars. A bell tone sounded again. Gilla blinked against the glare, and saw a circle of light pulse from the Heart, expanding outward. The thick band of light looked like it was traveling under the earth, illuminating the grasses from below. Moving fast, it climbed the rise and passed through their group.

Gilla turned to watch it go, bright and visible far into the distance. A second followed the first, with the same bell tone resounding through her bones.

She turned back and saw a third, and then a fourth, pulse issue from the Heart. As the fourth band of light and sound raced away, it was joined by the horses moving away from the stone in all directions, scattering the warrior-priests.

But the warrior-priests around her were staring at their hands and the ground, tears streaming down their faces. 'The magic,' she heard one whisper.

Ouse gasped. His hands were glowing, strong and bright.

'Cosana!' Lander shouted. 'El!'

Gilla jerked around and saw the spirit horses galloping straight up the rise toward them. Cosana was laughing, her hair filled with flowers. El looked sad as he rode past, his hand held up in farewell. Gilla raised her hand in return, and then he was gone with the other spirit horses. Her heart ached in her chest, but she knew he'd ride with her until the snows.

One last spirit rider came up the rise, headed straight for the Eldest Elder, a warrior-priestess with a very intent look, as if stalking prey.

Wild Winds couldn't quite see all that was happening, but the needle of light nearly blinded him. He felt the warmth of the waves of magic as they flowed over him even as the last of his strength faded.

His knees weakened, and he sagged in Snowfall's and Lightning Strike's arms. It would not be long now.

Another grasped his arm. 'Stand, Wild Winds. Stand and see.'

Wild Winds frowned, blinking at the sight of Twisting Winds at his side. 'Elder?'

Twisting Winds nodded, his wise eyes concerned. 'One last lesson, young one. Magic is a blade that cuts both ways.'

Confused, he felt a warm body tuck itself under his other shoulder. 'Stand, Wild Winds.' Summer Sky's face was filled with both joy and regret. 'One last dance, my friend. That which was taken is restored. That which was imprisoned is now freed.'

'Stand, Wild Winds,' Stalking Cat commanded, both hands on Wild Winds's shoulders. His fierce eyes forced Wild Winds to raise his head. 'One last battle, Warrior-Priest. Embrace the old. Preserve the new.'

'Oh, that's helpful,' Wild Winds grumbled, but Stalking Cat just gave him a fierce grin and shifted slightly. Wild Winds drew in a sharp breath as he saw Arching Colors racing toward him on horseback, her hand reaching out for him.

Gilla watched as the two who were supporting Wild Winds cried out as the warrior-priestess rode right through him. The woman threw her head back as the horse surged on, holding up something in her hand, her mouth open as if crying out her success in the hunt.

The two supporting Wild Winds lost their grip, and he slowly slid out of their hands and collapsed to the ground.

Gilla looked back at the Heart. The needle of light was still there, swirling, towering. The warrior-priests below were now running toward it. Just as one reached out to touch it—

It was gone.

Gilla blinked at the spots before her eyes, staring at the center of the Heart of the Plains. But it was empty, the stone once again gray and dark.

Ezren, Bethral, and Bessie were gone.

Gilla choked back a sob as Chell wrapped her arm around her shoulders. Lander and Ouse came over and hugged her tight. 'Tenna and Arbon live, Gilla.'

Gilla cried that much harder.

The darkness had descended, but the torches and firepits were still lit around the Heart. The female warrior-priest knelt at Wild Winds's side, but the male was pointing down at the Heart. 'Look. Something is wrong.'

The warrior-priests that stood about the Heart of the Plains were acting oddly. Some were standing, staring at their staffs. Others were kneeling, and crying out. Faint sounds of anguish rose in the air.

'Skies above!' The female by Wild Winds rose to her feet. 'Their tattoos! Eldest Elder, their tattoos are gone.'

Wild Winds started to laugh, a strong, healthy sound.

By dawn, they were all crammed into Wild Winds's tent, everyone eating and talking excitedly.

Gilla's friends had plunged her into the stream. She scrubbed every inch of skin twice as they sat on the bank and told her everything that had happened. They'd brought her gear, so she donned fresh tunic and trous as Lander and Ouse set up her tent for her.

Now they sat around her, all of them tucked tight in the front corner of Wild Winds's tent, at his insistence. He'd wanted to hear everything they had to say about the events that had led up to this moment.

For the warrior-priests and priestess that had followed him up the ridge had all been gifted with magic the likes of which they'd never seen. They were all eating fry bread and roasted gurtle, and drinking strong kavage. They were excited at their new powers, but there was also a deep worry about learning to use these new gifts. Wild Winds had asked Gilla and her friends to describe how Ezren Storyteller had torched his enemies when he'd lost control of the powers. As a warning, he said, of the dangers involved.

The tent buzzed with talk and joy, for Wild Winds sat on his chair before them all, sat tall and straight and strong. Healed, although whether by the magic or by Arching Colors's touch was a subject of much speculation and anyone's guess.

Gilla sighed, her belly full, her friends close. The future held many possibilities, but right now she just wanted to curl up in her tent and sleep.

One of the guards entered the tent and spoke to Wild Winds softly. Wild Winds frowned, then nodded. The guard went out, and a moment later the tent flap opened to admit an older woman. She was dressed in trous and her hair was in dreadlocks, but her face and chest were as pale as a babe's.

The tent went silent. Gilla craned her neck to see, but Lander squeezed her hand. 'It's one of the other warrior-priests,' he whispered. 'One that lost her tattoos.'

'Mist,' Wild Winds said gently, looking with sadness at his old friend's naked breasts and bare skin. It was so odd to see her without her tattoos. 'Enter in peace.'

Mist took two steps closer, the staff in her hand bare of decoration. She made no move to sit.

'Your skulls?' Wild Winds stared at her staff.

'The skulls shattered the moment the tattoos disappeared,' Mist said calmly. 'You have magic?'

'You can't see it?' Wild Winds gave her a sharp look.

'No,' Mist said, 'nor can the others.'

There were gasps at that, but Wild Winds raised a hand for quiet.

'The ground glows with power,' Wild Winds said. 'The Sacrifice has been made, and magic has returned to the Plains. But it appears that there are new questions now. New responsibilities.'

Mist gave him a sharp look, taking him all in. 'You are well?'

'Yes,' Wild Winds said simply. 'A gift of a future.'

Mist nodded. 'One I will not share.'

'I am sorry, Mist,' Wild Winds said. 'But you and the others will have to live with the consequences of your choices. Perhaps with time you can relearn—'

'We will not live long enough,' Mist said.

'Eh?' Wild Winds raised an eyebrow.

'We can no longer summon horses.'

Wild Winds stared at her, dumbfounded. The young ones around him gasped.

'See for yourselves.' Mist gestured outside. 'They are trying again, even as we speak. A small herd, down by the Heart.'

Wild Winds nodded, and the young rushed the flap, leaving him alone with Mist.

'We cannot call them. If we catch one, it will not let any of us mount. If we manage to mount, the horse is uncontrollable,' Mist said, her face grim.

'The Spirit of the Horse . . .' Wild Winds shook his head. 'You have offended.'

'We cannot hunt, cannot ride.' Mist sighed. 'The Sacrifice has his vengeance. Many have already sought the snows.'

'He sought justice, not vengeance,' Wild Wind reminded her. 'What of Hail Storm?'

'Cursing in my tent. He claimed to have other ways of wielding magics, but we have listened and have rejected his ways.'

'He is still a danger, then.'

'I doubt it,' Mist said. 'The wounds on his arms are swollen and puffy. There are red streaks growing up his arm very quickly, and he is fevered. He may not see it for what it is, but I do. If the fever does not claim him soon, I will give him mercy before I seek the snows.'

'Ah.' Wild Winds stood. 'I am sorry, Mist.'

'Do not be. I made a choice, and I live with the consequences. My decision is made. But I wanted to see how you were before I chose that path.'

Wild Winds pulled her into a hug. Mist stiffened, then melted against him for a moment.

'You could share my tent. I would care for you,' he whispered into her hair.

'No.' She pulled away and stepped back, her expression implacable. 'I'd offer you my skull, old friend, but I doubt my wisdom would aid you.' She turned, and headed out of the tent.

Wild Winds followed. 'I think the customs of the warrior-priests must change, including that one. But we shall see.'

They walked to the rise where the young ones had gathered to look down at the Heart.

'It's true,' Snowfall said as he stopped beside her. 'The horses will not aid them.'

Mist joined them and looked down at the group struggling to get mounts. 'Do you know what happened to the Sacrifice and his Token-Bearer?'

'No.' Wild Winds sighed. 'They vanished. But I wish them well, wherever they may be. As I wish you well, Mist.'

'Send your people to our camp later this evening,' Mist said calmly. 'No need for the tents and supplies to go to waste.'

'I will,' he said. 'Safe journey to the snows, Mist. And beyond.'

'May the elements be with you, Eldest Elder.' Mist walked toward the Heart, and Wild Winds silently watched her go.

Gilla couldn't believe her eyes. No matter what they did, those warrior-priests could not summon a horse. They had all stood and watched as that woman talked to Wild Winds, and then started to walk toward the Heart.

Wild Winds had watched her go, regret etched on his face. But then he shook his head, and turned toward them all.

'We all need sleep this day,' he said. 'We will finish our meal, and set watches.' The others nodded, and turned back toward the tents, talking among themselves.

Wild Winds held up a hand as Gilla and her friends started to move. 'Wait, Warriors.'

They paused, darting looks at each other at being addressed as warriors.

'I would ask that you remain with us for a time, before you make any decisions about your paths. The spring challenges will be held soon, and those who will challenge for warlord status will arrive shortly. I'd learn more from you about what happened here, if you would.'

They looked at him, then Lander pushed Gilla forward.

Gilla nodded. 'We would stay, Eldest Elder.'

'Good.' Wild Winds turned back to the tents. 'Let us talk as we eat. The rest can wait until later. Although' – he pointed ahead with his staff – 'maybe sooner than I think.'

There were riders before his tent, warriors of the Plains. Gilla blinked to see the one at the front, one of the largest, blackest men she had ever seen. He was dressed in fine chain mail, his sword on his back. His dark eyes flashed, and the gold earrings in his ears caught the morning light. 'Wild Winds,' the man said, his voice booming.

'Simus of the Hawk.' Wild Winds strode up and stood before the man, planting his staff next to him. 'How may I aid you?'

Those dark eyes flashed under raised brows. Gilla had the impression that Simus had noticed the lack of skulls on the staff. And the presence of young warriors in the group of warrior-priests. But the man said nothing about that.

'An explanation would be a good start,' Simus said. 'My evening pleasures were interrupted by a needle of light that pierced the sky, and a singer with an itch of curiosity.' Simus shot a glance at the man next to him. 'I had no choice but to leave my bed and seek you out.'

'Joden of the Hawk.' Wild Winds nodded at the big man with the broad face and light brown skin. 'You are a singer now?'

'No, Eldest Elder.' Joden shook his head with resignation. 'Not yet. I—'

'Pah,' Simus said. 'A small matter.' He fixed his gaze on Wild Winds. 'Well? What was that all about?'

'Please, Simus of the Hawk,' Wild Winds said, 'you are welcome to my tent. We have a tale to tell, one long in the telling.'

'You will tell it?' Simus demanded.

'Yes,' Wild Winds said.

Simus pulled his head back in surprise, then frowned.

Wild Winds lifted an eyebrow. 'What, is Simus of the Hawk struck speechless?'

'I am waiting for the sky to fall on my head,' Simus retorted.

'Which is how the tale begins, if you would hear it.' Wild Winds said.

Gilla smiled as Joden dismounted immediately.

'You think that warrior-priests cannot change?' Wild Winds asked Simus. 'Come and hear the tale, or not. As you choose.'

'Keir is going to gut me,' Simus grumbled, but he dismounted and joined his friend.

Wild Winds paused, and looked back at Gilla and her friends. 'You are welcome, but you can also choose to sleep, if you wish. Your part in this tale can be told later.'

Lander and Ouse followed Wild Winds, but Chell turned to Gilla, who was already yawning. 'I'll see you to your tent,' she said as she took Gilla's arm. 'You had the worst of it.'

Gilla nodded, and together they walked toward their part of the camp. She sighed, letting her tiredness overcome her. 'Do you think Ouse will become a warrior-priest?'

Chell shrugged. 'Who's to say? But if he does, I am glad it's Wild Winds that will teach him.' She looked back toward the tent. 'I'm glad Simus of the Hawk is here,' she added. 'I would serve under him.'

'Oh?' Gilla arched an eyebrow.

Chell flushed. 'He is a fine-looking man. And rumor has it that he is amazing in—'

'That can all wait for tomorrow.' Gilla yawned, her jaw cracking. 'I just wish we knew what had happened to Ezren and Bethral.'

Chell shrugged. 'Maybe we will someday. Who knows what story may come our way?'

Gilla sighed. 'I just want to know the end of that tale.'

'Here we go.' Chell lifted the flap of the tent. 'Sleep as long as you want, Gilla.'

Gilla nodded absently, then crawled in. The blankets looked so inviting, but there was a lump in the middle. 'What?'

A head lifted from the blanket, which was rumpled and gathered together. Yellow eyes blinked at her, then a mouth yawned, showing sharp teeth.

'Cat!' Gilla said with delight. 'You—'

Tiny mewing sounds came out of the blanket. Gilla reached over and pulled back a fold. She crowed with delight at the sight of five tiny bodies, each struggling to suck at their mother's teats.

'Cat, you are a warrior of the Plains now.' Gilla reached over and carefully scratched its . . . her . . . head. 'I just wish you could speak as to the fate of the Storyteller and his Warlord. What happened to them, eh?'

THIRTY-FOUR

Ezren lost all sense of time and self, as if the light was endless and eternal within the core of his being. The power danced through him, joyous and gleeful. There was a deep feeling of gratitude and urgency. As if he had to choose.

That was easy. He wanted his lady and his stories. More than that, he would not ask. The rest, they would build together.

There was a pause . . . a question . . .

His voice. The scars.

Ah. He hesitated . . .

No. His choice was made even before he had thought it through. *Change nothing*, he thought firmly, trying to make sure the wild magic understood. *Bethral loves me as I am, and those events made me as I am now. Change nothing.*

Laughter then, a wonderful, happy sound, seeming filled with an acknowledgment of wisdom hard won. Then the light and power twirled, and Ezren felt as though he was being tossed and twisted by the wild currents of time.

Slowly, his senses returned, and the world righted itself. While he still could not see, he felt Bethral's hand in his.

He tightened his grip, and her fingers clutched at his just as tightly.

The blindness faded, and as the world came into focus, he could see her next to him, her blue eyes wide. 'Ezren,' she said breathlessly.

'I am here,' he said, pulling her close, their hands still clasped tight.

The light surrounded them, covering them with a soft aura.

Bethral seemed to sparkle, her armor glittering in the light. 'Are we dead?' she whispered.

'If we are,' he said just as softly, 'we are together.'

But then Ezren felt cobblestones under his boots, and the glow faded away. He was facing Bethral, who looked dazed and confused, and beautiful. Bessie was behind her, shaking her head with a jingle of harness and barding.

They were standing in the center of the courtyard of the Castle of Edenrich, the sun blazing above them in a cloudless sky.

Ezren could not believe his eyes, but his lungs filled with the scents of the city, the familiar smells that spoke of civilisation.

Awareness hit Bethral's face as well, and she stared at him in disbelief. 'We're back?'

Ezren swooped her up with a great laugh, lifting her high in his arms, plate armor and all, swinging them both in a circle. 'The triumphant heroes return!'

'Ezren,' Bethral gasped, staring at him. 'Are you well? The magic?'

He stopped and stood there for a moment, bracing himself against her weight. 'Lord of Light . . . it's gone.' He grinned at her. 'It's gone!' He spun her around once again, in the opposite direction, laughing with delight.

Bethral laughed as well, her hands on his shoulders, her hair sweeping through the air. He rejoiced at the happiness in her eyes. With care, he set her on her feet, keeping his arms around her waist. 'I am going to peel you out of that armor and—'

Someone coughed.

Ezren jerked back, then spun, finally focusing on the people around them.

Queen Gloriana stood close to the back wall of the courtyard, holding a bloody sword in her red-gloved hands. Ezren narrowed his eyes at the sight of the gloves that were to be worn only in times of dire threat to the kingdom.

Gloriana's eyes were wide as she stared at them, her sword held defensively. 'Bethral?'

Oris lay on the ground behind her, his face slack. Alad was

next to him, propped up on an elbow, blood staining his chest. He was panting, his hand pressed over the wound, his face filled with fear and astonishment.

Bethral shifted, drawing Ezren's attention behind him.

Five men stood there, weapons out and ready. They were spread out, blocking all exits from the courtyard. Armed and well-armored, they all stared with the cold eyes of killers. Behind them stood a figure taller than the others, wearing a dark, hooded cloak.

The figure's eyes flashed in the depths of the hood. 'What in the name of—'

'Gloriana?' Bethral asked, her hand going to the handle of her mace. 'Who are these men?'

'Bethral?' Gloriana breathed, as if not daring to believe. 'Ezren?'

'They're traitors,' Alad gasped from the ground.

'Good enough,' Ezren said, and stepped back. 'My Lady?'

Bethral leapt for Bessie's saddle. With one swift move, she raised her mace and turned Bessie to face the foe.

'Kill them,' the cloaked man shouted, pointing at Bethral.

'Idiots,' Ezren muttered, backing closer to Gloriana. Her face was grim, and she jerked forward, as if to join the fight. 'No.' Ezren put his hand on her arm. 'Don't get in Bethral's way.'

Gloriana grimaced, but stayed where she was. Ezren knelt by Alad and eased him flat, frowning at the amount of blood. The blond tried to push him off. 'Lady Bethral.' Alad struggled to rise. 'She can't hope to—'

'Yes, she can,' Ezren said, glancing over at his lady.

Bessie snorted as Bethral settled in the saddle and they charged the first man to move.

The fight exploded around them. The five men tried to meet Bethral's charge, their shields and swords held high. But the warhorse crashed into the group, knocking one man to the ground, then using her hooves to make certain he would not rise again.

Bethral swung her mace as Bessie pivoted and kicked, a

whirlwind of death. Two more joined the man on the ground, helmets dented, clearly unconscious. The other two started to move back, eyeing the open gate.

There was a scrabble of boots on the cobblestones as Gloriana ran forward, charging straight for the leader.

The figure in the cloak backpedaled, shouting orders to the remaining men. 'Attack the Storyteller,' he snarled.

They started to obey, turning their backs on Bethral and running toward Ezren.

Ezren just stared at them, shaking his head. 'Fools!'

A bloodcurdling scream, and the nearest one stumbled and fell, a lance of the Plains piercing his chest.

The second man didn't stop. He turned and sprinted for the gates.

The second lance took him at the base of his spine.

Gloriana was fighting the leader, spitting curses as their swords crossed, her pretty face contorted in rage. Her opponent was barely managing to parry her blows.

Bethral turned Bessie, focused on Gloriana's opponent, and drew another lance.

The figure fled through the gates. Gloriana made as if to follow.

'No,' Bethral commanded.

Gloriana stopped, breathing hard, her sword at her side. 'But—'

'No.' Bethral slid from the saddle. 'You don't know – there might be an ambush waiting.'

Gloriana swallowed hard as she tried to pull herself together. 'I was praying to the Lord and Lady . . . where did you come from?'

'Explanation will have to wait.' Ezren knelt again. 'Oris and Alad need healers.'

'Where in the name of all the hells are your guards?' Bethral demanded.

Gloriana looked down. 'I didn't raise an alarm. I need to explain—'

Ezren didn't like the sound of that. But he looked down at a touch on his arm. 'Lord Ezren? Is that really you?' Oris lifted his head, his eyes dazed and distant. 'We thought you dead.'

Ezren put a hand in the middle of Oris's back. 'Stay still man, until we can get help.'

'Guards!' Bethral had dismounted, and was pounding on the doors into the castle proper. Whatever objection Gloriana had was being ignored, apparently. Guardsmen spilled into the courtyard, weapons at the ready.

Gloriana hurried toward Ezren. 'I never thought to see you again. Where have you been?'

'Later.' Ezren wadded up some of Alad's tunic and pressed it to his side to stanch the bleeding.

'I want to hear that tale,' Oris said.

'No fear,' Ezren said. 'I will tell the tale at our wedding feast.' He looked at Bethral, who was snapping commands to all and sundry.

Bethral paused, as if sensing his gaze. She returned his look, a smile dancing on her lips, before she resumed issuing sharp orders to the guards.

'About time,' Oris grumbled. 'You two were as thick as stumps about your feelings for one another.'

Gloriana snorted out a surprised laugh as she knelt at his side. 'Oris!'

'Well, it's true,' Oris said. 'And you! Where did you learn such language, young lady?'

Gloriana choked back a sob that turned into a laugh. 'Alad.'

'I never!' Alad protested.

The guards were gathering around, and lifted the men into their arms. 'To the healers, and quickly,' Gloriana ordered, and they left at a run.

Ezren turned to Queen Gloriana, who stood looking after her men, blood dripping from her sword. 'What happened here?'

Gloriana sighed. 'A long tale. But it—'

'Can wait,' Bethral insisted, looking at the guards that were dealing with the dead. 'Let's see to your safety first.'

'This way,' Gloriana said. 'One of these men can see to your horse. Once we're in my chambers, I'll tell you all about it. But you must tell me your story as well.'

'Of course,' Ezren said, but then he stopped dead. 'Lord of Light, I do not know what happened on the Plains or how the story ends!'

'Well, you know our ending,' Bethral said softly. 'It ends with a beginning. Our lives. Our love.' She held up her hand, displaying a silver scar that ran the length of her palm.

Ezren found the same scar on his palm. He drew a deep, satisfied breath as a sense of well-being swelled in his chest. He looked into Bethral's blue eyes and smiled, reaching out to pull her close. 'It does at that. We will start the story there, shall we?'

Bethral pressed her lips to his. 'Yes, love. I rather think we will.'